I0612631

IN THE BLINK
OF AN EYE

BEING AN ANTHOLOGY OF THE FURTHER LEGENDS
OF ELLICOTT CITY'S BLINK MAN

Edited by K. Patrick Glover

ROXTON PRESS
BALTIMORE

This Edition: Copyright © 2019 ROXTON PRESS

Individual contributions copyright their respective authors. An extension of this copyright page exists on page 271.

Copyright ©2019 Shelley Davies Wygant, K. Patrick Glover, William Couper, Matt Lake, Seth Adam Kallick, Jacob Le Doux, Patrick Storck, Josef Richardson, Megan Morgan, Paul R. Sieber, Steve Toase

Butterfly Kisses, The Blink Man, Peeping Tom, and related concepts

Copyright ©2019 Erik Kristopher Myers
ISBN (paperback edition): 978-1-7341530-0-2

Editor: K. Patrick Glover
Cover design: Ilan Sheady and Uncle Frank Productions
Interior layout and design: Matt Lake

Roxton Press
Baltimore, MD

fb.me/RoxtonPress

CONTENTS

Foreword by K. Patrick Glover

Postscript by Megan Morgan

Afterword by Erik Kristopher Myers

FOREWORD

By K. Patrick Glover

I first met Erik Kristopher Myers in a comic book store. I was there to sign copies of my latest book, a graphic novel called *A Wicked Little Town*. Erik was there signing copies of his newest film, a documentary called *Butterfly Kisses*. We were at adjacent tables and spent the afternoon chatting. We exchanged work, him picking up a copy of my book, me taking home a disc of his film. A couple of nights later, I sat down to watch it.

It focused on an urban legend called The Blink Man or Peeping Tom, a pair of students who attempted to make a film about him, and, ultimately, the tragic fate of Gavin York. The film intrigued me and I began digging into the facts surrounding the case. I kept coming across stories that deepened the mystery of Peeping Tom and the Ilchester Tunnel.

Unlike the events documented in the film, many of these stories cannot be substantiated. Some are hearsay, some not even that. One tale was found, hand-written, in a steamer trunk in an attic in Hagerstown. Another was found in the pages of an old journal in a thrift store in Ellicott City. Each story, on its own, represents an interesting piece of folklore, but together they paint a larger portrait of something dark and sinister in that Howard County train tunnel.

While investigation into the legend of the Blink Man and into what really happened to Gavin York are still under way, I felt it was important to get these stories out to the public. They provide important context in understanding the deeper mysteries here, and even if some of them prove to be apocryphal, at this point in time the legend is more important than the reality. It wasn't the reality of those stories that drove Sophia Crane and the mysterious Feldman to film their experiment, it was the legend of Blink Man.

It was that same legend that sent Gavin York on his tragic quest.

And it is that same legend presented here.

A wonderful group of authors has taken up the task of turning these tales into something both enjoyable and frightening to read. They have turned what in some cases was nothing more than whispers and rumors into compelling narrative. They have given shape to shadows and focus to what lurks in the corner of the eye. The stories here won't answer any questions, that's for another time and place. If anything, they will leave you with still more unanswered questions. Maybe that's better, maybe the questions here shouldn't be answered. Do any of us really want to know if The Blink Man is real?

What does it say about us, if we do?

THOM

By Shelley Davies Wygant

This is the least substantiated of the stories within the volume. Author Wygant has used her personal association with various historical societies to verify and flesh out the rumors that make up the core of the story. The best we can say at this point is that the story related here may have happened, and if it did, this is the narrative's most likely form.

The nights were always the same for Thom, especially once he began to spend his days with her. He would come home late, eat leftovers in the kitchen of the boarding house, and then collapse into a deep sleep that was haunted by dreams. Dark ones.

They always began the same way. He'd be walking into the mine with his dad, talking and laughing like they always did. They were good at their job and they loved doing it. There was a power and precision to calculating just enough explosive to carve out the next section of rock and coal but not so much that it would bring the mountain down around them.

But then things would change. As they walked further into the tunnel, toward the detonator, the lights in the mine began to dim and the laughter faded away into silence.

"Do you feel it, Thom?" his dad would ask. "Do you see him?"

"Feel what Dad? See who?" he questioned.

"The ysbryd. The dark thing that lives in the rock," his dad whispered. "The ghost that flickers in the shadows outside your line of sight. The thing that both beckons and pursues you. The dark thing you feel you must look away from but cannot."

Then came the flash of light and the explosion that made him bolt upright out of sleep and into an ice-cold sweat as the dawn began to color the sky blood red.

The light was starting to fade from the sky. Thom lay atop her and when he finished, he opened his eyes and looked down into hers. They were open and as blue as the vinca flowering on the steep slopes below St. Mary's seminary. He grunted as he rolled over to lie next to her on the soft blanket he'd brought and he pulled a bit of it over them. His bones were older than hers. Despite the warm spring weather, the air was cool behind the huge craggy rock that hid them from view.

Except for the first few times, they rarely spoke when they met here. The forest was dark and deep but voices carried easily across the valley despite the rush of the Patapsco River below. Mostly, they communicated through touch.

This time it was no different. He ran his fingers across the delicate skin of her hipbone and traced it up along her jawline. She turned to him for a last kiss. It was getting late. Evening vespers would begin soon and she couldn't be late.

Thom had no reason to hurry. Saturday supper at Franklin Cugel's boarding house in Ilchester was left on the kitchen table. Cugel's wife, Mary, wasn't much of a cook. Eating whatever she'd prepared cold tended to improve the flavor. So, he laid back and looked at her as she recomposed herself for the journey back to St. Mary's.

First the white linen undergarments. Then the heavy black wool stockings. She held on to a sapling to balance herself as she stepped into her black tunic and pulled the wide-bell sleeves up over her delicate shoulders. It was a process that took a long time. But it was time that he didn't mind spending.

By the time she finally smoothed her blazing blonde hair

under her white coif, righted her heart shaped veil, and tied the distinctive bow of the Sisters of Christian Charity under chin, the sun had sunk a degree or two lower in the afternoon sky.

With a quick wave, she mouthed, "goodbye", and stepped from behind the rock to make her way down to the trail that led to the river and back to the seminary. He listened to the rustle of her robes recede into the forest as he stared up through the trees watching the vultures spiral above, scouring the updrafts for the scent of death.

"Oh, you're back late," Mrs. Cugel said as he came through the door. She turned to look at him. "Guess you'll miss evening vespers. There's some potatoes and what's left of a roast chicken in the kitchen."

"Thank you. I went to mass this morning and was communing with the creator of cold beer and Maryland rye whiskey on my walk back from Catonsville," he joked as he grabbed a plate to take up to his room in the Cugel's modest but spacious home.

The four story stone building had been built in the 1830's by the son of one of the Ellicott brothers and used as a home, tavern, and hotel before he sold it to the Redemptorists back in 1866 and it became part of St. Mary's College. Frank Cugle worked at the college. He, his Mary, and their two young sons got to live there free and took in boarders like Thom to make extra money.

The handsome house next to the railroad tracks reminded Thom of his family home in Flintshire in North Wales. Like Ilchester, it was a town hewn into the living granite of the hills above a river. It was there that he and his brothers had learned the craft and strange alchemy of blasting from their father in the coal mines of Mostyn Colliery.

Thom had married young and foolishly. He almost did not get to reach his current ripe old age because of what happened at the colliery in 1884.

His father had always talked about what he called "the dark thing" that lived down in the stone bowels of the mine. He said he was drawn to it, or it to him. Just before each blast he had a moment where he thought the thing might grab hold of him and make him stay down there with it forever.

Maybe that's what happened that day when his dad detonated a massive charge causing the River Dee to break through the wall of the mine and completely overwhelm the pits. Thom and his brother barely made it out alive. The Colliery never reopened.

That was the end of his life in Flintshire. He and his young wife packed up their things and left for America with their young daughter Catherine. They settled in Scranton, Pennsylvania and, until his daughter fell ill, they had a good life. He made decent money as a master blaster in the Lackawanna anthracite mines. But after spending sixteen years risking his life for the company, he got into a scuffle with a foreman. And, well…that was that. His wife and their invalid daughter, who needed a lot of doctoring, couldn't be supported on a shop clerk's wages.

So, when the men from the B&O Railroad came up and started waving wads of money to get skilled workers to help build their new tunnel near Ellicott City, Maryland, Thom jumped at the chance. He roped in his friend Mike O'Hara to come along with him to join a crew of one hundred and fifty men who would be working night and day to blast a deep hole through a steep granite cliff on the banks of the Patapsco River.

The first time he saw her, he was on his way up Jacob's Ladder, the sixty-six-step stone staircase that led from the Ilchester train station to the seminary above. She was on her way down. Her face was flushed and her habit billowed out around her as she hurried down the steep steps. He tipped his tall, stovepipe hat and quickly got out of her way.

"Who's that?", he asked Mike after she disappeared around the corner at the bottom of the hill.

St. Mary's College was a seminary that prepared young men from all over the Baltimore region to enter the priesthood, so the sight of a young woman on the grounds, and a pretty one at that, was unusual.

"Oh, that's Provincial Licking's new assistant," replied Mike. "She's here on loan from the Sisters of Christian Charity in Baltimore. Think Sister Margaret is her name."

"Well Jesus, Mary, and Joseph, she's a looker. Never had nuns who looked like that growing up in Flintshire," Thom mused as they continued up the stairs to the back of the Cugel's house.

Little did he know, Thom would be seeing a lot more of Sister Margaret.

A few days after he passed her on the stair case, a fellow blaster miscalculated the percentage of glycerin for the explosive charge. When it went off at the bottom of one of the narrow shafts that the automatic steam and compressed-air drills had bored into the top of the hill, it sent a geyser of granite shards 50 feet in the air.

One of them clipped Thom just above his right eyebrow. He was out cold for almost three days. When he came to, everyone was astonished that not only had his brain not been addled like an unwanted duck egg, but after two weeks, he was able to walk. The B&O Railroad sent a doctor to look at him who said it would be at least another month before his hands would be steady enough to set a charge.

The Cugels were kind. They'd seen Thom wire nearly his entire paycheck to Scranton every week and knew what that money went to pay for. Frank assured him he could rest up and recover rent free, but that wouldn't pay the bills that kept coming back in Pennsylvania.

A day or so after the doctor made his pronouncement, Frank came to Thom and asked, "You can read and write, can't you? I seen the letters you send to your wife. Sometimes they're two and three pages long. Maybe there's a way you could make money that way?"

Thom chuckled, "If I could make money writing letters to my wife, I'd be a rich man ten times over by now."

"Nah, not writing letters. Office work," he said. "Licking's got a whole bunch of young fellas up there on the hill helping him tend to whatever church things he has to tend to. Obviously, there's a lot to do. That's why he's got that pretty nun working for him."

Cugel worked his hand on his mouth and went on, "I know a lot of things that happen up there...don't ask me what...but I think I could get you in. Lemme see what I can do."

Less than a week later, Thom was trudging just slightly unsteadily up the covered "chute" that lead to the massive cupola-topped upper college and the office of The Very Reverend, William Licking.

Sister Margaret greeted him at a desk outside the Provincial's walnut paneled study. When he awkwardly reached up to remove his hat, he fumbled and it fell off his head and rolled across the floor. They both reached for it at the same time, and when their hands touched it felt like a 60% nitroglycerin charge going off up his arm.

She blushed crimson. He mumbled something and then was quickly ushered into Licking's office where the Provincial was seated behind an imposing desk. He was flanked by Father Hild, professor of Morals at the college and the Prefect of Students, the

Reverend John Hausser.

The interview was over in less than five minutes. He'd be paid $3 a day and would be helping Sister Margaret with filing, correspondence, and anything else that wasn't too physically demanding. Three dollars was far less than the $5 dollars a day he'd been earning as a blaster, but his rent was free and he'd get to work alongside the prettiest woman in Ilchester. He shook the men's hands and agreed to show up for work the next day.

When he got back down to Cugels, he thanked Frank, saying "I don't know what you did, but that was the fastest I've ever gotten hired in my life."

The work was easy and working alongside Sister Margaret brought him a joy he hadn't felt in years. But in his state, it was still exhausting. The dreams were still there, and they troubled his mind.

Although Thom and Maggie, as she'd asked him to call her, worked side by side filing student records, sorting correspondence, and replacing books on the library shelves, small talk was kept to a minimum. Father Hild would frequently glide through the warren of studies and nooks near the Principal's office, his eyes glittering with the suspicion of Thom's attraction to Sister Margaret.

In one of their rare times completely alone, he asked her what everyone in Ilchester who saw Sister Margaret wondered. Raising his eyebrows and gesturing to her veil and the pert bow of the Sisters of Christian Charity order under her chin, he asked smiling, "So how did all this come about?"

Her smile faded and her expression darkened. After a few awkward moments, she said, "There was a baby."

Taking a minute to consider what he'd just heard, he said, "Ah, I see..." And then after a beat, asked, "The father?"

"James McCarthy. Class president at Boys' Latin. Never spoke to me again after I told him," she said lowering her eyes.

"How'd your parents take it?" he asked softly.

"About the same as James did. Packed me off to Villa Louise, and left me there," she said, biting her lip. "They moved away to the Eastern Shore. Just couldn't bear the shame of it."

"So, how old were you?" Thom questioned.

"Sixteen," she sighed and looked away. "After the baby was born and adopted, I just stayed. James graduated and went on to study at Johns Hopkins. I heard he married a debutante from Guilford. I never heard from my parents again."

Thom sucked air through his teeth, "Well, that's a pisser...um, forgive my language."

"It's okay. I've heard worse," she smiled wryly. "Anyway, the sisters were nice for the most part and it just felt like the closest thing to home that I might ever have."

"Hiraeth," he said knowingly.

"Hee-drythe?", she questioned.

"Welsh word. Don't worry about how to pronounce it, because you'll never get it right anyway," he chuckled softly.

"Okay then, just tell me what it means," Maggie replied, with mock annoyance.

"It really can't be translated. Close as I can come is that it's a bittersweet feeling. A longing for home. Something that's gone. It may have existed at one time in real life or only in imagination," he said. "It describes how I feel when I think about my Dad and our life back Flintshire."

"Hee-drythe...hee-drythe", she repeated, even though she knew she was mangling the word and then paused a long moment.

"Can you ever satisfy that longing? I mean it sounds so sad," she said slowly, pausing again. "Can you ever get it back? I mean maybe by making another 'home'?"

"I dunno," Thom said wistfully. "I never really tried."

She reached out to touch his arm. He pulled back with a start. That electricity again.

Thanks to the restorative powers of Mrs. Cugal's nursing and the relief from the hard labor in the tunnel, Thom began to recover enough to resume his custom of walking the 4 miles into Catonsville for lunch on Saturdays.

Getting there involved a bit of a workout. The route from the Cugels house, across the bridge and up Hilltop Road to Frederick Road was as steep as any that he'd hiked in north Wales. The scenery was achingly similar. The road wound up the hill, past clusters of the tidy stone homes where the workers at The Thistle Mill lived and then into deep forest above the Patapsco before it dead ended at Route 144 that lead to Catonsville.

One day as he was helping Maggie file a newly delivered batch of Our Lady of Perpetual Help prayer cards, he mentioned his weekly walks.

"Oh, I love walking", she said. "I often stroll on the trail down along the Patapsco. I know a couple of places where you can find morel mushrooms higher up in the woods when the Redbud trees bloom in spring."

"You hike in that get up?", Thom shook his head in amusement.

"Oh yes, Sister Margaret is our little billy-goat," said Father Hild over his shoulder as he brushed past them on his way to Rev. Licking's study.

After Hild disappeared, she turned to Thom and whispered, "Maybe I'll run into you sometime on one of your walks."

His heart stopped for a moment.

She went on with feigned casualness, "There's an outcropping of rock just down from the crest of Hilltop Road that shades my secret morel hunting spot. The Redbuds will be starting to bloom soon. I usually make it up there by 2:00 PM on Saturdays."

And so, it began.

Thom would walk up to meet Mike for an early lunch in Catonsville, and then on the way back he'd slip into the woods to meet Maggie.

By late June, the Redbud blooms and the morels had disappeared, but their hunger for each other remained and seemed to get stronger every time they met. Most of the time, the silence of the forest blanketed them. But occasionally, they allowed the sounds of their coupling to be drowned out by the roar of a passing train.

Thom had recovered enough from his concussion that the railroad doctor cleared him to go back to work. The final blasting work on the Ilchester Tunnel was going to be next spring. To celebrate his return, the foreman and crew agreed that Thom would have the honor of doing the last detonation that would connect the two ends of the tunnel into the one continuous 1,405 foot passageway.

His return to work on the tunnel meant the end of their daily meetings, which made Saturdays all the sweeter. When the weather cooled, they moved their trysts to one of the many abandoned cottages in the woods. He found one with a working fireplace and stocked it with enough wood to last the winter.

Thom knew that as much as he cared for Maggie, his relationship with her would have to end at some point. When the tunnel was completed sometime in May, he would be heading back to Scranton, while she would be returning to Villa Louise and the Sisters of Christian Charity in Baltimore. It would be sad, but it would be a natural and inevitable break.

So he was surprised when they were back at their hideaway, behind the boulder, the next spring, and she told him something that that would change what was left of their lives forever.

After they'd fallen away from each other, sweaty and exhausted, they laid there looking up at the vultures lazily swirling in circles above them. Softly clearing her throat, Maggie broke the sacred silence with a simple sentence.

"I have to tell you something," she whispered.

His heart froze. This time not with desire, but with some dark premonition that filled him with dread. What seemed like an eternity passed before she spoke again.

"I'm pregnant," she said with obvious happiness in her voice.

Not waiting for his reply, she rose on her elbow to look at him, the silken strands of her strawberry blond hair falling down around her pale face, and let the words tumble out in a breathless string.

"I know this is something neither of us planned on. But it could be a good thing, Thom... Your job on the tunnel is almost finished... I'm supposed to be leaving soon too... We could run away together somewhere... and make a new life with the baby," she said. "Oh Thom...it'd be hee-drythe... hee-drythe, for both of us..."

Her words hit him like the chunk of granite that had almost killed him last spring. He knew what he had to say, but his lips seemed to be paralyzed.

So, he took the coward's way out. He let his silence speak the words he didn't have the courage to say, "...wife back in Scranton... not in love with her ... have a daughter... she's sick... if things were different, we might, but I can't. I just can't."

Although Maggie couldn't hear his unspoken words, Thom's silence said everything she needed to know. She wasn't the school girl she was ten years ago. She was stronger than when she told

James about their baby and had collapsed at his feet sobbing in anguish as he turned away.

She waited and drew in a deep breath and said, "Well, all right, then."

Her stockings, veil, shoes, and heavy habit were neatly folded beside them. Naked, she stood up and scooped them into a ball. Without another word, she turned her back, and disappeared behind the rock that had shielded them from the world and walked into the forest. Steeled with resignation, she didn't care who saw her. She'd recompose herself elsewhere.

When Thom got back to the Cugels, the black-edged envelope was waiting for him on the kitchen table along with the remains of Mary's meatloaf supper. He picked up the envelope and sat down. Based on the post mark and the black border, he knew it was bad news from his wife in Scranton.

Thom almost felt too wrung out to face it. But he opened the envelope anyway, set aside his dread, and began reading.

"Dear Thom, I have been crying since last Tuesday when it happened..."

Winter rarely loosened its icy grip on Scranton until May. His invalid daughter, had caught a chill that turned into grippe. In her weakened state, Catherine was no match for the illness. It dragged her into the grave in a matter of days.

"...it happened so fast Thom, and she needed me so much... there wasn't time to send word for you to come home... And to be truthful, somehow I didn't even want you to..."

The ill-advised rush into marriage, the distance between them, and now the death of their daughter had finally put an end to what never should have been.

"There's nothing here for me now", she went on. "I've booked passage home at the end of the month. Your things and a few of Catherine's are packed up in the apartment for you... I wish I could say more, but we both know there hasn't been anything more to say for a very long time..."

There was nothing to go back to in Scranton.

A combination of grief and relief washed over him. He'd deal with everything... the loss of his daughter... Maggie... the baby... whatever might be... tomorrow. Right now, he just wanted sleep untroubled by dark dreams followed by a dawn of what might be a new future.

But that was not to be.

The found Sister Margaret's body in the Patapsco River just before sunrise. She was dressed in her habit face up, eyes open, her black sleeves flapping in the water, spinning around in a slow circle in an eddy above the Thistle Factory dam. The novitiate who stumbled upon Sister Margaret immediately raced up Jacob's Ladder to tell Rev. Licking. Wanting to stay as far away from this unpleasant event as possible, he sent Father Hild and Frank Cugel to deal with the situation.

The fathers arrived within an hour of the seminary student's grim discovery.

"Oh dear, it looks like our pretty little hillbilly, slipped and fell on one of her walks," Hild sniffed derisively. He stepped back from the river's edge and sat on a rock as he watched Frank Cugel wade in to retrieve Sister Margaret's body.

Frank grasped one of her thin white wrists to draw her out of the eddy. Her young, slim body should have floated easily toward him. But something held her firmly in place. Frustrated, he grabbed her under both arms and pulled. It took some effort to finally get her up out of the water and onto the bank of the river.

When he did both Father Hild and Frank Cugel saw it. There was a rope tied around one of Sister Margaret's delicate white ankles. When Frank reached down and pulled on it, he dredged up something that made his heart go cold. It was a heavy, iron ring the millworkers used to tie up horses at the Thistle Factory.

Father Hild arched his eyebrow as he looked at it. "Well I guess we don't have to worry about having a funeral mass at the chapel for this one."

"I think maybe you will," Cugel said ominously as he cut the rope off her ankle and tossed the tie into the deepest part of the river just behind the dam. "You know that I know about things that you and Rev. Licking wouldn't like to have come out."

"I don't know how long you think you can play that card, Frank," remarked Hild. "You and your family live at the Ellicott House rent-free. That could change."

"As long as I have a breath in my body and you want to keep what you're doing up on the hill private, it won't," he shot back. "Now go send for some help to get this poor girl up to St. Mary's."

The full funeral mass for Sister Margaret was open to the public. She had been a popular figure around Ilchester having helped out with the Catechism classes for the children. Many fondly recalled her cheery waves and gifts of delicious mushrooms she brought back from her walks along the Patapsco.

Thom and Mike O'Hara attended too. Ashen faced, with his tall stovepipe hat in his lap, Thom recited the liturgy along with the rest of them but he didn't go up to communion. He hadn't been to confession for a long time.

Rev. Licking and Father Hild had made noises about having Sister Margaret buried somewhere in Baltimore. Frank Cugel had other plans. He made sure that the Easton Sons hearse took her body to be buried in the newly opened St. Mary's Cemetery high up on Ilchester Road.

After Maggie's death, Thom's dreams about his dad and the thing living in the darkness of the rock grew more and more vivid. But now when he and his dad faced the ysbryd in his dream, it seemed less menacing. It seemed to know him. In his waking hours, deep in the shafts at the tunnel site, Thom sometimes he thought he heard it whisper his name.

When the time came for the final blast to unite the two ends of the tunnel in May 1902, the B&O Railroad foreman remained true to his word and assigned Thom to do the final blast. The narrow 10-foot wide shaft where the charge would be placed had been bored 100 feet down from the top of the hill.

Thom stepped up to the edge of the shaft and looked down into the darkness. It was pitch black. Blacker than the coal mines of Mostyn Colliery. He could hear the slightly faraway sound of the band playing on the Ilchester end of the tunnel opening. This was a big day for the town and the railroad and a crowd had gathered to watch the spectacle.

Thom had carefully prepared the 60% glycerin charge that was calculated to be enough to obliterate the last layer of rock and open the tunnel. But just in case, he added a little bit more, earlier in the morning. 65%. 70%. 75%. Just to make sure.

He lowered the charge into the shaft by its long fuse and waved the crew back from the shaft. Typically, they would use a safety fuse which burned at a rate of a foot minute. At 100 feet that would take almost an hour and a half. The crowd was impatient and the railroad men wanted to put on a good show. So, instead they used a much faster pipe match fuse that would race the flame down to the charge in less than a minute.

Thom was an expert blaster, but a dare-devil, and despite being almost middle-aged, a pretty fast runner. He figured he'd give the boys a show by lighting the fuse and waiting until the last minute to get out of the way. So, at the appointed time, he waved the crew back, pulled out his lighter and lit the fuse.

He looked down into the shaft where the sparking, sputtering flame on the fuse was speeding toward the charge below. It was just about then when he heard the voice whisper his name.

"Thomas," it said, "come."

This time, it wasn't "the thing" calling him, it was his dad. A wave of sorrow, nostalgia, and yearning washed over him. Flintshire. Maggie. Catherine. Hiraeth.

He turned and nodded to the crew. Then, whispered "Yes, it's time. I'm coming," and stepped down into the dark thin air of the shaft.

They say that people as far away as Fort McHenry heard the blast. A roar went up from the crowd in Ilchester as the last curtain of rock exploded in a spray of grit and powdered granite revealing daylight from the Baltimore side of the tunnel.

The band began to play. The railroad men took their bows. Picnic baskets were opened and sarsaparilla flowed like the Patapsco after a summer rainstorm.

The Baltimore Sun reported in the May 5, 1902 edition that "The two openings came together the other day with wonderful precision, without the deviation of an inch sideways or up or down."

The only people who knew what had happened were the crew, high on the hill, far from the celebrations below. There was nothing to be done for Thom now. They'd tell the railroad bosses tomorrow after the bunting and the bandstand had been taken down and the crowds dispersed back to their homes in Ilchester, Catonsville, and Ellicott City. They picked up Thom's tall, stovepipe hat, which had blown off when he jumped, and headed down to join the festivities.

The Ilchester Tunnel, and perhaps something more, had been opened.

Thom had pretty much kept to himself, so when word got out that he had been killed in the blast, the towns people "tsked" that it was a pity but not much more was made of the event. The Cugels, of course, took it harder than most. They had grown fond of the odd Welshman and would miss his dry sense of humor as well what they took as his appreciation for Mary's cold leftover suppers.

The B&O Railroad management notified Thom's wife of his death. But since there was no body to be collected or buried, she didn't come. His passing wasn't even reported in the papers. It was bad publicity that the railroad thought would spoil the news of their success.

The crew gave Mike O'Hara Thom's hat, but he had no use for it. He ended up giving it to Frank Cugel, who had always admired it despite its oddness. It was just as well, since a little more than a year later, Mike was killed by falling rock while working in the tunnel in June 1903.

Once it was finished, the Ilchester Tunnel accommodated dozens of trains running night and day. Had it been built fifty years earlier, it might have made Ilchester the bustling town Benjamin Ellicott imagined it could be.

In the years after it was built, the tunnel became a magnet for sightseers and teenagers looking for a thrill. The kids would creep themselves out by peering into the tunnel imagining they were conjuring the ghost of Thom.

Frank Cugel's oldest son Philip was among them. One Sunday before mass at the Seminary chapel, he confessed what he and his friends had been doing.

"I told you to stay away from that place. With the trains running at all hours, it's dangerous," said Frank.

"I know, but all the kids are doing it," the teen said. "I actually think I saw him last night."

Frank scoffed, "You did, did you now? What makes you think that?"

"I was staring into the tunnel and then, all of the sudden, I saw him. I knew it was him because he was wearing his funny hat," said Philip pointing at Thom's old stovepipe hanging on the peg by the door.

"And Dad..." he paused as he anxiously glanced out the window toward the tunnel below, "...I think he followed me home."

IN THE COURT OF THE YELLOW KING

By K. Patrick Glover

This story was sent to me from a woman in Boston, claiming to be the great grand-niece of the woman who narrates this tale. She says that this was sent back scribbled on a stack of loose pages, along with the other personal effects of her Aunt. The pages themselves are certainly of the time period described, but as no mention of the author's name is included, they are difficult to verify in any meaningful way.

The house was painted a dull yellow, as if it had been left too long in the sun and all of its vibrance and life had faded away. It sat far back from the road, alone. Forest surrounded it on three sides, but even the trees seemed to keep their distance, leaving a barren space of dirt and twigs around it. The windows were cloudy with decades of grime that obscured everything within except for the faint glow of the lights and the battered and broken window blinds which were always pulled half-way down. The house had no neighbors to speak of. It sat on a seldom used road, three miles north of the Ilchester Tunnel, so to say that no one ever saw another human being enter or leave the house isn't saying much, but still.

No one ever saw the solitude of the yellow house disturbed, not by man or beast. It was better that way. The things that happened in that dull yellow house were never meant to be seen. Not by human eyes. I wish with all my heart that I was not the exception that proved that rule, that I had never seen that house, that I had never set foot upon its land, much less inside the dreaded thing. Wishes are devilous things, they often come far too late, and they are granted only by things better left in the recesses of imagination and the corner of the eye.

Even knowing that, if I had the opportunity to make such a wish now, if I could turn back the clock so that I had never come down to the state of Maryland, I would offer up any sacrifice necessary. I would never have opened the letter from St. Mary's College, never agreed to come and provide a guest lecture in the folklore that was my specialty, if I had known any of what was to follow.

I suppose I should have been concerned with the specificity of the request, the origin of an otherworldly phantom known as a flimmern-geist and the details of the dimension it inhabits when not being brought forth into our own. I had to forage through quite a few arcane books from my private library to find any answers as the flimmern-geist is an obscure spirit even in my area of expertise. After pushing past several brief references in various guides, I found a more detailed explanation in a volume by a sixteenth century alchemist named Jakob Bohme.

Bohme was a Lutheran Mystic of the time and much of his work involved blending folklore with religious dogma. He believed that a flimmern-geist was the spirit of someone who had died a violent death and spent eternity in a place just beyond the edge of our vision. His work was unclear on just what that place might be, although there was some allusion to purgatory or someplace very like it.

That brought something to mind and sent me digging for another volume that I had obtained some years previous. It was without a title and badly translated from Arabic, but it mentioned an ancient and cursed city on the shores of a Lake Hali that lies just beyond the edge of our vision. The phrasing, in translation at least, was exact. It could be coincidence, but my mind leapt with excitement at the connection, a feeling that perhaps only dusty old academics like I would understand.

With these finds, I had enough information that I could feel comfortable speaking on the subject, but more importantly, the request had left me with the impression that I might learn even more if I could exchange thoughts with the group that had requested my lecture. In the end, it was my own thirst for knowledge that had me sending an affirmative reply and packing my bags for the train ride down from Kingsport, Massachusetts.

It was still early into the new century and even though 1910 felt like a progressive new time to us, the faculty at my college were concerned about sending a female professor off on such an adventure on her own. But we were a small institution and I was paying for the trip out of my own funds, hoping to replace the hole in my account with the offered speaking fee, so in the end, I left in my own company.

When I arrived in Ellicott City, I took a room in the Howard House Hotel, a towering structure built into the side of a granite hill, overlooking Main Street. The train ride had left me exhausted, so I had an early dinner there at the hotel and went back to my room to sleep. There I dreamt of black stars over a still lake. I awoke in the morning feeling refreshed but uneasy.

St. Mary's College was just over two miles from the hotel, but it was a pleasant spring day and I decided to walk there, hoping that the Sister Haversham who had written me would be free to talk upon my arrival. I was in no hurry and my walk was a leisurely one, and yet I found myself becoming anxious as I went. The people I passed were outwardly friendly, but I sensed something else, an undercurrent of suspicion, or perhaps something darker.

I would have dismissed it as mere paranoia, brought on by my journey and the strange dreams that followed, were it not for what happened when I arrived at the college. There was no Sister Haversham there, they had never heard of her. I showed them the letter that had been sent and, although it appeared to be on authentic stationary, the folklore class that it mentioned did not exist. It all appeared to be an elaborate practical joke, one that had cost me a great deal of money.

I walked back to the hotel in a dazed silence. The loss of the funds that I had expended thus far was upsetting, but not debilitating. While I was not a wealthy woman, my grandfather had left me enough money that I could live comfortably as I pursued my academic interests.

It was the mystery behind the entire thing that nagged at my mind. My initial thoughts about being the victim of a joke seemed less likely the longer I considered the matter. The knowledge required to compose that initial letter was so arcane that even I, an expert in world folklore, had to research what was described. The very idea that a layman would have such information at their fingertips was ridiculous.

I was greeted back at the hotel by a message that a Mr. Cornelius Haversham was in the lounge, awaiting my return. It appeared that I would get some answers after all. Mr. Haversham was a large man with a bushy beard and hands the size of hams. He rose from his spot to greet me and as he took my hand I found his touch to be light and his voice surprisingly gentle.

"My sincere apologies, Professor. I had hoped to catch you before you left for St. Mary's, but it appears that I missed you by a quarter of an hour."

"I see," I said, curtly. "I suppose that effort is at least somewhat commendable, but it doesn't excuse the false claims that brought me here."

"No, I suppose it doesn't, but those claims are not as false as they appear. Please, join me, and I'll try to explain."

I sat down, hoping that I appeared reluctant. In truth, I was finding the whole thing utterly fascinating and I could not wait to hear more.

"I represent a private organization with a great interest in certain elements of folklore. Everything in the letter that we sent to you was of genuine interest. We very much do want you to speak on the subject and we will happily pay you for your time. We just thought that you would take our request more seriously if it came from the college."

"A private organization?"

"Yes. We call ourselves the Knights of the Yellow Court."

"And the letter I received? I would imagine it to be foolish to declare a written hand to be definitely masculine or feminine, yet I have a hard time imaging your heavy hands producing so delicate a script. Is there, indeed, a Sister Haversham?"

He smiled, briefly, and, I think, almost laughed. "I don't think anyone would mistake dear Margaret for a bride of Christ, but I do have a sister and it was she who wrote the letter, or at least it was in her hand. I suppose we all composed it, by committee, as it were."

"And just what is your committee's interest in flimmern-geists?"

Haversham's face changed, almost imperceptibly, as if he was trying carefully to remember a well-rehearsed speech. "There's a local story, a legend. About a man named Thom. It's said that he was killed in the final blast that made the Illchester Tunnel."

"Said?"

"No body was ever found. No trace at all, no blood, no bone, nothing.

"What do you believe happened to him?" I asked.

"We think he was blown into another world. That he became a flimmern-geist.

"Existing just beyond human vision?"

"Yes. Visible only through the corner of your eye," he said.

"Have you ever heard of Carcosa?"

"It doesn't sound familiar."

"Strange is the night where black stars rise
And strange moons circle through the skies
But stranger still
Is lost Carcosa."

I thought of the black stars over the lake in my dream and a shiver ran through me. "I think," I said, "that you should take me to meet the rest of your yellow knights."

Haversham shook his hefty head. "I wish that I could. For one, our meeting hall is under construction at the moment. There was a minor flood, it caused some structural damage." Then he laughed, nervously. "And most of the others aren't around right now. They didn't believe you'd come."

"I see."

"But Doctor Henning is in town. He's our chief officer. He has a home up on College Road. It's a sizeable place, we could gather those who could come and meet there."

My enthusiasm for the subject was getting the better of me, but an undercurrent of unease had settled in and taken hold of my heart. I could feel it pounding, not in excitement, but in dread, somehow understanding the danger of my situation in a way that my conscious mind did not.

If I could have seen the faded yellow house where Mr. Haversham was suggesting we meet, I think, even not knowing what lay ahead, I would have turned him down, enthusiasm be damned. Such was the power of that place, that it made clear it's horrible intent with just a glimpse.

But here, in the safety of the hotel lounge, my undefined discomfort was not enough to dispel my curiosity and I agreed to meet with the remnants of his group that very evening. We settled on a time and it was arranged that Margaret Haversham would be at the front of the hotel with a carriage to take me to Doctor Henning's home, where I would give my initial presentation to the few members of the Court who were available to gather.

I spent the rest of that afternoon napping, and I dreamt once more of the black stars over the still and quiet lake. This time, on the distant shore, I could see the silhouette of a man, tall and thin, wearing a tall hat. He stood perfectly still at the edge of the water, but I could sense that he was waiting for something. In the final moments, before I woke, I heard a horrible voice whisper to me.

"Don't close your eyes," it said. "Open the door."

I awoke in a fevered sweat, and took my time preparing for the evening's work. I bathed there in the hotel, although the water felt old to me, and somehow unclean. I dressed neatly in the finest outfit that I had brought with me, one that my students back home had called matronly, but in an admiring way. I was just three years shy of my fiftieth birthday and I had never married. Few men had ever called me beautiful, but matronly, to my ear, sounded respectful, if not complimentary, and it was, I suppose, what I felt was a well-earned description.

Satisfied with my appearance, I sat at the room's elegant desk and studied my notes until the agreed upon time. It wasn't until I was headed down to the lobby that I even considered food. There was no time now, I could see my carriage waiting on the street outside. I almost turned back then, telling myself it was out of hunger and not fear, for the very sight of the carriage had set my nerves afire. But I was a distinguished academic with the greatest knowledge of folklore on the eastern seaboard, and I would not be frightened off by a missed meal and a little girl's flutters.

Margaret Haversham was waiting for me in the carriage, a stern looking woman of about my age, perhaps a few years younger. She nodded at me, but remained largely silent during our journey. I tried to engage her in conversation, but got little more than indifferent mutters in reply. If she had any interest in my presence or in what I had to tell her organization, she hid it well.

It took our carriage just over half of an hour to reach the yellow house. I looked at it, sitting there in the woods, in all its malevolence, and I felt my resolve seep away. It looked old and in disrepair, but that couldn't account for the atmosphere of sheer horror that surrounded the place. As I stepped from the carriage, I found myself shivering, as though the temperature had dropped significantly during our ride.

I looked to Margaret, hoping for some sign of encouragement, but found instead a face void of emotion, flat and disinterested. I looked back at the house and saw it, not through the fog of my initial response but simply as it was, a small, yellow house that had seen better days. Indicating, perhaps, an impoverished organization with a dwindling membership, like so many similar historical organizations back in New England. Not frightening, I told myself, but sad. And having convinced myself that my misgivings were just a leftover effect of my eerie dreams, I made the biggest mistake of my life.

I stepped inside.

The group that waited for us within was small, just three men including Haversham, and one woman. The neatest and most professional looking of the men turned out to be the house's owner, Doctor Clifford Henning. He greeted me and introduced the remaining members, a husband and wife named Frank and Dorothy Copper.

The living room was set up for an informal presentation, with the five members of the Court taking their seats on a pair of well-worn settees, positioned in a 'v'-shape. A coffee table sat before them and several glasses sat upon it, half drunk. The doctor and Mr. Cooper both reached for their glasses as they sat. At the front of the room was an old lectern, and I stepped behind it and took a deep breath, attempting to steady my shaken nerves.

A woman whom I had not seen before, and assumed to be Doctor Henning's house keeper, stepped into the room and brought me what appeared to be a glass of spirits. I took it, gratefully, and took a sip before I began, savoring the smoky taste of the whiskey. I talked of flimmern-geists for over an hour, drinking two full glasses of whiskey in the process, to calm my nerves. I covered the history of the term itself and the legends surrounding both how a flimmern-geist was created and where it resided when it was not menacing someone on the earthly plane. That was the area that seemed to spark the most interest in the group.

"This place they inhabit," Doctor Henning asked, "is it accessible from our world?"

"The method of doing so varies according to culture," I replied. "But certainly. One medieval European tome references human sacrifice. More recent volumes suggest some sort of ritual, usually involving vision."

"Vision?" Mrs. Copper inquired.

"Yes. Because the flimmern-geist exists in a realm visible from the corner of the eye, finding a way into that realm inevitably involves entering through that vision. A Germanic volume from the 15th century suggests removing the eyes altogether, but Jakob Bohme believed that you could open the doorway by staring, unblinking, for a period of time."

"For how long?" Again from Doctor Henning.

"A significant but not impossible amount of time. It's not specified in the work, but these sorts of stories are usually vague. I suspect that it's more important that the length is meaningful to the practitioner. Folklore suggests that ritual or spell is more about achieving a state of mind than following a precise set of instructions. Perhaps an hour would be appropriate, but I imagine that even an hour would be close to impossible to actually achieve."

Now that my presentation itself had drawn to a close, I could feel the whiskey going to my head. I wanted nothing more than to ask Margaret Haversham to return me to my hotel, but my audience still had questions they were determined to ask.

"Where would such a ritual have to take place?"

"I think that would vary depending on the flimmern-geist you were attempting to reach. The best place would be where the spirit had met its violent end, I suppose. Could I sit down, I really am feeling very light headed."

"Of course you are," Henning said, taking me by the arm and guiding me to the couch. "That would be the laudanum." I tried to pull away in alarm, but my muscles no longer seemed to be responding to my commands. The faces of my hosts seemed to be distorting in horrible ways, shimmering and dissolving in the gaslight.

"Please," I mumbled, but found myself unable to finish the thought. I sought out Margaret's eyes and found them to be smiling in a hideous fashion. It was there, in her eyes, that I finally realized the full implications of my peril, and knew that there was absolutely nothing I could do to help myself. I was falling into the deepest blackness I had ever experienced and the last thing that I heard as I fell, filled me with an exquisite terror.

"Prepare my surgery..."

I woke outside, unable to move, my entire body racked with pain. I was strapped to a wooden framework, standing before a dark tunnel. The skin around my eyes felt unnaturally tight and I found that I couldn't close them. A wooden block was pressed against either side of my head, so that I couldn't turn my neck to look around.

I tried to voice a question, to ask where I was, what had been done to me, but all that came out was a harsh croak. A voice spoke softly beside me, the now chilling voice of Doctor Henning.

"Don't try to speak. You are dehydrated from the procedure. You'll just do yourself further harm."

My eyes ached and itched and I tried desperately to force my lids closed, to no avail. Henning walked around in front of me and smiled.

"Let me." He held up a glass dropper and let its liquid fall into my eyes, each in turn. It felt soothing, and I fought back the ridiculous urge to thank him for his kindness. "You are probably wondering where you are, yes?"

I nodded as best I could with the confines of my restraints.

"This is the entrance to Illchester Tunnel, finished by the B&O railroad just seven years ago. It is where Black Thom is said to have lost his life, in the final explosion that cleared the tunnel. It is Thom that haunts this place, Thom that brings us here tonight. There is a story that has begun to circulate, that if you can stare into the mouth of this tunnel for an hour, as you yourself suggested, unblinking, then you can open a doorway and let Thom through. Once you've seen him, though, well, he becomes attached. Each time you close your eyes after that, he gets just a little closer. The only way to hold him at bay is to refrain from blinking completely."

There I heard Mr. Haversham laugh. "You don't have to worry about that part, Professor," he said. "The doctor has sown your eyelids open, you see. You cannot blink. So, Thom will not be able to harm you."

I became aware that the rest of Henning's murderous group was there, unseen, behind me. I couldn't see anything but the tunnel in front of me and I wondered how long I had left, how long I had been staring into the darkness.

My body tensed and tried to recoil in horror, but it could not move. What felt like leather straps bound me expertly to the wood. I could only see in front of me, down the darkened tunnel, but my vision was adjusting to the darkness, and with the full moon in the sky it seemed that I could now see through to the other side.

"You are wondering, why?" Henning asked.

I mouthed the word 'yes' as carefully as I could, and the Doctor nodded.

"Of course you are," he said. "It must seem unfathomable to you. We have no interest in meeting Black Thom, we shall leave that pleasure for you. Our interest is entirely in what lies on the other side of that doorway. You spoke briefly with Mr. Haversahm, I believe, about lost Carcosa. It is an ancient city on the shore of the black Lake Hali, not far from fabled Hastur. During the day it is lit by twin suns, and by night it is circled by strange moons. It is ruled over by a King in Yellow, whom we have served faithfully for many years. It is our destiny to join his court in Carcosa, so we have searched for many years to find the way there."

"You shall open the doorway for us," Margaret said. "When Thom comes through, we shall slip past him, into that ancient land."

I fought hard against the dryness in my cracked throat and managed to whisper, "why me?"

"There seems to be one more vital component to the ritual. Belief. We have tried this experiment twice before, but our offerings didn't understand, they didn't believe the gateway would open, therefore it did not. We decided that our next attempt should be someone who understood the ritual in a way that would brook no disbelief. Your background as an expert in this sort of folklore made you the perfect candidate."

From that point onward, Henning fell silent, like the others. He stepped back from my view and left me to my own horrified contemplation. Every few minutes, he would step forward and drop liquid into my eyes, to keep them from drying out in the night air. The world nearest me seemed to fall from focus and the end of the tunnel become sharp in my vision. I could see the trees gently moving in the breeze outside the end of it.

What felt like an eternity later was marked first by footsteps, then by the blurry sight of the five Knights of the Yellow Court making their way down to the far end of the tunnel and taking up their places alongside its inner walls.

I knew then that it wouldn't be much longer.

It started as a shimmering, like a dark reflection on a pool of water. Then I could see the lake from my dreams, and the darkly gleaming city beyond. A figure stepped forward, no longer on the far side but on the closest shore, and water dripped from his tall, tilted hat as he stepped into the tunnel.

He stood there, in the pale light, and as the Knights stepped through the doorway the world seemed to blink, in and of itself. They were no longer stepping onto the shore of Lake Hali. Now the vision through the end of the tunnel showed me that damned yellow house, and as the Knights stepped through, they screamed in horror, a scream unlike anything I had ever heard, a scream I felt in my very bones and organs.

Thom stood there in the tunnel, unmoving, as I watched Doctor Henning and his friends torn to bloody shreds by nothing, watching the blood and meat fly from their bodies like bits of mud and tree branch in a storm. Even amidst all the flying gore, the house remained untouched, it's yellow color almost iridescent now, in the darkness.

Some time after that, the world darkened. I lost consciousness along with the last of my hope, and fell into a dreamless nothingness. I don't know how long I was gone, but the world was bright when I woke, and I was on the ground along the side of the tunnel. It was a train rumbling through that woke me and I watched it in utter disbelief that something so normal could still exist in this world.

My body was no longer bound! Someone (or something) had loosened my straps and freed me, although my eyes were still held firmly open and had dried out to the point that my vision was cracked and painful. I got to my feet and stumbled away from the tunnel, but not before one final look down that menacing tunnel.

In its darkness, I could still see the shape of Black Thom, standing there, waiting patiently for me to blink.

That was two days ago. I'm back in the yellow house, now. It was a three mile walk from the tunnel, but I encountered no one along the way. Not that it matters, no one could help me now.

I expected to find the housekeeper here, but she is gone. The place holds no signs of life but mine own. My eyes remain open and will stay that way until the end. It's the only way to keep him out there, at the edge of my vision. I apply the drops as frequently as I can remember, but truth to tell, it no longer seems to matter. The damage seems permanent.

I leave this record to warn others. I don't know how long I'll be able to maintain things as they are. I expect I may have another day or so, but it may be only hours. Once I'm gone, I think Thom will return to the other side, as long as no one is foolish enough to repeat the ritual. But I've been looking through Doctor Henning's papers and it looks like there are other disciples of the Yellow King, and I can only hope they read this before trying to find their way through to lost Carcosa.

The King in Yellow is a mad king, do not follow him into the darkness. Let Carcosa stay lost and let Black Thom rest under the black stars.

THE FLIMM

William Couper

This tale was passed to us verbally by the Henry family. It was presented as if the family themselves didn't believe it to be true, but they had heard of the research we were doing and they wanted to pass it along. Author Couper interviewed several members of the family in order to best reconstruct the following events.

The truck sputtered and wheezed as Willard passed the town limits. The gas he had traded for a couple of days ago was almost gone, the engine must have been running on dust and sand for over a week. He grumbled and pleaded with the truck as it shuddered and slowed down. The power waned, and it trundled to a halt with a final cough.

Women walking along the street gave him strange looks. He knew he did not look like he belonged there. Tall, wiry and drawn, as he was, his skin leathery. His tatty, dusty coveralls and distressed shoes were a stark contrast with the women's flowery dresses and shiny footwear.

He kept his eyes on the ground, yet he could not ignore every gaze or each time a woman would cross the road to avoid him. He wanted to tell them he meant no harm, but he was afraid trying to talk to them would attract more attention. That kind of attention could escalate, and he did not want to attract the attention of the police. He had no good answers for their inevitable questions.

His trudge along the street brought him to a general store and he stopped. There was no money in his pocket, the last time there had been any money in his pocket was somewhere in Kentucky.

Since then he had traded his skills as a laborer for food and other supplies. It was sparse and difficult, but better than the alternative.

He stared at the shop, unsure of what to do. His plan had been to carry on through the town, but the truck's plans had not included that. What he was contemplating was a bad idea. He walked in.

Two women browsing the shelves looked round and treated him to horrified expressions, before they scurried out of the shop.

The shopkeeper, who had been adjusting the merchandise behind the counter, turned and looked confused. His gaze fell on Willard and he pursed his lips.

"You spooked a couple of my regulars," he said, but he did not sound angry.

"Sorry, sir."

"You are about as not local as can be, aren't you?"

"I've come a ways."

"That's the truth. Looking for anything in particular?"

"Not as I can think."

"You're not a good liar, though."

"What?"

"You've been eyeing these cans like a dog who's gonna snap one up in their mouth and run."

Willard said nothing.

The shopkeeper laughed. "Don't worry, I'm not going to tell anyone your secret. Looking at you, I don't think it's much of a secret."

"Are there any jobs going?"

"The biggest employer around is the old mill, but I don't think they're hiring right now."

"Thank you kindly, sir. Sorry to have bothered you."

"Now, now, don't take it on so, young man. I didn't say no one in town was looking to hire someone. As a matter of fact, I've been considering it."

Willard narrowed his eyes at the shopkeeper. His journey from Oklahoma to Maryland had shown him many things, but few to give him faith in the charity of strangers, especially employers.

"I think I'd best go," Willard said.

The shopkeeper rushed from behind the counter in what looked like a practiced move. "Hey! You're not one for trusting, are you?" he said. He looked around the shop and looked along the street. "Things will be quiet here for a while. Come along."

The shopkeeper guided Willard out of the store by the shoulder and locked up. Willard hesitated, but the insistent pressure of the other man's hand on his shoulder moved him along.

"You're obviously a man in serious need of vittles. When was the last time you ate?" the shopkeeper said, between occasional waves to people on the street.

"A couple days ago."

"I've got some stew on the stove, a bowl of that will have you right as rain in a jiffy."

"Won't your boss be aggrieved you closed up his store?"

The shopkeeper laughed. "Old Mister Henry won't be a problem. Because I'm old Mister Henry. Jacob Henry," he offered his hand.

Willard took it and replied, "Willard Jenkins."

"Pleased to make your acquaintance, Willard. My family's run that store since we came over from the old country going on a century now. Ellicott City's become my family's seat, you could say."

Willard allowed Jacob to guide him further through the town. A short while later they walked up to an impressive-looking stone house. Not quite a mansion, it was one of the larger homes Willard had seen.

Inside was quiet and chilly. There were several mirrors

hanging on the walls and more as they went through the house, into the kitchen. As Jacob said, there was a pot sitting on the stove, and from the stove came a soothing warmth. A sturdy table with one chair sat in the middle of the room.

"Have a seat," Jacob said.

Willard looked around the room, marveling at the electrical devices. His gaze was drawn to an object on the table. He wanted to touch it but was too fearful in case it was fragile.

"Don't you have a wife to do that?" Willard said.

"I was married once, for a while. It didn't take. She's long gone now," Jacob replied with a shrug. He kept stirring the pot.

In a few minutes Jacob put a steaming bowl of meaty stew in front of Willard. While Willard slurped down the food, Jacob retrieved another chair.

"I don't get many visitors these days. I should dig out some more furniture," Jacob said.

"Oh, I couldn't impose."

"You're not imposing. You'll be earning your keep in the store. Most of your money will be coming back to me. Eventually you will have enough money to get yourself a little place. For now, you stay under my roof and come with me to work in the store."

"That's mighty kind of you, Mister Henry."

"Well, you look like a hard worker who needs a chance to get back on his feet."

Willard looked down into his bowl and his appetite fled him. He kept spooning meat and vegetables into his mouth, but the savor was gone. He thought of the strangled farm, desolate after years of producing crops. The day he and his family left. The camps. The fights.

His gaze was drawn back to the camera.

"One of my little indulgences. I like to photograph things," Jacob said.

He picked up the camera, stood up, took off the lens cap and aimed the lens at Willard. A snap and Willard was blinded by white.

"Sorry about that. The flash takes everyone by surprise. Once this roll of film is developed you'll be part of my collection." Jacob grinned. His eyes darted to look above Willard's head. "I've been gone from the store long enough. I'll be back in a couple hours. Can you read?"

"A little."

"There are books in the den if you like. There might even be a newspaper around somewhere. Make yourself comfortable."

After Jacob left, Willard sat in the kitchen, drumming his fingers. He explored the first floor. Most of it was open, except for two doors. One, he guessed, went down into the basement. The other door had a symbol carved on it, a circle with a line through it running up and down. Right across from this door was another mirror.

He stepped away from the door, eyeing the symbol. As he walked to the den, he realized the mirrors were placed in such a way that the reflections showed the symbol. Even in a far corner of the den, the symbol was inescapable.

There were a few books in the den, some of which he was comfortable enough to pick up and start reading. After a while he kept being drawn to the symbol and what comfort there had been ebbed away. It felt like it was watching him. He roamed the house, even breaking through his fear of going upstairs, and found there was nowhere to escape the reflected symbol.

Upstairs he found another curiosity. There were framed photographs. In some of them was a pretty, blonde woman in her late thirties or early forties. All these photographs were taken outside, at different times of the year. One feature was prominent in all of them and in most of them became the true subject. A tunnel. He had seen many like it, some much longer. A railway tunnel cut through a hill, nothing out of the ordinary, yet with each new one he saw, the more upset he became. With the symbol looming everywhere he looked, he was certain he had to get out of the house.

He rushed downstairs and pulled on the front door. It did not budge. Jacob had locked him in. He ran to the other side of the house, where he had seen another outside door. This was also locked.

As he cast around to find something to smash the glass on the door, the front door opened. Jacob walked into the kitchen carrying a box of groceries.

"Why did you lock me in?" Willard said.

Jacob held his free hand up, smiling. "Take it easy, fella. It wasn't anything to do with you, just a habit I have. I've been living on my own for a long time. Sorry to give you such a scare."

"There's something unnatural going on around here."

"You've well and truly spooked yourself there, friend."

Willard made to walk past Jacob. Jacob stood in his way, laughing. Even though Jacob was shorter than Willard, he was broader, and what Willard thought was fat, he now realized was muscle. Willard had underestimated men like this and been on the hard end of a beating. There were weapons nearby and he wondered if he could lay a hand on one.

"Get out of my way," Willard said.

"I'll let you go once you've taken a few breaths and told me what's got you so riled up."

"Your house ain't right, sir."

"It's a little large and can get a mite cold from time to time."

"The mirrors. The mark on that door back there."

Jacob laughed again. He was beginning to annoy Willard. He had to stay in control of himself, he had no convenient way to escape this time.

"The mirrors are a thing my mother and my grandmother did," said Jacob. "I've always found it comforting, but you're not the first to find it a little strange. I'm told you get used to it. That's what my wife said, anyway."

Willard tried edging to the kitchen door. Jacob, without seeming to notice, stayed in front of him.

"The mark," Willard said. He cast a quick glance at the front door, it seemed to be miles away.

"It's from the old country. Some superstitious claptrap about the Flimm. That came from my great grandparents, I'm told. It's harmless nonsense, I can assure you," said Jacob and indicated the dining table. "Please, relax. Tomorrow will be a big day for you and we need you to be at your best."

"You're not going to lock me in again, are you?"

"No. And to be certain, I will have another key made for you. We can't have my newest employee trapped in the house, can we?"

Willard stood, eyeing the door.

"Go if you like. I don't think you'll easily find someone as accommodating as I am. I've seen what local law enforcement do to drifters."

Willard knew too well what law enforcement in a lot of places did to drifters. He still carried bruises from nightsticks. He sat down at the dining table while Jacob unpacked the groceries.

"Speaking of the old country. You've given me an excuse to make something my grandmother used to make," Jacob said.

Willard, unwilling to trust Jacob, nibbled the dish made from potatoes, onions and sausages put in front of him.

Jacob studied Willard once they had both finished eating. His smile had taken on a thoughtful look.

"My grampy said you could trust a man with a good appetite. I've always found it true. There's an honesty you can't hide in someone who enjoys food," said Jacob.

"I haven't eaten like this in months, Mister Henry."

"It's some tough times for sure. With what's happening where you're from and all this strangeness in Europe, I think some common human decency is just the ticket."

"I haven't seen much of that in even longer, Mister Henry. Present company excepted."

"We should get you a sensible bedtime and washed up."

Jacob boiled a kettle and filled the fanciest bathtub Willard had ever seen. Once Jacob was gone, he settled into the warm water. Aches and hurts he had become used to died away, soothed by the warm water. Accumulated dirt sluiced from his skin in grey waves. He allowed himself to smile and close his eyes.

There was a shadow in the corner of the room.

He gasped and faced the corner. Empty. He had been certain as day that a tall man with a top hat was there. The door was closed, as was the window. He stared at the corner.

The good feeling gone, he got out of the bath and dried himself off with the towel Jacob had provided. Jacob had also taken away his coveralls and shirt, leaving him with a clean nightshirt.

He checked the bolt and it was in the locked position. It did not look like it had been tampered with.

Jacob was waiting for him when he came out of the bathroom.

"Let's get you into bed. I imagine it has been quite some time since you last lay in a proper bed," Jacob said.

"I've almost forgotten what it was like."

Willard tried to sound cheerful, but he was distracted by the photographs of the tunnel. He was curious about the constantly repeated pictures, however, the warmth of the bath had seeped into his mind and the drowsiness overwhelmed him. He would ask Jacob about them in the morning.

The bed was simple, the covers white, the mattress on a metal frame. It was far nicer than the cot he had slept in on the farm.

"I hope this will be good enough for you," Jacob said.

"It's just about the most beautiful thing I've ever seen."

"Well, you get a good night's sleep. I'll wake you bright and early tomorrow, and we can get to work."

"Thank you kindly, Mister Henry. I'm sorry I acted so earlier."

"Don't give it another thought. We can both agree you've gone through some rough times. You'll settle in just fine. Goodnight, Willard."

"Goodnight, Mister Henry."

Willard collapsed onto the bed and the last thing he heard as he fell asleep was the snap of the light switch.

His wrist hurt. Both wrists hurt. Willard woke up to find the room still in darkness. He was not alone. Someone grunted near his feet. More pain flared in his ankles.

"Wh–what's going on?" Willard cried.

"You woke up earlier than I had expected. No matter," Jacob said.

Willard tried to move, but his arms and legs were restrained. Coarse rope bit into the skin around his wrists and ankles. Jacob was not the only one in the room, or so Willard thought, as the tall silhouette standing behind him vanished in a moment.

"The Flimm has chosen you. You should feel honored. He took to you very quickly. He ignored Marsha for the longest time. I thought I was going to have to take her to the tunnel, but he understood what I was trying to do."

"Mister Henry, I don't understand."

Jacob loomed over him, eyes and teeth glinting in the low light. "We don't need to understand the Flimm. My family hasn't understood him since he appeared in our lives, around the turn of the century as my grampy told me, we simply knew what he was. He isn't even demanding, as long as he gets something occasionally. You don't need to go to the lengths those foolish yellow people went to. Terrible business that. Made some fine property unusable."

Jacob retreated. Willard blinked. The silhouette, the Flimm, stood next to his bed and vanished. His gaze went to the ceiling and he screamed. Etched into the plaster were dozens of circles with lines through them. He writhed against the restraints. He was held fast.

Blink. The Flimm leaned over him the way Jacob had. Before it vanished, he saw the black pits for eyes, tunnels to a terrible.

Jacob stood at the bedroom door and giggled.

Tears streamed from Willard's eyes and he blinked again. The cold, pale face was almost touching his before it disappeared.

He squeezed his eyes shut tight. He did not want to see that grinning face again. Something touched his eyelids. A rough brush. Willard groaned. Another unpleasant brush, scratchy. He tried to pull away. The bristly caress happened again. And again.

Too much, he opened his eyes. The eyes and mouth were opened impossibly wide. The darkness was even more terrible than he first thought and he screamed as it consumed him.

THE SHADOWGHAST

By Matt Lake

Author Lake explains below how he came to possess this piece, but it is worth noting one thing. Although he has redacted the name of the woman who sent him the piece, he did pass it to my team for verification. We can find no evidence of her existence and the address from which it was sent is now an empty lot.

Every so often, a story really gets under your skin. This is especially true when you stumble into the world of local folklore, and it's even more especially true when you pride yourself on doing serious research. That's why the story of the haunted trestle in Ellicott City has been bothering me so much lately. I heard a few mutterings about it a decade ago—at least I think I did, though I don't know how much of that comes from real memories and how much from false memory syndrome. Anyway, I couldn't find enough solid material on the subject to justify further research. There's nothing unusual about that—I could say the same about dozens of leads that never panned out—but this one keeps coming back and biting me in a big way.

Strange goings-on in Maryland have been a passion of mine for as long as I can remember, but when I was commissioned to compile a bookful of them, it became...well...not an obsession exactly; let's call it an abiding passion. I assembled thick piles of research for *Weird Maryland*, and was handed a massive dossier from the publisher too. I sent out feelers among my friends, their friends, and their friends' friends, and was deluged. It was a wild ride, a whole lot of fun, and a whole lot of work. And more than a decade ago, I met my deadline and moved on to the next project.

Then my book came out and to my bemused surprise, it became very popular. Libraries and bookstores and schools called me to make appearances to talk about the stories I'd covered. At these events, most people told me what they liked about the book, though some were more keen to point which of their favorite stories I'd either gotten wrong or missed out altogether. Some of those armchair critics appeared at book signing events. Some of them collared me while I was out with friends. One of them even showed up at my front door with a documentary crew once and got aggressive about it. (I wasn't too happy about that, as anyone who saw that documentary could probably tell.) But some of them wrote old-fashioned letters and mailed them to my publisher, and I have held onto them because it seemed like a respectful thing to do for anyone who would pony up the price of a postage stamp.

It was one of these letters that jump-started my interest in that old legend recently. I was sorting through my old letter files, and it caught my eye because the whole manila folder felt like a throwback to the last century. The letter was type-written on a kind of translucently thin paper that I'd not seen since the 1970s. The uneven indentation of the individual letters told me it had been banged out on an old manual typewriter by someone who had learned to touch-type and wasn't too strong in the pinkie fingers anymore. The shaky signature at the bottom of the page looked like the kind of loopy cursive that they stopped teaching some time between the world wars. And as if that wasn't evidence enough that this letter came from an elderly person, the writer introduced herself as a 93-year-old widow.

But the real kicker to this letter was that it described that old railroad trestle haunting, and it came with an unusual attachment: A photocopy of a narrative poem that described the legend in detail.

<Address redacted>
Ellicott City, MD 21043
January 11, 2007

RE: Weird Maryland

Attn: Matt Lake

Dear Sir,

We were given a copy of your book for Christmas this year. It was fun reading about the places and things that we have lived with all our lives. I haven't even finished the book yet, but one item came to my mind as I browsed, and since I am now 93 years old, I figured that if I want to add to the mix, I had better tell what I know now.

I am referring to a story that a cursory glance at your index shows is not in your book. I live in the town of Ellicott City, having returned here in my widowhood to share an old family home that used to belong to my uncle. As I was growing up, my uncle used to tell us ghostly stories about a haunted railroad trestle on the edge of town. The details of the legend were always a little fuzzy to me, because I would plug my ears as I was genuinely scared by the tale. I never made a pilgrimage to the site. In fact, I would not have remembered the tale at all, were it not for a recent purge my granddaughter made of the contents of our attic.

My uncle was something of an amateur printer, and in a box in the attic, my granddaughter found his old letterpress. Now I'm sure that a man of letters like yourself will know about letterpresses, for they were a popular hobby in the 1920s among people who liked to write. It is a table top device bigger than a typewriter which can print one page at a time from a plate of moveable type. They are now becoming popular among collectors. In fact, when my granddaughter sold my uncle's letterpress in her antique shop recently, it fetched a pretty penny, let me tell you. Even the old print samples she found in the box alongside the press have raised interest among some collectors.

It is one of these print samples which prompted me to write to you today. I have had it Xeroxed and attach it with this letter. It is a poem which my uncle must have printed out long ago, which tells the tale of the haunted trestle on the edge of town. The poem as printed did not have a title, nor do I remember the name of the ghost who was supposed to haunt the railroad trestle, but for some reason, the name THE SHADOWGHAST springs to mind, so that is what I call the poem and the ghost which is its subject.

I do not know whether my uncle wrote the poem, or whether he himself transcribed it from a newspaper or book. Whatever its origin, I hope it provides an avenue for further research for your future ventures into the weirdness of our state. Perhaps you will include this legend in a future book.

Thanks for listening,

Sincerely,
<name redacted>

The photocopied pages that came with this cover letter looked old. The grain and rag of the original pages were clearly reproduced, and so was some obvious yellowing around the edges. They looked like loose pages ready to stitch and glue into an early Victorian chapbook, but something about the phrasing and content of the poem seemed a little more up-to-date. I've not studied narrative poetry since high school, but this one felt like something a smart journeyman writer might bash out for a quick paycheck in the 1920s rather than something a Keats or Browning would write. Or perhaps, as the widow who had sent it to me suggested, the poem was an amateur piece written by her uncle sometime in the 20th century.

Whatever the poem's origins may have been, its contents grabbed my interest immediately, and kept it until the last line.

The Tale
Of A Creature Not of This World
But Beheld In Dark Places

CANTO I
The Night of the Challenge

The wind was cold and at our backs;
We stood at midnight on the tracks
And stared into the tunnel, waiting for a sign.
I thought it was a schoolyard dare
That brought us standing, shivering there
I thought, "When it's all over, we'll be fine,"
We both ignored a chill at our spine,
"When it's all over we'll be fine."

They challenged us at the schoolyard gate
They called us afraid—that's a word we hate—
They said we lacked the courage to behave like men.
They told us where to go when the sun went down—
To the trestle on the freight line, two miles out of town
Where the trains cross the river and the road, and then
Plunge into the tunnel running through the hill.

They said that brave boys go there, and it's quite a thrill.

They said that men had died there, on the rails long ago
When the rains were so heavy that the ground began to flow
And dragged a mudslide in the path of a speeding train.
The men that died that day were mourned
And the railroad company, roundly warned
That the town could not endure another instance of such pain.
So they engineered a sturdy tunnel through the hill
And the tunnel and its trestle both remain there still.

"Stand at midnight at the tunnel's mouth
Make sure that your right side is facing south
And stare through the tunnel till the clock strikes one.
Don't breathe a word and never blink
Don't pray or laugh, or even think.
Just stare through the tunnel till the ritual's done."
We assumed that this whole venture was all in fun
And that is how the creature won.

"Something will appear," they said as we walked by,
"You'll see him lurking in the corner of your eye,
And as soon as you see him, then all will be revealed.
For cowards, this secret will remain unknown,
If you learn it, then we'll find out
just how much you've grown"
So we accepted their challenge and our fate was sealed.
And so we stood there, wretchedly cold,
Hoping that our darkest fears would never unfold.

The clock tower chimed in the middle of the night
As the twelfth chime echoed, the tunnel seemed so bright
But not from hidden magic; we had grown used to the dark.
The staring and the cold made our eyeballs sting.
We stood and stared and waited for the final ring

THE SHADOWGHAST

Of the clock-tower, chiming one o'clock,
when we could leave our mark,
Secure in the knowledge we had passed the test,
And possessed a hidden secret unknown to the rest.

We stood almost an hour before that man-made cave
The only sounds were wind, and the river's rippling wave
And the clattering of teeth in my companion's mouth.
The fear began to rise as minutes passed by.
The shivering increased and we knew not why.
The wind suddenly dropped,
and in the distance from the south
We heard the clock tower chiming one:
The signal that our ritual was finally done.

We blinked our eyes in silence and began to walk,
Feeling far too idiotic to resort to talk.
We felt those youths had played a prank
on gullible young boys
and so we walked in silence on the road to town.
Our eyes, still sore from staring, cast in sadness down.
Our footfalls and the stream,
they were the only background noise.
We walked along in silence deep
And longed to be at home, asleep.

CANTO II
The Break of Dawn

The morning sun sliced through a chink in the curtain—
A shaft of light and dust—and I could not be certain
That our night-time escapade had not been a dream.
But I felt my heart lay heavy, there in my chest.
My limbs all ached; I yearned to have more rest,
Yet the time had to come to rise, and make it seem

That our adventure had been real—and a real mistake—
And so, to chase off sleep, I gave my head a shake.

The shaft of light and dust from the curtain's crack
Shimmered slightly as I rose and yawned
and stretched my back
And cast a moving shadow across the wall.
"The limb of the old birch, shaken by a gust,
Casting leafy patterns on the wall ... It must
Be that," my sleep-soaked mind surmised, and all
I thought of then was the morning chores:
The soap, the toothbrush, walk to school,
and sundry other bores.

I missed my friend on the walk to school.
Not wanting to be late
I walked alone up to the lurkers by the schoolyard gate
And could not resist the chance to raise a shout
"We stood at midnight on the track
We weren't afraid and never looked back
I guess that you don't know what it's all about."
The lurkers at the gate just smirked and said
"You'll see him soon enough, and you'll be dead."

"What do you mean by that?" I almost cried,
"A ghost appears to folks like you,
and all who've seen it, died."
Those lurkers at the schoolyard gate
had done it one more time
They taunted and they won, because we fell for it.
They measure you and judge, and they can tell you're fit
For mocking; so they perpetrate their crime
Make sure there are no witnesses, and then
Go on to find more victims, and taunt them over again.

THE SHADOWGHAST

It was then I thought I saw him, through the edges of my sight,
My companion from the ritual on the tracks last night.
And I knew these taunts upset him more than me.
So I set out in his direction to lead him a different way
But as I turned to face my friend, well, what more can I say?
The image of him vanished—there was nothing left to see—
I turned back toward the school gate, and realized my fears:
The lurkers had another chance to pelt me with their jeers.

They day went by but my friend did not come
I missed him, of course, but my senses were numb
From too little sleep and too much aggravation.
So I resolved to visit him as soon as I could
Though I needed to rest, I knew that I should
Take that walk uphill from the station
Take a left turn and a right, and knock on his door
Give him homework, and leave, and nothing more.

But at his door, his mother waved me off, and turned away
"He's ill," she said, "Too ill." and that's all that she would say,
Then shut the door in my expectant face.
She said the same the next day, and the next day still.
Her face was drawn with worry, and she herself looked ill
But every time I turned away, for a second, in that place
In the corner of my eye, I swear I saw him leaning
A little closer every time. And now I know the meaning.

CANTO III
The Shadow Falls

The wind was cold against my face
This evening. I increased my pace
Along the street that led to my friend's home.
I knew his folks would send me back again,
And claim he was still ill, and then

Demand I turn around and trudge back home alone.
But not tonight! I would not turn around.
No, not tonight. Tonight, I'd stand my ground.

The street was busy for that time of night
At almost every door a person stood,
at the edge of my line of sight
But I forged straight ahead to see my friend.
I reached his door, but instead of making sound
I quietly tried the handle, pushed the door,
and stood my ground.
The door swung open to a hallway; at the end
Of which a tall thin shadow faced
Me, dark and featureless, and my heart raced.

I flinched and blinked and gaped, and then
He wasn't there. My heart still pounded. I looked again,
And told myself I'd fallen into fear just like a child.
Those lurking taunters at the schoolyard gate
Had done their work; those people that I hate
Had planted fear inside my head; a fear that so beguiled
Me, it lodged an image inside me:
I was seeing things I could not see.

So I stepped across the threshold, crept along the hall,
Careful not to make a sound, I barely breathed at all
Until I reached the foot of the stair
When I heard voices, but could hear no word
A muttered conversation that could not be overheard
So of course, I paused and strained my ears there
But all I heard was "cannot see,"
A phrase that made no sense to me.

So step by silent step, I climbed the stairs
Crept past the reading nook with its cushioned chairs

And to the room in which my friend was lying
At the door I heard no sound
So I turned the handle, looked around
And opened up his door.
His eyes were red from constant crying
His face was pale, his mouth was strained
Into a caricature of a scream of pain.
"It's only me!" I hissed at him "I'm here!"
His eyes half-closed, which pushed out a tear
That slowly welled into a drop that slid
across his face and lost its form.
"He's here too," his gurgling voice sobbed out
"Can you see him too?" He cast his eyes about
As if his mind, unhinged, could see a swarm
Of hostile creatures all around.
He flinched at all these phantoms,
cast his eyes down to the ground.

He blinked. Then abject terror etched across his face.
He thrashed his body all over the place
And gurgled from some place deep inside.
His family's feet were hard upon the stairs,
His mother's voice was chanting Catholic prayers,
My back against the wall, I tried to hide.
"Oh GOD!" he shouted, choked, and finally sighed
"He's reaching out!" and muttered as he died.

CODA
Twilight in the Corner of my Eye

This place is cold. I don't know how I came
To be here, but I'm lying here just the same,
And looking all around me.
I dare not speak or even think
Or look away or even blink

I don't know how or why, but he has found me.
He is hiding in the shadows everywhere.
I cannot see him, but I know he's there.

And that, as they say, is all she wrote. I wish there were more, because the contents of this old folder raised many more questions than it answered. Just as it was back when I was on a tight deadline for producing books of Maryland lore, the tale of this haunting is frustratingly hard to pin down. Is it fiction or nonfiction? Folklore or fake lore? It's just too hard to verify.

Did the legend inspire the poem? Or did the story originate with this poem, and become attributed to the uncle's local railroad tunnel? Or are the two completely unrelated but similar enough that one old widow lumped them together under one heading?

I wish I knew. By now, the widow who wrote to me is probably dead; she's certainly not at the address she provided in her letter. Nobody that shared her last name seems to have ever lived in Ellicott City. And name searches through national databases are also coming up blank. Also elusive is the origin of the poem: It's not attributed to anyone—heck, it doesn't even have a title—and I can't locate it or any mention of it in the anthologies and databases I usually turn to for answers.

So this story is still sticking in my craw after all these years. Most of the lore that crosses my desk I can either verify or ignore. Usually, a little digging—or the passage of time—will turn up answers to mysteries like these. But not in this case. This one keeps coming back, with a few more details added and a lot more questions raised. Some day I hope I'll have enough solid research to plant this story, either in a proper nonfiction book or in the ground, but that day hasn't come yet. I'm beginning to doubt it ever will.

DEAD IN VEGAS: ONE NIGHT ONLY

By Seth Adam Kallick

This story was found, more or less as is, in a steamer trunk in an attic in Hagerstown, Maryland. The trunk appears to have belonged to the figure referred to in the story as Curly Joe. The name has been changed because it was associated with a very wealthy family of some standing in the community. How the appearance of that character in the story reconciles with the actual name provided is hard to imagine, but lawyers have advised us not to include it here without hard evidence.

I want to tell you a story about John and Jane, a love story if you will. Oh, I'm no poet I swear, in fact you should bear in mind that, despite it being Valentine's Day, I remain humbly cynical about the whole affair.

Damn, there I go again, forgive me.

They weren't your typical high school sweethearts, no one introduced them at a young age. Love had not blossomed some Spring afternoon where the sun was a particular shade of orange sherbet, the smell of flowers did not float on the breeze to be remembered at every special moment in their lives. Their path to togetherness was not some fine woven tapestry that you could cozy up with in the wintertime, more like a security quilt frayed and stained from years of anguish that you can't seem to ever part with. I lost my first tooth when my mother ripped my yellow blanket from my hands. The corner part I liked to chew on had these loose strings that sometimes would get caught in my mouth. She had insisted it was time to throw in the towel, so to speak, and proceeded to separate me from my favorite thing. Instead my tooth flew into the air like popped corn. Mama was so excited she forgot to throw it away.

See? Now I'm getting side-tracked.

That's what love does to you, it makes you get all googly-eyed, you start blabbering on and on about this and that all while the poor waiter just wants to take your breakfast order.

"Oh, so and so only takes their eggs over-medium so they can sop up the runny bits with slightly burnt white toast, they are a terror without their morning coffee."

Barf.

Whatever you read about love, whichever movie you like to compare the journey your heart has taken over the years, the recompense for being so damn lovable? Hollywood bullshit machinations at their best. Trashy romance novels, gripping Euro-lit post-war rekindling of child-hood sweethearts, yuk. Dumas knew what he was talking about when he charted Edmund Dantes transformation in the Count of Monte Cristo. Spending his remaining years in solitude after having told his absolute love to take a long walk off a short pier, they weren't getting back together after 17 years of wrongful imprisonment. He wasn't rushing to her side after he'd vanquished his arch-nemesis who had taken his intended as his own. Only in some cotton-candy imaginary world would anyone let that shit slide.

Now, songs?

Well, we all know that music's core DNA is made up of two types of songs, love & the loss of love. Somehow music is the only medium that can capture true beauty, actual feelings transposed into a colorful loom of pain and joy. That long car ride after you break up with someone, oh that is the fucking worst. Every damned song seems like it was meant to point out all the failures, the cheating, the sorrow, a personal attack finding you no matter which station you change the radio to. However long it takes to get over that special one, that song will always carry the pain, instantly transporting you back to that same moment in time.

How come it always hurts?

One thing that is for certain, no matter how much you may fall for someone the return investment will never be equal for love is an ever-shifting amoebae, mutating daily for better or worse. That kind of uncertainty can cause some extreme reactions, mental and physical. Ask any cop how many domestic dispute calls they answer in one evening and I'll bet you it equals the amount of doughnuts eaten in one sitting. When love starts taking this kind of turn, blaming the power of it as an excuse to commit heinous acts, well history is littered with those stories.

"Crimes of Passion" they're called.

The old Charles Atlas ads vowed to "Make You A Man!" in only seven days. In that time you could build your weakling physique up to He-Man proportions to eventually beat-up the galoot that stole your lady. What the ad never showed was our hero, having vanquished the bully and won back his love, summarily strangled her to death for being unfaithful with his powerful new muscles.

Isn't that how all good love stories end?

Lights.

All twinkling under an onyx blanket hidden away in the middle of the desert, they could be seen from a hundred miles away, a beacon of wonderment shining hot in the cold night. Some flickered, others flashed, even more blinked in unison with the heartbeats of those who came to seek their fortunes. The kaleidoscope of reds and greens, the white arcing tracers, aqua and long, swam freely to the low din murmur rising up from the palm tree lined boulevard. Hints of perfume, sizzling steaks bloodying a cutting board buffet hung in the ether, seeking purchase in the nooks and crannies of the Nevada city.

It was unlike anything John had ever seen.

Sipping his cocktail, gin martini extra dirty three olives, an overwhelming sense of nostalgia passed over him. John shuddered, arm raised as he sipped from the martini glass, careful not to spill the precious medicine. Moving delicately along the tarred roof of the Dunes hotel casino he sat down on the edge careful to put his drink down before dangling his feet like a kid over a train bridge. John picked up the martini going straight for the skewered olives, popping one into his mouth and savoring the briny explosion. The memory flooded into his head once again.

His grand folks had taken him to the circus one summer. They had saved for quite some time to take young John. This was before the bad times. Enthralled by the clowns, mesmerized by the flying acrobats his young imagination had been truly awoken. Then he saw them, majestic and beautiful. John could see the wisdom in their eyes, he could smell their sadness. That and their shit.

The elephants wore jewel encrusted saddles, ornate face masks reflected the high beam lights throwing twirling swirls of color upon the big-top's tent. John had fallen in love with elephants that day. The thought of them brought him joy like no other, so much so he had one tattooed on his left bicep, well the skeleton of one anyway. It was a reminder that even the most regal of creatures ends up taking a dirt nap eventually. John touched his arm where his elephant lay dormant. Under his shirt, beneath his suit coat, he could feel it pulse with that of his heart's beat. Another sip of the martini and the moment passed giving way to insight. The lights and costumes of the circus weren't enough to wash away the smell of animal feces. It did nothing for the look of sorrow written plainly on the dancing bears, the beasts of burden pretending to be content.

It felt just like that here.

"Las fucking Vegas."

He drained the remainder of the martini wishing he had brought the shaker with him before sauntering out on the roof to admire the town. John rubbed his other shoulder, the one with her name inked forever into his flesh. He smiled then burped satisfyingly into the warm air. Down below dreams were coming true. On the street under his dangling feet millions were being both won and lost simultaneously in the blink of an eye.

"Shit!"

John dropped the glass, its shattering lost in the buzz of the town, a pain racked his temples. Somewhere behind his eyes there was a bright spark of something then it was gone. He shook his head a few times placing the palms of his hands against his face. He would need another drink to cure what was most likely a combination of jet-lag, exhaustion and relief. His sleep had not come easily of late and he had given up the urge to pass out when the bell-boy locked the hotel room behind him. He chose rather to take some of the dusk atmosphere into his lungs and some liquor into his belly.

John's head had begun to clear thanks to the gin. He was breathing a little easier now, finding it more and more difficult to shake the weird vibe he had noticed. It had started a few days earlier, no surprise considering the events that had transpired. Maybe he was feeling guilty? The headshrinker who had been sitting next to him in 3B had suggested this on their way from Dulles.

"Is it true that everyone wants to screw their mothers?" John asked.

This simple question set the good doctor off on a crash-course into modern psychiatric medicine of which John was captivated. Soon he was casually chatting about his love-life.

"Can I make a confession, doc?"

"Well, it doesn't quite work like that, John. Although if you give me a dollar bill it would fall under doctor/patient privilege, assuming I decide to take on a new one that is."

John reached into his wallet careful not to let the doctor see the wad of cash he was carrying; he pulled a bill and gave it over.

"And as long as you don't tell me about a crime, otherwise I need to report it to the proper authorities," the doctor chuckled.

For a moment John thought the jig was up, that here even before he opened his mouth the truth was known, exposed by this wizard. No, that couldn't be. He was a charming man, people enjoyed getting his attention. His coolness had a touch of bad-boy which had never been a problem with the babes and oddly enough men wanted to know him, to impress him somehow. John had a knack for getting what he wanted. A real snake-charmer.

"I did just kill my wife," he said grinning.

His new psychiatrist looked lost, eyelids opened wide as he took in John's words. He summarily chuckled shaking his finger.

"Ha-hum, you certainly are a wisenheimer, John!" he said, laughing.

John made a face like he was a kid caught reading horror comics late at night by his father.

"I like you, doc," he said, giggling.

The last hour of the flight was spent in silence. Doctor Slocum, as he was introduced, had spoken about repressed guilt and that it didn't matter how long ago something occurred, the human sub-conscious kept detailed records. Hence dream interpretation has been a link in identifying crippling psychological pain that the mind has seemingly forgotten about. He prescribed Valium for John and good rest, then he went about his paperwork leaving John to his own thoughts.

Soon they would be on the ground and John would need a stiff drink. She would be meeting him at the hotel. His heart swelled at the thought of her healing spirit, not to mention her lips. John closed his eyes, picturing the last time he had seen her. When he opened them he was no longer on the airplane.

The baggage claim was empty, no one was waiting for luggage. John spun to a shadowy figure.

"You lost, buddy?"

John jumped a mile in the air. The security officer did not look amused, it was late and he was almost ready to settle in with a 12-pack of beer.

"I, a-aaaa, I was on flight 179 f-fr-from Dulles," John replied jittery.

"Lemme see your ticket."

John produced his ticket stub padding himself down to make sure he had everything on him, he grabbed his crotch to make sure that was still there.

"This flight got in an hour ago, guy."

The security officer was sizing up John. If he didn't figure out what was going on soon this lug might call the actual cops and no one needed that.

"Yeah, I had some bad fish on the plane. It's coming out of both ends if you know what I mean? I guess I'm just dehydrated."

The officer gave back him his ticket. He grabbed John by the shoulder escorting him towards the office.

"Let's go find your bags, sir and then we can get you some water."

John stopped.

"Actually, I think I need to hit the head again," he grabbed his stomach.

The officer agreed to bring his luggage, promising to return in a jiffy. Waiving acknowledgment John scrambled to his namesake.

A man was standing in front of one of the sinks in the

bathroom, his shirt and jacket were crumpled in a heap by his feat, a sodden white tank top held a moderately large belly, poorly, exposing hairy flab. The man looked at John as he barged in, casually wiping his armpits with a towel.

"You best be careful, my friend or she will chew you up and spit you out," he said.

John's chest began to tighten.

"Beg your pardon?"

The stranger continued his cleaning ritual.

"This friggen' place, am I right? Vegas, she is one fickle bitch."

John ignored the last remark, instead heading to the urinal to take a most satisfying leak, his nerves calming down as his bladder emptied. The heavy ammonia smell that lingered on the surface of the airport bathroom was enough to make his eyes sting. It kept the hidden reek at bay with gallons of bleach. It was head-ache inducing. With burning vision, John flushed his waste and returned to the wash basin to rinse his face, taking inventory of the cuts and scrapes he wore on his hands.

A viscous sneeze, loud and wet, ripped through his body and sprayed phlegm against the mirror in splotches. John waited for the inevitable second one, (his always came in two's), when he caught his reflection. However, it wasn't the red flecks of blood that worried him nor the missing second sneeze that shook his bones to their core.

Someone had been right behind him.

John splashed water on his face, bags the size of half-dollars had set-up permanent residence there. A five-o-clock shadow darkened his visage hiding childhood acne scars. Gone was the hot-headed rebellion, the Romeo of the East Coast who roamed the open road on a chopper. Instead, a mediocre insurance salesman looked back through the same eyes. He hardly recognized himself.

DEAD IN VEGAS: ONE NIGHT ONLY

Eyes pinched wide John inched his face as close to the mirror as he could, desperate for the stinging feeling to go away, trying to chart the movement of the red lines that wove back to his baby blues and craving a dirty martini.

He couldn't see shit.

He produced a comb from an interior coat pocket, using the same amount of strokes he had used for years. John was ready to collect his luggage and the get hell out of this god forsaken airport for good. A small scratch, the shape of a crescent moon, had appeared just under his left cheek. John was too busy daydreaming about being locked behind a secure hotel room to notice. Hurrying to leave, seemingly unaware of his surroundings, he slammed into the janitor who was only trying to mop up the last bathroom on his way to clocking out. Both men took a spill, landing on their respective asses.

"Jumpin' Jeebus, mister you seen a ghost?" asked the janitor.

John sat up, shaking his head in frustration. He blinked his eyes in embarrassment. When he opened them the bell-hop was standing before him, hat in hand. The young man in all red coughed politely into his white gloved hand.

"Oh, oh yeah... sorry," John said, reaching into his coat pocket to produce a dollar tip.

He couldn't remember getting to his room nor leaving the airport and yet here he was, checked in and walking over to the makeshift bar. Pouring the martini, John tried to retrace his steps from exiting the plane. Try as he may it was like peering through heavy fog with only a small flashlight to guide the way. Gulping the drink in one large swallow, John made himself another before taking a stroll through the luxurious hotel suite.

A set of cozy bathrobes hung on a rod next to the enormous tub, equipped with jets guaranteed to soothe and massage aching muscles. He fantasized about her washing her delicate skin with a soft cloth, smoking those little cigars she loved. Cigarillos, she had called them. John had thought it was sexy, to see her blow little smoke rings up into the air. He lit a cigarette before taking his drink to the roof.

So many lights.

The colors were fading, arcs of blues and oranges coursed their way up to the heavens where they kissed the blanket of darkness slowly making its way across the sky. It looked like sherbet in a bowl from where she was sitting.

"What a view," she said to no one.

She would be with her lover soon. Savoring the deep smoke from the little cigar she was puffing on, Jane relished in the comfort of the ritual. Finally over the stench of the things, she understood why people took such pleasure in the act of flooding their lungs with toxins, despite ads stating that smoking was the "It" thing to do. Jane liked the way she could bite down on the finely rolled tobacco leaf, getting a little buzz from the juice. It made her feel powerful.

Lately her senses had been thrown off course, a boat at sea without sail nor oars subject to the whims of Poseidon. Odysseus she was not, although her journey had followed her through the lonely island of marriage, fighting a beast greater than any cyclops, boredom. There had been this feeling once long ago, like capturing lightning in a bottle, when Jane had been young and impressionable. Invigorated by the raw energy, frightened by these foreign feelings, she'd stirred for the first-time in her young soul the unharnessed passion only read about in stories.

He had been casually sitting back on his motorcycle holding court, as he was known to do, in front of the Uncle Wigglies. The mid-afternoon sun cast a long shadow as he espoused his wisdom to the gathered ice cream store patrons, some listening intently, desperate to lick the melting dessert from the cone. Others were snobbishly worried his greasy hair and foul language would somehow make the rum ripple less enjoyable.

John.

Oh, how he had seemed so wise, so old compared to her fifteen-year-old self. At nineteen he had already lived through so much, as was his claim, apparently running off to join the circus when he was only nine. He had resurfaced a decade later, howling into town on a black chopper, leather jacket, bad-attitude, a regular rebel. Since his return there had been wide-rumored speculation to various degrees of absurdity about his missing whereabouts.

Jane cared nothing for the jealous whispers, he was everything the world said was bad, and that suited her desires more than she cared to admit at the time. She studied his movements, holding her history book close to her chest, the way he took a puff of the Lucky Strike, holding the thick white smoke in his open mouth only to shoot it out his nostrils like some mythical creature.

A living dragon prince.

They would fly away on his shiny motorcycle, cruising the open road with only the wind in their hair, she clutching his leather jacket, arms wrapped around him for life. All who witnessed their love would become jealous knowing that they would never be that happy themselves. For Jane, life was about finding a partner who could change you, bring out the very deepest person you always were meant to become. Life was too short to be speculated on, who we are and where we are going, all that talking about shit? Nah, it was better to burn out then fade away in Jane's estimation.

These dreams of fancy could be traced back to her unshakable fascination with the notorious Barrow Gang, more specifically the legend of Bonnie & Clyde. She had come across a magazine detailing their exploits, a sort of comic book, it had re-creations of their most famous last stand, bullet riddled and together. This love, this togetherness through living hell, this is what Jane fantasized about. Not so much the robbing and killing but the sheer force of nature driving these two lovelorn kids to a life of self-sustaining crime.

After Bonnie & Clyde were finally brought to justice and summarily executed, local newspapers began to circulate a poem that Bonnie Parker had penned entitled "The End of the Line," a haunting foreshadowing of events to come. She initially had given it to her mother who had then passed it on to a reporter, thus perpetuating the legend in newspapers around the country.

For Jane's twelfth birthday, an occasion which seldom brought joy, she received that very poem. Preserved carefully it had been inserted into a brown wooden frame that her step-father had made.

Normally not one to show too much affection, Jane couldn't keep a gruff exterior, especially when presented with such a thoughtful gift. She jumped into his lumbering arms thanking him profusely while planting little kisses upon his bearded cheek. Her step-mother looked on in disbelief, having never wanted to adopt the little brat to begin with. Her relationship with them became semi-normal as now she referred to him as Pop, choosing to hold a little resentment by continuing to call her step-mother, Betty.

The poem hung above her bed in the same spot that had once hung a cross.

Daydreaming, fantasizing about John had become her primary goal during the summer of 1948, which blossomed during a particular jovial Sunday matinee of "Abbot and Costello meet Frankenstein." In the balcony section of the old theater, her crush sat cramming popcorn into his mouth giggling like a school-boy. After all her reconnaissance and all of his showmanship, here now in the glow of the film screen did his inner-self shine bright and hot. He had been sitting all alone, so invested in Bela Lugosi he didn't notice her slip into the seat next to him until their hands met going for a handful of popcorn.

That's all it took.

They made arrangements to meet again the following weekend to catch "The Treasure of Sierra Madre." John had bought her snacks, marveling at the young woman that he was beginning to fall for. She endeared him afterwards, sharing pie and talking about the film at the local diner, and when she did a dead-on impression of Gold Hat, he laughed so hard milk came out of his nose.

"We don't need no stinking badges."

Laughing off the nostalgia of a time long lost, Jane reached for the book she was currently reading. It was called, "I Am Legend," and it was about the last man on earth. Flipping to about the half-way point, folded neatly between the pages was a piece of paper. Jane pulled this out and tossed the book back onto the little table sitting next to her chair careful not to spill what was left of her drink. She would need another.

Gently she unfolded the old newspaper clipping making sure not to tear any of the edges.

You've read the story about Jesse James
of how he lived and died;
If you're still in need
Of something to read
Here's the story of Bonnie and Clyde

The sixteen-stanza poem was as moving and poetic as the first time she had read it. Words held the true power over us, that and our emotions. Funny how things work. When Pop and Betty had died in a random boating accident, Jane's rage had consumed her. Just when she had been making some progress coming out of her shell, the only people who had given two shits were wiped out of her life forever. Jane had thrown the framed poem against her bedroom wall shattering the glass, sending chunks of wood every which way. She still bore the diamond scar along her right wrist from an ill-attempt at cleaning the mess up.

Her heart ached in sadness. The past is a dangerous place to swim, there's never a life-guard on duty, and you can sink into the deep end at any given moment. Bobbing and floating in the depths of first kisses and forgotten birthdays, sure you'll only spend a few minutes there, maybe clear up some long-lost grief. Most likely you'll spend the remainder of your life living in the past and before you know it you will look up and it will all be over. It always ends.

She longed for her love. Soon they would be together and the pool of the past would be drained and cemented up forever. There was only the future and the dimming sunlight signaling the end of day and the beginning of night.

Perhaps it was the jet-lag, disorientation from propelling oneself through the air to reach a far-off destination in record time. It could've been the martini gulped down in a quickened pace on an empty stomach. There was something about the stench of fish being served in an airplane cabin, whoever came up with that idea should be locked in the luggage overhead compartment with said fish. Just the memory of it was enough to send a gag reflex straight to John's mouth.

The dry Nevada air was a far cry from the frozen tundra of his native Baltimore. The weather when he touched down was a cool 82 degrees, not anywhere like the mid-drift snow he had abandoned. February in Maryland was wet and cold with sporadic bursts of warmth, just enough to piss you off.

The hairs on John's head stood at attention, someone had walked over his grave. That's what Sandy, the bearded lady from his circus days used to say while brushing her face with a wooden brush. Whatever it was called, it was starting to scare him. A serious case of the heebie-jeebies had crept up on him, sending his sense of time in all directions at once. John turned his neck quickly, sensing someone behind him.

"Oww, shit!"

The pain shot up his left side leaving his shoulder and neck throbbing and numb. He had almost forgotten he had been in a car accident. His heart dropped at the thought of losing her, his baby. How she used to look in the sunshine after a bath, sexy sexy. The Studebaker had been brand spanking new, candy-apple red with a tan hard-top. That he had sprung extra for the top was the only reason he was still breathing. The vehicle had flipped over several times as it plummeted down the embankment. This was all told to him afterwards in the hospital. He had suffered a torn rotator cuff, bruising on his arms and various cuts along his hands that appeared defensive in nature. After a few hours John was given some aspirin and sent home with instructions to stay awake for at least twenty-four hours lest his mild concussion prove to be more than just that.

John was hopeful that the Las Vegas trip would be a getaway. No one knew him here and money was the talk of the town, before he even landed he was already on the plus side rich. Another thing to get used to. He would have to make use of all the amenities the hotel had to offer, he deserved to be happy. Life had not quite gone according to his plan. The nostalgia machine had been turned on full and memory lane was cluttered with wrong decisions. The one bright spot was Jane, she who had tried to be so coy about shadowing him that summer oh, so long ago. He could tell that this was no ordinary teen-aged girl. Something inside her burned wild yet it was raw and untested.

Could this be the one true-love that was often spoken about in song?

John had continued to live care-free that summer, riding his chopper, swimming in Loch Raven reservoir, taking in movies. He had loved going to the movies every Sunday. A flask of whiskey hidden in the pocket of his leather jacket, popcorn in hand, he would ascend to the balcony taking solace in the dark where no one could bother him. She had followed him one particular day pacing herself at least one block behind him. John would casually turn around as if to notice a building or a particular storefront. Catching her out of the corner of his eye she would dart into an alley to avoid being seen.

With courage she had sat down next to him, careful not to interrupt the movie. When his hand made contact with hers, grabbing the popcorn, he had felt a little spark of lightning. She had sensed it as well because they both smiled at one another before settling in to finish the movie in silence. John couldn't remember how many movies they had seen together. It had begun a ritual for the two of them, lasting years. Time was wonky. John could remember that first movie and the last movie they had seen, particularly because Jane had screamed at him walking out of the film, stating she didn't appreciate the subject matter.

Black Widow, 1944, starring Ginger Rogers.

John had thought it was fascinating, staying to watch the credits and then again during the next showing, almost like he was taking mental notes preparing for some grand plan. A mark in time preserved in his thoughts and taking purchase at the Senator Theater. It was when he left the movie, walking home, John first had the thought that he could kill his wife and get away with it.

He needed another drink.

John picked up the white courtesy phone and punched "zero", casually rubbing his shoulder which had begun to hurt more and more.

"Front desk," the woman sounded pleasant.

"Yes, this is room 2004. Could you please send up a bottle of gin, vermouth, some olives and a rare t-bone with ketchup?"

"Certainly sir, we'll have it ready before you can blink."

"Wait...what?"

The line went dead.

John began to have a mild panic-attack, though he wouldn't know what it was, continuing to chalk up his behavior to all the wrong reasons. Never did it occur to him that fate was finally catching up with him. The bathroom light flickered before it turned on, buzzing something awful, like a thousand bees in a holding pattern above the world. The cold water felt good on his face. Looking at his eyes in the mirror, the blood-shot red would be less obvious in Vegas, he would fit in with the other hoople-heads.

Sin City.

Legend says whatever happens in Vegas stays in Vegas. It doesn't mention anything about the emotional baggage that comes attached with each doe-eyed individual hoping for a lucky roll of the dice, just one good hand of poker and then nothing but a check with a couple of commas to live off of forever. You have to admit that's quite the advertisement. Odds on changing your circumstances for better or worse seemed like a coin toss, a fifty-fifty shot is better than most will get on their best day.

Best to forget and move on.

He was already pacing around the room when the knock came.

"Room service."

John opened the door allowing the young man to wheel in the

cart, pushing past his suitcase which lay unmolested in the middle of the room. The bell-hop lifted the silver lidded tray revealing a bloody steak big and juicy, steam tendrils wafted to the high ceiling. John took a deep smell, closing his eyes to savor the aroma. When he opened them the vertigo was overwhelming. He found himself standing on the ledge of the roof's hotel. He dropped to his knees, careful not to step over the edge. They were only on the third floor, certainly a fall wouldn't be fatal, maybe a broken neck or ankle, still the black-out was enough to scare the shit out of him.

John's gut locked up causing a convulsion of sorts in his stomach. He leaned over the side of the hotel and proceeded to purge its contents. Undigested chunks of steak rained down upon Las Vegas boulevard hitting the concrete with a rat-tat-tat-splat.

"Hey!?!"

Someone shouted from down below apparently taking collateral damage in the onslaught of the martini meat hailstorm. John fell back upon the roofs tar-lined expanse. He coughed several times, concentrating on the stars above to help settle his breathing. There was something very wrong with this, it had to be the concussion right? He overheard a guy talking at the bar just days before about falling down his stairs just before Christmas. Blacking out, the guy had forgotten the next two weeks of his life, fragments returning only later on. He had quit smoking cigarettes and now had the habit back in full-swing, not remembering when he had started up again.

"Yeah, it's just a concussion. Get a hold of yourself, John."

The taste in his mouth was like hot death. Afraid to lurch once more, John thought it best he head back inside. She was certain to knock on his door any moment and it would be very derelict of him to be seen in his current state.

Drawing the water in the bath to an almost scalding

temperature, John slipped into the tub releasing a sigh of pain mixed with exhaustion. The water felt like heaven to him as he focused his mind on the events of the last few days, desperate to shake his dread.

The tag on their brand-new living room set was still affixed to the silver chair-leg, $189.00. A fortune spent on a couch and some chairs, what a waste. Looking around the cozy living room of her two bedroom house, Jane felt a twinge of sadness. Plopping herself down upon the bright yellow couch it felt too quiet. Nothing was happening, nothing ever did happen. Life had become boring. The most excitement they had was their weekly card game with their neighbors Dick and Donna, gathering over wine and rummy. Gossiping about local scandals, dishing on the who's who of the Howard County Maryland elite.

It was what Jane would've referred to years ago as a regular barf-fest.

The holidays had always been the easiest way for her to fit-in. Truthfully she enjoyed all the pomp and circumstance associated with Christmas. Caroling, the lights, the genuine smell of snow and fir trees. Add a nice glass of tawny port and you had one fine time. New Year's 1955 had come and gone and when the holiday hangover crept in it looked like this year would be just like the last and more of the same since they'd gone ahead and tied the knot.

Jane had little to want for in the realm of possessions. John was management at an insurance adjuster, utilizing his charming ways to make quite a name for himself among the salesman, ad guys and money barons. They had a new Studebaker convertible, something called a microwave which had delighted John and everyone who came to witness the magic of frozen dinners. Luckily the bar was always fully stocked, they did enjoy their alcohol. Her husband's fondness for martinis was another thing that had stuck in Jane's craw. This was a man who used to have a sip of whiskey then rage on into the night.

She reached for a bottle of brown, her go to called Macallan. It was a single-malted scotch of which she dumped three fingers worth into a crystal rocks glass before taking a big gulp. The smooth burn began in her esophagus, trailing off to settle in her empty stomach. Jane could feel the scotch course its way through her bloodstream, producing a calming effect on her nerves. Returning to the couch the day would be about napping and drinking and reading her new book, I Am Legend.

There was a knock on the door, shave-and-a-haircut.

"For Christ's sake," Jane said, closing the book with a hint of despair.

She checked herself in the mirror. Just because she was unhappy didn't mean she would let it betray her looks. Social customs dictated she wasn't to entertain strangers without her husband present, especially at home. She was dressed casually in red and yellow separates, her black hair pinned up in the back. Frankly the whole world had gone insane. What would Bonnie Parker say?

She cracked the door open, it was Jimmy the postman. He was buck-toothed and very nice. "Sorry to bother you Jane," he said with a shyness that betrayed an obvious crush. Jane was flattered, she welcomed any chance to smile.

"No bother, Jimmy. Just reading about the end of the world."

"I knew you would like that book, I hope someone makes a movie about it." He had removed his hat and began fidgeting.

"I promise I'll return it when I'm finished," she said with a smile.

"Oh, no-no, it's a gift. Always give a book away after you've read it. That's my motto."

"Well it sounds like a good way to look at things, thank you Jimmy."

"You're welcome," he said, walking away.

Jane couldn't believe this was the only reason he had interrupted her daily boredom. Almost as if on cue he snapped his fingers, spinning around on his heals.

"Jeepers, where's my mind? I almost forgot why I came."

He reached into his mail-bag producing a small package wrapped cleanly in brown paper. It had no address but simply printed on the front was her name, handwritten.

"I know it's tomorrow but I didn't want to intrude. Happy Valentine's day."

Before she could say anything Jimmy handed her the package and ran off to finish his rounds.

Jane watched Jimmy run across the street. Almost getting run-over by a car, he spun around and shot off like a top down the block. She shook her head giggling. He was so sweet and awkward it reminded her of the innocence that came with youth. Closing the door, she went into the kitchen and sat-down in the booth at the breakfast nook. The package was wrapped and folded with such care she hated the sound of it ripping. The frame was brown-wood, not at all special, but when she flipped the wood over to reveal the picture it was holding, the urge to cry hit her like a ton of bricks. She had only felt this way about a gift one other time.

Staring back at her through cigar pursed lips was her hero, Ms. Bonnie Parker. She was leaning

on the hood of a black car, stolen, with one arm, and in the other she held a revolver. Her hair was pulled back under a beret of some sort and she wore sensible shoes. The picture had gained notoriety at first glance when published. Women didn't smoke cigars, they sure as hell didn't hold guns or rob banks. It was the most wonderful present she had ever been given. Jane tried to think back when she must have told Jimmy about her love of Bonnie and Clyde but the gift was too powerful and she decided to lie down instead.

Up the stairs, past the photo gallery of people she hardly recognized, top of the landing, second door on the left was the bedroom. With picture-frame in hand Jane fell back on the bed relishing in taking up the entire surface area. John slept on the right-side yet always ended up on her side of the bed leaving her less than her body's width of room.

Selfishly, she cursed her luck. How she could have made such a bad calculation?

The first few years with John had been everything she imagined it would be. They rode his motorcycle across the country and then back. They slept under the stars, made love in the fields, once they even robbed a little gas station just for kicks. Promising never to do anything like that again they pissed away the money on booze, gas, and huge steaks. Whenever John brought up the idea of getting hitched, Jane would always change the subject It was easy with him, mention something he liked and he was off on a tangent.

She was able to deflect his wishes for settling down only for so long. The constant buzzing of the motorcycle seat had begun to take a toll on her thighs. She didn't think they could continue this path, food cost money, living cost money. She wasn't a criminal at heart and never did he mention the robbery or a life of crime as an alternative. John was a rebel but he was a different kind of crook. No, it would be a real job for him, entry-level learning about the insurance business. They rented an apartment, Jane taught sewing lessons on the side, a talent she never spoke of. Those were good times, the salad days as she would refer to them.

John got a promotion and then another one, so the next step was to get married. Jane didn't want a fuss and with no parents to object to their union they made it official on February 14, 1950 at the "Tunnel of Love Chapel," in Atlantic City, New Jersey.

Valentine's Day.

What better date to seal their love than on the holiday invented for celebrating it?

Looking back it seamed hokey and a completely square thing to do yet for the next year their love bloomed stronger than before. Jane was certain that she had made the correct life choice. When the honeymoon period was over, John was rarely home. His job now required him to travel, leaving Jane alone for weeks at a time. He bought her a new house to decorate, filling her time choosing between aqua-blue and tweed-yellow bed-spreads and the like.

Then one day she looked up and it was 1955. She was twenty-two years old and already felt like an old crone. John had long since changed from the rebel without a cause to a regular schlub. His belly had begun to grow. Their love making had slowed to a turtle's crawl with pressure from friends to produce a child. Jane had no desire to bring a new life into this world.

She looked at the picture, her Valentine's day present from her crush, Jimmy the postman.

Jane put the picture under one of the several pillows adorning the bed and closed her eyes, she would need to figure out how to tell John that she would be leaving him.

"When are you going to get rid of your wife?"

He had just closed his eyes. The sex had made his head hurt and now he had to deal with this, always this. If he had known it was gonna be like pulling teeth he never would have started with this broad, all he needed was another nag in his life.

"I'm fucking serious, John. You promised me we would go to Vegas."

He prayed that she would assume he was asleep and let the subject go. A nice quick nap would set him straight for dealing with the rest of the day. Not likely, the pillow came down fast onto his face scaring him more than anything.

"For fuck sakes, Jill. Are you a child, can't you see I'm trying to catch a few winks?"

She put up her fists like she was gonna fight him. On their knees they wrestled around for a minute or so, John maneuvering the small woman on her stomach so he could smack her ass.

"Now are you gonna behave or is daddy going to have to punish you?"

"Not if you call me daddy you pervert!" she said laughing.

John began to tickle her. They rolled around on the bed until Jill got her leg caught in the bed-sheet, she fell off the bed with a thud.

"Ahhhhaaa---haaaaah."

"Stop laughing, asshole. It's your fault," she said, trying hard not to laugh as well.

"What the fuck did I do?"

"I'm serious, John. When are you going to leave that spinster?"

"Jill the broken-record. Look, I told you, tomorrow is our wedding anniversary, okay? I can't leave my wife on fucking Valentine's day, it's bad form."

She laughed sarcastically.

"Bad form? You're screwing your secretary, my apologies Saint John."

Jill went into the bathroom, slamming the door. John grabbed a cigarette from her pack, lighting it with a silver Zippo. He exhaled the smoke and laid back on the bed. He was stringing Jill along, he had already been thinking about how he was going to leave Jane. Briefly he had entertained the idea of smothering her with her pillow in the middle of the night, that or one of another hundred ways he had learned about from investigating death claims. He would never mention that to Jane nor Jill for that matter. Never let them see your hand.

"Are we still meeting for drinks later?" he asked through puffs of nicotine.

"I haven't decided yet," answered the closed door.

"Well if you decide to grace me with your presence, I can be there around four."

The door did not offer a reply and John didn't wait around to receive one. Instead he got dressed and left her apartment. He would need to go back to the office and shower before heading home later. The last thing he needed was a confrontation of this magnitude and although it would expedite the process entirely, tonight was not the night to lay waste to the only person he had ever loved. Even though she had long stopped resembling the rebellious woman who had stalked him like prey all those years ago, John still loved her.

Enough to take out a $500,000 insurance claim against her life.

Perhaps he had been planning something all along. John was the type to play a hundred angles with confidence. One would work out the way he wanted in time. Getting into his car, the new smell still permeated it despite those nasty cigars that Jane loved smoking so much. He had begged her to not smoke them in the new sports-car but she had brushed him off as a bourgeois asshole, pointing out that old John would never have cared about the smell of her cigars.

Back in his office John showered in the executive washroom. He had several clean shirts in his closet, he chose a pale-blue button-up and sat down in his chair. The office was modest, several awards for sales adorned the wall, a painting of a sailboat took up a good chunk of the other. On his desk he had two pictures, one of him from his circus days, a group portrait of the carnies, the other of he and his bride, smiling on their wedding night. He hardly recognized the couple and turned the picture over.

Jane awoke from her unexpected nap refreshed if somewhat confused. That's the problem when you fall asleep during daylight and awaken in the dark. The body needs to acclimate itself to its surroundings. For Jane, her own bedroom felt more foreign than when she had seen it devoid of furniture on the day they moved in. All the make-up, the clothes, the jewelry, none of it was really her. In the closet, buried in the back in a dry-cleaners bag was her old leather jacket. Jane pulled the jacket off the hanger, burying her face in it to inhale the smell.

It was like coming home.

She put the jacket on over her shirt, remembering to take the framed photo with her as she made her way downstairs to the kitchen. It was nearly four o'clock, John would be home around seven and she wanted to start preparing dinner for them. Tomorrow would mark their fifth wedding anniversary and it was also Valentine's Day. A double-whammy of a gut check washed over Jane, she felt nauseous. Knowing that she would be walking out on him, actually preparing to do it was a whole other affair. Where would she go?

What would she take with her?

How would she get there?

The thoughts flooded her mind as she focused on preparing dinner. The garlic, butter, thyme, salt, and pepper steak was her specialty. In a pan, medium-rare, it had a wonderful crust from the sear. Jane always like the way the meat hissed when dropped into the buttered hot pan. She had bought two sixteen-ounce strips as an anniversary present. Her husband loved a good steak. She would boil some potatoes, making a mash. She couldn't decide on sweet carrots or corn. In the end she went with the carrots to break the flavor combination.

Jane turned on the radio. It was a fire-engine red Westinghouse tube radio, last year's combination present from her hubby. John was a big fan of insisting both holidays be celebrated at once, it was more romantic when really he was just a cheapskate. My how things changed.

> Life could be a dream (Sh-boom)
> If I could take you up in paradise up above (Sh-boom)
> If you would tell me I'm the only one that you love
> Life could be a dream, sweetheart

The lyrics didn't give Jane any comfort. It was almost like she was living through the emotional break-up before actually ending the relationship. It was true, John was her life and had been for the past seven years. She would have to go far away, establish a new identity. There was nothing more scorned than a divorced woman in her circle of associates. One of theirs, a lovely gal named Harriet, was left with a son. Divorced and still residing in her ex-husband's house, she had been quietly disinvited from all social gatherings following her separation. Jane always thought that was bullshit. Harriet was a sweetheart who taught English and spoke Spanish fluently.

Jane hummed along to the radio as the pot of water began to boil. She dumped the potatoes in, lighting up a cigarillo with the flame from the gas stove. John hated them and secretly she smoked them to piss him off. Lately their behavior together had been calculated to irritate one another. It was Jane's intention to spend the holiday with her husband as one final chance. If he proved that all his past behavior was just because he was also unhappy, well she would reevaluate her situation. His job was slowly killing him and yes, he made really good money but they never got to go on trips or relish in the good life like many of their friends.

Instead Jane had settled for crockery and television, drinks at brunch, weekly card games, barbecues and leisurely strolls around the neighborhood. That was her routine, that's what all the money bought. She relished the poor times when they had nothing but each other to keep warm, the real love only heard of in stories. If only life were a dream.

"Another drink, buddy?"

"Huh?"

The bartender was not amused, he hated repeating himself.

"Do...you...want...a...drink?"

This time it was John who was not amused. Cheeky bartenders were the last thing he wanted to deal with right now, he needed to think long and hard before going home. How would he dispose of his wife without arousing suspicion? Essentially, he needed an exit strategy and a way to cash in on Jane's life insurance policy, it had to look like an accident.

We're sorry for your loss, and on Valentine's day to boot.

It's also my fifth wedding anniversary.

You poor man.

John assumed it would go something like that. He wouldn't have any trouble collecting on the policy since it was issued by his firm, nothing weird about a husband wanting to protect his family. He could argue the point all day long, it's what he did for a living.

"Martini, please," he added. A pissed off bartender could be bought for a nickel, although there was nothing strange about drinking at four o'clock on a Wednesday. The bar was uncharacteristically slow for this time of day. It was him, Mr. Personality bartender, and one other vagrant looking type guy a few stools over from John.

Main Street, Ellicott City was a bustling hub of people always coming and going, a mecca for shopping, eating, and drinking. One could easily take the number 9 trolley from downtown Baltimore, arriving in the quaint country-side, far enough away from the dreariness of the city to actually breathe the clean air. You could look up and count every star if you wished, something that the drab city prevented. John had moved up in his firm, Rueckert & Associates, which was located down on Paca Street, in the city. He had opted to live in the county in order to maximize their position in an up and coming neighborhood.

The advantage of being unknown, far away from his wife's prying eyes, didn't hurt. There he would be free to socialize with whomever he wished as his job often demanded the wining and dining of clientele from time to time. John was an expert schmoozer, always quick with a joke or to light up your smoke, his wide-grinned smile won over Men and Women alike. Casual flirting came with the territory, then he met Jill. At this very same bar they struck up a conversation about movies, both claiming Abbot and Costello as their favorites. From there it was to a motel room off of route 40.

John's first illicit affair left him energized yet deeply saddened. Never did he dream of hurting Jane but lately she had lost all of her pizzazz and instead spent the days drinking. Their sex life had paid the price, more of a routine pipe cleaning than anything resembling love. He kept her happy with clothes and all of the newest gadgets for the home. Why she was so miserable he couldn't comprehend. She acted like a spoiled child, she never left the house, and he was left to bring home the bacon. He longed for the days of old, the circus, the open road, thirty pounds ago when he truly felt alive.

It would be easy for him to uproot. The house was in his wife's name, her policy would pay off a cool half-million which he could sit on or piss away at his leisure while cavorting with his mistress. No one would begrudge a widower another chance at being happy. They would encourage him to find love elsewhere, an eligible husband at 26 should not be alone, left unattended to his own misery.

The bartender returned with the martini taking his sweet fucking time, John hated their kind. Just make the goddamned drink, set it down and shut-up. He cared less for the history of vermouth and even less about striking up a friendship. Even still it was impossible to sit at a bar alone and not be bothered by someone. As if on cue the stool next to him became occupied, she was very late. He hated waiting for people especially when he needed to return to the homestead for dinner. When he turned to regard his mistress, he was taken aback by the missing tooth grin of the shabby looking fellow who only recently was minding his own business.

"You look like a man with a dilemma."

John gave the man a once over. Upon closer inspection he wasn't as homeless looking as he once thought, just dirty and aged. He must work in a factory somewhere, John thought before deciding to humor the old goat.

"As a matter of fact, tomorrow is my wedding anniversary, five years."

"Well congratulations on that achievement, young feller. On Valentime's day to boot."

John cringed at the mispronunciation, bullshit holiday or not. He nodded in agreement.

"If you don't mind me saying, you don't look too happy about the affair."

"What affair?" John asked, paranoid.

"I mean the marriage aspect; you don't look like the marrying type."

"Excuse me?"

"Now, now young mister, I mean no offense. I have seen my fair share of wandering lovers as I spend my nights drinking in bars, so old Curly Joe picks up a few things along the way. Just saying."

Curly Joe moved back to his original stool, not wanting a confrontation. He had learned that in bars as well. John felt like an asshole and took the seat next to Joe.

"I'm John, sorry. It has been a rough go of it lately," he admitted.

"Well that's alright, why don't you buy me a drink and we'll consider ourselves friends from here on out."

John waived over the idiot bartender and decided he would confide in this Curly Joe, a drunkard was not a reliable witness and therefore could be told virtually anything to be disputed should someone come calling for the information at a later date. Truthfully, he hoped this stranger would provide some much-needed clarity on his future choices.

"You ever been married, Joe?"

"Me? Hell, no. Not the marrying sort. Never did find anyone to match my crazy," he sipped his National Bohemian. "Had a few close calls but nothing major."

"Here's to crazy," John raised his glass to which Joe returned the gesture.

"C'mon pal, it can't be all that bad?"

"Trust me Joe, it seems like it's been years since I've been happy. I think it's time to move on." John found himself mildly relieved. Saying a thing out loud brings you that much closer to it being real. Evil thoughts found purchase in the nooks and crannies of his soul. He was traveling down a dark path of guilt and ruination from which there was no return. He realized these dark feelings were always inside, the need to rebel, his early raucous upbringing, the way he thumbed his nose at society. That is what drove John to marriage in the first place. It made sense, the life of crime so fantasized about by Jane in the guise of Bonnie and Clyde, her reason for loving him was a sham.

John blamed the marriage on Jane. She was always pushing and prodding to be the next famous lover/gangsters, that they would both go down together in some blaze of French kiss laced gunfire. Buried side-by-side for eternity, their love would stand as a testament for all the wide-eyed hopeless romantics to come.

"Fuck that," John said to himself.

"What's that?"

"Hey, Joe what's your story? Here I am being a selfish prick and I never once asked you about your life."

"I could tell you my story over another brewskie?"

John ordered another round for the both of them. Joe took a big slug of his beer upon its arrival and cleared his throat.

"I used to work for Bethlehem Steel down in the city. Mainly we done all the steel for the B & O Railroad line right up the way, so naturally I became a denizen of this fine establishment. I was not but fourteen when I left Chicago for the east coast. Came here with twenty-five cents in nineteen-ought-seven, wandered around for a while before I got caught up in some trouble. Ran away straight to the steel mill and hid there for forty something years.

"That was up until last year when I was supremely retired not of my own volition. Seems I have a big mouth and some of the upper-management didn't take too kindly to the things I was saying. Souring the reputation of Bethlehem Steel and such and such. Cocksuckers took half my pension and sent me packing, which is why I sit here today conversing with you. The end."

Joe chugged his beer. The belch he produced was juicy and reeked of horseradish.

"What kind of things were you saying, Joe?"

"Oh, you know, us conspiracy nuts say all sorts of shit. Only when you hit on some truths does someone come a knockin', looking for an explanation. I says, 'How many more people need to die at that tunnel for anyone to give three shits?' Needless to say, this was not falling on virgin ears as to my estimation, clever cocksuckers knew and didn't care."

"Tunnel?"

"Ilchester Tunnel, just up the way. Crosses over the Patapsco river just across from the college, big train bridge. Suckers carved right into the living rock."

"Sounds beautiful," John said.

"Oh, it is, truly a sight to be seen. But you don't want to go there, John, and I say this as your new friend."

"Why would I want to go there?"

"Well you look like you were thinking of some magical spot to take your missus for your special day, picnic of sorts. Maybe head on out to the tunnel, most folk around here treat it as a park and ride, if you catch my meaning?"

Joe winked.

"But you said to not go there," John answered confused, "So why even mention it?"

"It's not my place to interfere with free-will, something I absolutely cannot do. Now I can say that the place is utterly haunted and that some folks don't find their way home so good. The road is dark and winding, a car could easily crash into a tree. Especially a Studebaker."

"How did you know I had a..."

Before John could finish, Joe pointed to the car parked in front of the dingy bar.

"Saw you come in fella."

John was beginning to understand that Curly Joe was offering him a solution to his problem. How and why would not become clear until it was too late.

"Shit!"

John had forgotten all about the time, he was going to be late for dinner. He grabbed his jacket and finished his martini.

"Thank you for all of your guidance, Joe. I have to skedaddle."

"But wait, I haven't even told you the rest."

"Gotta go, see you around," John clapped the old man on his shoulder and made for the door.

"One last piece of advice, young feller."

John waived his hand in the air. He had all the information he needed, best to get home and begin laying the groundwork for tomorrow's big night. The door behind him closed shut with a slow shooshing sound. The faint words of Curly Joe crept through the small opening, gently fading as the words drew closer to John's ears. He was in the car and on his way when he forgot them entirely.

John pulled into his driveway twenty minutes later. He turned the car engine off and sat there for a moment. The sun had gone down for the day, the night already consuming the air around him, time was odd. John couldn't believe his eyes when he looked at his watch and it read 9:30pm. There was no way he wasn't going to get the third degree from Jane. If he was lucky, he would only have to deal with her for another twenty-four hours, give or take.

That was a comforting thought.

He was about to head inside when something large and brown hit the windshield with a splat.

"Jesus H. Christ!"

John grimaced in pain as his shoulder slammed into the Studebaker's hard-topped ceiling. He rubbed his neck trying to work out the knot that was already starting to form. The windshield of the car was streaked with grease, the culprit slowly inching its way down the gentle slope of the glass. The brown piece of meat that was supposed to be his dinner came to a rest in between the duel wiper blades, hanging there depressed and sad, a fitting example of his current predicament.

The assault from above continued with the next course of mashed taters, careening down in giant globules, not concerned for where they were aimed. A hail-storm of glazed carrots followed him as he briskly made his way into the house. He was met at the front door by his wife. Swiftly, he ducked out of the way as the stove-pot missed his head. She had nearly made contact and was rearing up to smack him with a wooden spoon. John grabbed her wrist, twisting ever so much that she dropped the would-be weapon.

"Are you out of your fucking mind?"

"Says the son-of-a-bitch who's three hours late for dinner. Take your hands off me!"

Jane wrestled free and they both took to separate corners of the living room, he covered in his dinner, she breathing heavily on the verge of tears.

"Okay, look, I'm sorry I was late. It was business, I was working," he pleaded, picking potatoes out of his ear.

"That's your excuse for everything, 'I'm working.' It's bullshit and I am done pretending everything is okay."

"What do you mean by that?"

"What do I mean? What do I mean? Damn, you sure turned out to be a dimwit."

John raised his hand as if to strike her then realized how far off the rail he was acting and shamefully put his hands in his pants pockets. Jane was horrified that he had even made the attempt and retreated upstairs to the bedroom. John pursued but the locked door of their shared room prevented his entry. He banged on the door several times with a closed fist.

"Goddammit Jane, open the door! Let's talk about this."

From behind the door he could hear her rustling through the closet.

"There's nothing to talk about, you abusive asshole."

"Jane, I'm sorry. Really, it wasn't me. You know I would never hurt you." His voice was soft.

"Bullshit," she barked back. "All you do is hurt me."

He resumed his banging until his hand was red. Certain she would not open the door, John gave-up and went into the bathroom to take a shower. This was all going wrong. Any neighbor with ears would've heard the ruckus, the steak was still affixed to the hood of the car. Husband and wife get into a fight, she dies under mysterious circumstances, his chances of a clean break were slim to none. She was nuts if she thought she was walking out on him that's for certain.

John finished his shower and put on his bathrobe before heading downstairs. One glance at the still closed bedroom door answered his current question. He grabbed a Swanson frozen dinner out of the ice-box, Salisbury steak with gravy. Ripping off the plastic wrap, he tossed it into the microwave, where he punched five minutes into the machine before making himself a drink.

What a long day, he thought, crunching down on an olive. He would need to remedy this situation immediately. His biggest worry was that Jill, who had already ditched him at the bar, would show up at the house pissed off. John suspected more than dinner would be thrown his direction should that happen and he was determined to win back his wife, if only for one more day.

How hard could that be?

He was Mister Charming, the smooth talker who could enter

a room, sizing it up before his first cigarette was down to a nub. He sat eating his dinner in silence and when finished he deposited the container in the trash, no clean-up.

Easy-Peasy lemon squeezy, thank god for the small things.

Jane had intended to pack a suitcase to leave. She changed her clothes to something a bit more subtle, a pantsuit grey and white striped, then being a consummate rebel made her way out the bedroom window, scaling the trellis until she reached solid ground. The steak winked back at her. She felt horrible about the cow that had given its parts for a wasted dinner. Jane picked up the piece of meat from the car and tossed it into the bushes aligning the concrete driveway. She plucked the extra key from her pocket without a second glance and drove off into the night.

John was unaware as he had fallen asleep to dreams of train tunnels and raining food.

So please turn on your magic beam
Mr. Sandman, bring us, please, please, please
Mr. Sandman, bring us a dream

The radio sent the sweet music bouncing around the interior of the car producing a calming effect. Music could always cure whatever ailed Jane. There was something about the instrumentation, the exact placement of notes and chords culminating into a song that transported her away. The Chordettes were wishing the sandman would provide a true-love, some Romeo for the lonely. Jane had loved the song but now thought the premise totally unrealistic and switched the radio off. She had seen an evil side in John, something deep down in him that scared her more than she cared to admit.

She drove around and around, not really paying attention to where she was headed, a fugue state of motor system functionality keeping her body going while her mind slipped into the past. She remembered countless movies seen as a couple, the laughing and love making. Why is it we always try to dwell on the happy times instead of focusing on the reality of misery we live in? Jane figured it was the soul's way of not giving in to desperate loneliness. Pushing through the trip down memory lane, she found herself parked in front of a bar on Main Street proper. She had always loved the quaint Ellicott City town, having spent many a carefree afternoon browsing the many shops and boutiques.

For some reason or another she had never seen this particular bar before, the sign only indicating that they were open. Suddenly she felt the need to drink. Locking the car, she pushed her way into the drab air and pulled up the nearest stool. The smell of peanuts and bleach was unnerving but not enough to drive her to the street in disgust.

"What can I get you, miss?"

"Macallan if you have it, one ice cube," she answered.

"Coming right up," the bartender said, shuffling off to pour the drink.

Jane took the opportunity to survey the bar. A new Wurlitzer Jukebox shined from one corner. Several bar denizens, deep into their drinks and sorrow, occupied various low tables strewn around the room. A pretty blonde was sipping on a red drink a few seats away from her. The bartender returned with her scotch.

"That's a mighty interesting choice of beverage."

The blonde woman was holding her glass high in salute. Jane did the same then drained the glass.

"Damn, I only ever knew one person who could slam the brown like that and I had to call her Mom," the blonde stranger said, moving over to where Jane was sitting. Jane pointed to the empty glass and the bartender refilled the drink.

"Put that on my check," she said.

"I can't let you do that," Jane answered.

The blonde leaned over and Jane smelled Vanilla.

"Too late, I like you and when I like someone, I buy them drinks."

"What should we toast to?" Jane asked.

"Well, since it's almost V-day and we are both here, alone, how about to the end of men?"

Jane thought that was a most wonderful thing to toast to.

The two of them sat drinking, unaware of the comings and goings of the bar patrons. Like school girls, they giggled and gossiped, becoming quick friends as those who have similar sorrow usually find solace in other lost souls. They had quite a bit in common including their love of cigarillos. Jane had nearly fallen off her stool when her new friend offered her one, squealing in delight. She hadn't felt this alive in years.

When you're in a deep conversation with someone you have just met, that's the only time you are truly paying attention to the other person. Each new reaction will either be points in the positive column or in the negative, depending on one's views and interests. Jane had fallen for John with the tally marks overwhelmingly pointing up when instead he was merely a downward arrow. He had been fooling people for so long she wasn't even sure he knew who he was anymore.

It was the saddest thing.

This interesting woman at the bar was the real deal. She talked the talk and walked the walk with an ass that Jane appreciated, for the first-time stirring feelings of an almost human nature. The minutes ticked by folding into hours and when Jane looked up, she gasped.

"Holy shit, I need to go," Jane got up to put on her coat.

"Lemme pay the check, I'll go with you."

"That's nice of you, but I need to get home," Jane said blushing.

An uncomfortable silence dragged onward slowly. Jane remembered why she came to the bar in the first place, to leave her husband. She felt a dizzy spell, slumping back onto the stool to catch her breath she was caught before toppling over. When she had regained her composure, a toothy old man was smiling back at her.

"You alright miss? Don't worry, it has happened to me on many occasions," he tipped his derby.

Jane cocked her head.

"Thank you, yes. I just had a little spell," Jane admitted.

"We did put on a good show of it," the blonde said, rubbing Jane on her shoulder in comfort.

"Curly Joe at your service, in the affairs of the heart accept no substitute."

"Affairs?"

Both Women looked at each other, having said the same thing at the same time.

Jinx.

"Nah, with Valentime's day coming up, I just figured it was trouble with your husband brought you out to the bar."

"How did you know I was married?" Jane asked worriedly.

"Forgive me for taking liberties but earlier in the day there come in a feller driving that same car, although his had less grease on it. He was soaking his sorrow in martinis."

"That's him, miserable prick."

Joe took to sipping on his beer, the seed had been planted.

"You know I think I will stay for another drink," Jane announced. "Bartender?"

Jane grilled Curly Joe on his interaction with John, plying him with beer. The blonde woman sat speechless, there was nothing for her to interject, so she sipped on her French 75, uncomfortably nervous.

"Now I tell you this only because you have been so nice to Curly Joe and he has taken a liking to you. A warning, don't blink."

"I do like you Joe and I thank you, but I don't understand. Don't blink?"

"I believe your husband means you harm, perhaps an anniversary accident is one way of getting rid of the problem."

Jane was getting agitated; this guy was having a laugh.

"What fucking problem Joe, spit it out!"

Joe was taken back, he produced a wicked grin and leaned in.

"You Jane, getting rid of you."

Blink.

Lights, too many of them. It was difficult to focus, the world had become a blur of shadows and voices, the myriad of sound spun its way around in merry-go-round fashion becoming softer then louder. There was a steady beeping noise keeping time in the otherwise quiet abyss of the cold vacuum that was all enveloping. It was strangely warm as feelings and senses began to re-arrange themselves taking familiar forms, re-connecting pathways that illuminated the dark. Another voice, this time his.

"A-aam I dead?"

More rustling, followed by a piercingly bright light.

"Am I in Hell?"

There was a soft chuckle.

"No, I'm afraid you are stuck with us a little while longer on Earth. Now if you really want Hell check out those hacks over at City hospital."

Some more giggling.

John regarded his surroundings gingerly. The light from a pen size flashlight bounced from each one of his eyes ensuring his motor functions were still intact, the beeping sounds of the EKG monitor blinking in rhythm with his heart. A deep itching came out of nowhere but when he tried to scratch his face his arms would not work.

"John, my name is Dr. Rushman, you are in the hospital."

"What happened, why can't I move?"

"You have been in a serious car accident, the restraints are precautionary measures. You're lucky to be alive."

"My face itches."

"Yes, there are some deep scratches underneath your eyes. Aside from bruising and various other scrapes you will make a full recovery."

There was a hint of deception in the doctor's voice, deep down he was hiding something.

"Where's Jane?"

The doctor looked plainly at John, removing his spectacles to clean them.

"I'm sorry, she didn't make it."

John's heart sank.

"It seems she was thrown from the vehicle and died instantly. For what it's worth, she most likely didn't feel anything."

The doctor put a reassuring hand on John's shoulder.

"You are going to be sore for a while, after some more tests you can go home. Is there anyone you'd like us to call?"

The doctor's tone had become somber and sad, there was nothing worse than breaking bad news to a patient.

"I'd like to get in touch with my office, the number is on a business card in my wallet."

The doctor went to the bedside table producing John's wallet.

"I don't think we will be needing these any longer," the doctor said removing John's arm restraints. He handed him the telephone and left to leave his patient some privacy. John sat for a moment; his head was killing him. His entire body was numb and sore. Assuming he was on some sort of pain-killers, he knew the worst was yet to come. Picking up the receiver he dialed his work number, holding the phone to his ear while he itched the spot on his face that now bore deep red scratches.

"Rueckert & Associates, how can I help you?"

"Hey, it's me."

"Oh my god, John! Where the hell have you been? Floyd has been going mental over-here trying to make sense of the...." she was cut-off.

"I'm in the hospital, I'm okay don't worry. Jane is dead," he scanned for any eavesdroppers, "Everything is going as planned."

Blink.

"Even though I walk through the valley of the shadow of death, I will fear no evil, for you are with me; your rod and your staff, they comfort me. You prepare a table before me in the presence of my enemies; you anoint my head with oil; my cup overflows. Surely goodness and mercy shall..."

The rain was falling in a coldly deliberate sideways slant that made it nearly impossible to angle the umbrella. No matter how you positioned it you were destined to get wet. For John the water was refreshing, like cleaning out a deep wound or being baptized. He knew he should feel relief but standing in the rain there in the Greenmount cemetery, surrounded by work friends and neighbors alike, the sorrow took hold of him. Deep-rooted and sincere, John wept for his wife.

Since the accident, which had only been a day ago, he had

been losing stretches of time. How he had left the hospital, made funeral arrangements and bought a new suit was a mystery to his bruised brain. The doctor has said he should be aware of a possible concussion and that short-term memory loss was often a side-effect. He was assured the memories would come back in the future.

When John had first decided he was going to kill his wife, cash in her insurance policy and then abscond to Las Vegas with his girlfriend, never did he imagine he would be feeling true unhappiness. For all her faults, all her nagging, Jane had been his true-love. The rambunctious teenager who had spent all summer trying to win his heart now lay in a cedar box about to be lowered into the ground, never to be seen nor heard from again. It was all so final. John's girlfriend had a connection with the funeral home and thus the entire process was handled for him expeditiously.

John itched his face, wishing the doctor had given him some topical unguent to alleviate the burning. It was always there now, a reminder of the accident. He hadn't expected to escape so unscathed. During the planning of the caper, when John was doing reconnaissance, picking out the exact spot where he would swerve off the road to initiate the accident, he was certain the car would be slammed up against a tree when it had in fact flipped over several times coming to a stop upside-down in a ditch.

He had opted to not see Jane's body in the morgue. The guilt was still something real that he would have to process and he thought it would be better if he didn't have to look at her dead face. He was afraid she might open up her eyes like in a horror comic. He wore dark sunglasses to conceal his grief, but really it was so no one could see the joy he could easily betray. John had killed his wife, making it look like an accident by actually getting into one. No one would question his motives until it was too late and then it was a slim chance as Jane had no living relatives to pursue vengeance.

The plan moving forward was to go home and pack, his flight to Las Vegas was scheduled to depart at 4:30pm, a reservation already waiting and confirmed at the Dunes Casino Hotel. Dean Martin was performing over the weekend and John had reserved two tickets for the show ahead of time. She would be meeting him later, arriving on the red eye to avoid arousing suspicion. John had been telling people he had an Uncle in Nevada who had offered to give him a job on his worm farm, the dry heated climate and change of scenery was what he needed during this crisis.

No one had questioned him. It was so easy.

When the service had ended, John stood by his rental car smoking a cigarette. Occasionally he would shake someone's hand as they offered him their condolences.

She was such as striking beauty, she was so young, are you going to sue the automobile company?

John smiled politely, thanking each mourner by name. He was relieved when the service was over. He wanted a moment with Jane. Walking over to the fresh grave he got goose-pimples except this time he was walking over his wife's grave. He leaned down on one knee.

"You always were the wild one. You would have ridden on the back of my motorcycle forever if I hadn't been scared of living. It's not what I wanted; domesticity be damned. I never wanted you, I was afraid of being alone and you were the only one who came calling. One blink and your whole life changes. No more living in the past for me, adios senora."

Blink.

That weird time shift thing happened. John looked up from the gravestone and into the face of his boss, Tim.

"Anyways, we all are just so sorry for you, buddy. Everyone loved Jane, she was a spark-plug that's for sure."

John couldn't remember leaving the graveyard. His clothes were changed and his face still itched something fierce.

"You okay, John?" asked Tim.

"Huh? Oh, yeah...sorry. Still a bit wonky from the accident. Say, there isn't anyone else here is there? I thought I saw someone out of the corner of my eye."

John's voice was shaky.

"Just us buddy-boy, we're the only two idiots that ever come in to work on a Saturday," Tim laughed.

"Right, listen Tim..."

"Don't worry about anything, I already processed the claim. Management has its perks, I should be able to wire the money to you in a few days. The Dunes was it? Fancy schmancy."

"Just looking for a little relaxation before I go to my Uncles." John was being coy.

"Say hi to Sammy for me, babe."

Tim launched into an impression as bad as his breath.

"Thanks for everything Tim, I..."

Blink.

".....says, 'That tooth's gonna have to come out', the woman says, 'I'd rather have a baby' so the doctor goes, 'make up your mind lady, I gotta adjust the chair,' Hahahaha."

"What the fuck is going on?"

"You see the doctor says..."

"Shut the fuck up!"

"Hey, guy...no need for that kind of talk, it's just a joke."

John was sitting in a bar at the airport. He knew it was the airport because the same annoying message kept coming over the loudspeaker, the woman's voice was vaguely familiar.

"The white zone is for loading and un-loading only. There's no parking in the white-zone."

John found his bag next to him on the vacant bar chair and made his way toward the information board which would tell him what time it was and what gate his flight was departing from.

"Hey asshole, you forgot to pay for your drinks!"

The bartender was standing with his hand out expecting money. John thought he recognized him but couldn't place from where. He pulled out a $100 and slapped it down on the bar.

"Gee, thanks, mister. Jane was wrong about you, you're not selfish at all."

John swung around feeling a spasm in his shoulder ignite.

"What did you just say?"

"I said thank you, it's a shame other people aren't as generous," the bartender winked.

John became dizzy. He stumbled backwards into a small-table of foreigners, spilling their drinks. He couldn't understand their insults. He was losing his shit. Itching his face, John's hand pulled back to reveal blood on his fingers. He thought he could hear whispers over the din of the airport hustle and bustle. Pointing and snickering, they knew, they all knew!

John tried to get his bearings but the room was spinning fast. Whether it was in his mind or not, too many things were vying for his paranoia. If this was what remorseful guilt felt like, he had vastly underestimated his constitution for committing murder. But it was an accident, truly. Even the doctors had said so. John really hadn't done anything illegal. He thought he heard a familiar voice before he lost consciousness, the chills took over and he knew no more.

"The dead-zone is for loading and un-loading only, there's no blinking in the dead zone."

Blink.

"3B."

"I'm sorry?"

"3B is me, you're sitting in my seat," the man said.

John was looking out the window of an airplane. Someone in an orange vest was driving a little buggy with several baggage cars attached. John got up allowing the man to take the window seat assigned and visited the plane's lavatory. He slid the little locking mechanism indicating the toilet was occupied. The light was dim, the bulb pulsing low, in need of replacement. John looked at himself, the scratches on his face were thin and red, his face pale. He sat down on the toilet after washing his face with warm water.

"Get a hold of yourself, John. Don't lose your shit now, we are almost to the finish line."

The knock at the door scared him silly.

"Please return to your seat for take-off," the flight attendant's voice was sweet and calm.

"Just a minute!"

John flushed the toilet. Spinning the toilet paper, which was back to front loaded, he grabbed a wad before stuffing it into his inner jacket pocket. He made sure his fly was zipped, combed his hair...

Blink.

"Is it true that everyone wants to screw their mothers?"

Blink.

"This flight got in an hour ago, guy."

Blink.

"Las fucking Vegas."

Blink.

The thing making its way up the corner of the room was built from the shadows. The candlelit reflections that licked off the bathroom's wall, the jagged edges of flame that flickered on the edge of darkness, formed a figure immense and deadly. Its prey lay asleep in the bathtub unawares. Hungrily, the shadow creature wailed, silently desperate to feed, it had been so long. From somewhere horrible six serpentine mandibles gently floated across the tiled floor, inching their way upward and around the bathtub's clawed feet. Around and around they wove themselves until they hovered merely inches from John's face. The thing on the wall eclipsed the room's light while its barbed tentacles, blood-red and razor-sharp, ever so gently continued their digging into his face just under his eyes.

John gasped. Shooting up from the bath like a rocket, he stood naked, shivering, certain there had been someone else in the locked bathroom with him. He scratched his face and looked around. The flickering candle, almost down to the nub, made his vision spotty. Carefully, John got out of the tub. The last thing he needed was a broken neck. He flipped the light switch on. The figure in the mirror wore a black hat of sorts, with horrible teeth looked like railroad ties, and the chasm of its mouth went on and on.

"Ahhhhhhhh!"

Blink.

The knock at the door, shave-and-a-haircut, increased its ferocity.

"Sir, it's Bob from the front desk."

John tied his robe tightly, convinced he had lost his mind for good. What the hell was that in the mirror? He opened the door, the man was bald and bespectacled, he was holding a letter.

"This just arrived for you sir," Bob the bell-hop said.

John took the letter.

"Would you like me to send the doctor up to look at those cuts?"

John slammed the door in Bob's face. The word "asshole" could be heard uttered in the hallway. John regarded the letter with his name and went out to the balcony to read it.

"Dear John, if you're reading this then I am dead..."

Blink.

Blink.

When Jane had gotten home from the bar, she found John asleep on the couch. He looked so peaceful. She spat on the floor. Upstairs she unpacked her suitcase, brushed her teeth and went to sleep.

It was their 5th wedding anniversary.

It was Valentine's day.

In the morning she would apologize to John, she would say it had been hard on her these last few years and she knew he was feeling the same. She would suggest they take a picnic that night to watch the stars, cozy up in blankets and sleeping bags. They could eat and drink in peace, knowing no one else would dare be outside in mid-February. She even knew of a romantic spot that was special. It overlooked the Patapsco river, on a train trestle. She would suggest they camp out on the railroad line, the threat of an oncoming train enough to add that little bit of extra excitement reminiscent of their early years together. She would tell him that the Ilchester Tunnel had a notorious history of which only a few knew.

Jane would leave out a few minor details, like that she'd

drugged the bottle of wine with sleeping pills. He wouldn't be able to see her spitting the wine out and back into the glass in the dark and so he would drink his fill. Once passed out she would wait until midnight before forcing her sleeping husband's eyelids open for an entire hour while he unknowingly stared into the dark tunnel.

Curly Joe had been very specific about the timing, it had to be just right. Afterward she would drag him into the car, struggling as he weighed a good two-hundred pounds. The accident would be easy enough to fake, putting him into the driver's seat and wedging his foot on the accelerator.

She had met someone who was willing to help, with connections to a local funeral home. Jane would fake her death. Knowing her old life was gone and a new one beginning was easier than it sounded. She relished the opportunity to rid herself of John. The only thing she wished more was to see the look on his face when he realized what had happened. Either way she would be long gone and he would be dead, as far as anyone would know they both would be, just like Bonnie and Clyde.

Isn't that how all good love stories end?

From the hotel room near the airport on house stationary, Jane wrote a letter. It would be found but at this point no one would be the wiser and frankly she would be around the world by then so good luck finding her. She sealed the envelope with a kiss before sending it in the mail. She wanted to stop by her funeral, curious as to who would be genuinely heart-broken and taking notes as to those who seemed less than saddened.

At the airport, Jane used the payphone.

"Hi, it's me. It's done. I'm on the next flight, I'll see you soon. I love you," she said hanging up the phone with a smile. She would spend the flight sleeping peacefully, having a cocktail or two without anxiety about living the rest of her life on the beach.

It was best Valentine's Day present one could ever ask for.

She slept like the dead, missing all of the scenic views the pilot was notably pointing out. Arrival had been peaceful, traveling made easier as she had practically no luggage opting instead to buy all new things once the wire transfer had come through. She had been brilliant with John's hotel information; her new friend had been instrumental in facilitating that little scheme. Half a million dollars, there was no way she could spend that in a lifetime.

Once she was checked into the hotel she took a shower and put on a light satin gown. It was white and hugged her hips quite well. She resembled a movie star, people in the lobby stopped mid-sentence to see her walk by, a women catching her husband's wandering eye slapped him silly across his face. Jane made her way out to the beach where several low reclining chairs were positioned with little tables. A waiter came by and asked her for a drink order. She put down her copy of I Am Legend, the poem snug and safe between its pages. The sun was setting, throwing colors and shapes across the heavens.

"What a view," she said to no one.

Dear John, if you're reading this then I am dead...well, not entirely. The old Jane, you know the one that followed you around all summer long? She has been dead for a long time. In her place, a shadow of the woman you claimed to love existed, a walking zombie forced to subscribe to a life that she never asked for, never wanted. That Jane is deceased now as well. You have seen to that with your clever little scheme. Insurance fraud, really John? I had you pegged so differently, I put my money on the wrong horse, I coulda been a contender. Did you really like my impressions or was that all a lie, too? I was so stupid, thinking that you were Clyde Barrow to my Bonnie Parker. Oh, how cruel the blind eyes of love can be.

Speaking of eyes, you seeing anything strange yet? I wasn't so sure about Curly Joe's stories of the tunnel, you remember him, don't you? The old man at the bar tried to warn you but you are a stubborn fool John, and you like to impress strangers by never shutting up so he had no qualms about giving up your intentions. You see, I am a real snake-charmer, too.

I learned from the best.

I was genuinely horrified to learn that you had been unfaithful. It broke my heart, John. Even though we had some bad times, I still loved you, I trusted you. Schmuck as you are, I never thought you capable of infidelity. None of that matters now. I'm sure you're in Las Vegas at some swanky hotel, waiting for your mistress who will never arrive. I saw to that as well.

Angry yet?

I would be really pissed off if I were you.

Anyway, I have to run. Lots of money to spend, thank you for taking out that generous insurance claim. One thing I won't ever be able to know and I will regret this for the rest of my life, is what your face looks like right now. The look in your baby blues, the shock. The scratches on your face? Do they itch, hurt? Is he getting closer to you or you to him? There really is no concrete evidence to support any of this but I have a gut feeling that you are answering these out loud in your high-pitched, anal retentive voice.

Gotta go now, babe. Say Hi to the Blink Man for me. Yeah, isn't that a weird name? There are like a hundred or so names he goes by, but I like that one the best as I feel it is fitting for our situation. Enjoy whatever time you have left on me, the bar tab has been taken care of in advance, consider it a late Valentine's day gift.

Some advice if you want to stay alive longer?

Don't blink, John.

Until death did we part,

Jane

Ps. I realized that I AM Clyde and thanks to you I have found my Bonnie.

Pps. Burn in Hell, fucker!

John ripped the letter into scraps. The pieces flew off the roof, blown away by the cool Nevada air. His chest began to throb, maybe he was having a heart attack? The lights, so many of them now spun faster and faster. John waved his hands to steady himself shrieking as he touched something warm and oozy. The thing known as the Blink Man reached out with iron hands, gripping him by the shoulders. The shadow monster lifted John up several feet in the air. John's eyes remained closed tightly, he could feel little ticklers on his face taunting him to open his eyes, to see his doom.

John blinked his eyes open; he saw cold death. Falling off the roof of the hotel he was dead before he hit the ground, his neck cracking as his lifeless body struck the street with a thud. Someone screamed. Various tourists gathered around the body, snapping pictures with their Kodak's. Later these same people would be disappointed that none of the film from their trip to Las Vegas could be developed thus proving that whatever happens in Vegas most certainly stays.

The night moved on, Dean Martin crooned his first song from the bar, Sammy Davis Jr. told a joke that sent the room crying, money was won and dreams were crushed. It was another night in the sin-city. The Sunday morning edition of the Las Vegas bulletin had a page three article with an unusual headline:

DEAD IN VEGAS: One Night Only

Las Vegas – Sin City is used to its share of tragedy, this is a place where you can bet your life-savings on one roll of the dice, you may strike it rich, or you may just lose everything. Much as our ancestors prospected for gold in these exact hills traveling dangerous roads with no sure thing guaranteed, pursuit of riches comes with a price. Local police were called to the Dunes Casino Hotel last night after reports of a suicide came in just after 1am. The body was identified as one John Doe of Baltimore, MD. Mr. Doe's luck had taken a sour turn, having recently lost his wife in a car accident mere days before. The grieving husband was pronounced dead on the scene. Las Vegas PD closed the case, citing it as suicide. Foul play was not suspected.

"What a view," Jane said to no one.

"It's not as beautiful as you."

Jane turned her head. Walking up the beach was the blonde from the bar.

"Hello, lover," she said, planting a kiss onto Jane's lips.

The blonde sat down on the chair next to Jane.

"Have you been waiting long?" she asked.

"Time is so weird right now, it couldn't have been for too long. Plus, it just made this moment that much more enjoyable," Jane blushed.

The waiter came over to take their order.

"I'll have another martini, what would you like, Jill?"

Jill took Jane's hand easing into the chair, she closed her eyes.

"I'll have what she's having," Jill said.

The waiter took his leave returning quickly with the drinks.

The two lovers sat on the beach together, finally. Their story was just beginning and as the sun set on their old lives, a sense of peace washed over them, calming nerves. The martini's helped.

Jane thought about what had happened. It seemed like a lifetime ago she had decided to kill her husband. Funny how things turn out. The future was filled with nothing but time and relaxation. Jane and Jill forever.

It wasn't until Jane blinked that her heart skipped a beat. Had someone been lurking behind them, spying on them. Seeing two women together was bound to cause a scene back home, here it was normal. This was more ominous. Jane chalked it up to nerves, biting into the olive from her drink, she savored the flavor. She scratched the spot under her eyelid which had only begun itching recently.

She thought she remembered something that Curly Joe had said about the tunnel, some piece of information she was supposed to remember. She could hear the words, his raspy voice whispering in her ears, the last thing he had said to her.

Terrified, Jane screamed loud and long, her vocal cords gave-out and yet she still wailed. The horror had set in and with no voice left she wouldn't be able to warn Jill. It looked like they would both go down together after-all.

It took the medics thirty minutes to calm Jane down, by that time she had dug deep grooves into her cheeks. Jill remained by her side crying for her lover, confused as to what was happening.

Jane thought she saw something, a face dark and solid before she passed out. The echoing voice of John throbbed in her head until she bubbled and frothed at the mouth before her thoughts went black, those two words the only imprint on her mind before she lost consciousness.

So, there you have it kiddies, a Valentime's Day story to warm your cold blood. A tale to re-energize your dead-end life, a yarn sure to leave you rotting in your grave. Love burns, love hurts and love kills. If you don't believe me, and I know what you're thinking, old Curly Joe has been spinning yarns as a drunken fool, unreliable narrator and such and such, just a bunch of horse-crap.

If you haven't learnt nothing from this here little tale, I invite you to check her out yourself. All you need to do is come to Ellicott City, Maryland. Wander on down to the remains of Saint Mary's and you will come across the Ilchester Tunnel. While you are there you might could mention old Curly Joe sent you. Although you may not have much for a voice when the Blink Man finds you, and he will, he always does.

One other thing, I would be remiss if I didn't give you one more piece of advice, no one ever takes it...guess they're too busy dying.

Don't blink.

BUTTERFLYKISSES68

By Patrick Storck

This tale was given to author Storck by a member of the clergy who wishes to remain anonymous. It is taken from a series of notebooks kept by the protagonist of the tale and is presented here largely as it appeared there, with unrelated day-to-day events removed.

BUTTERFLYKISSES68
by Patrick Storck

The windows were down on the AMC Ambassador as it drove through Wilde Lake on an oddly humid April afternoon. From the passenger seat, Anthony Cornuto took in the peaceful scenery amid a flurry of construction, trying to reconcile it with the Baltimore he grew up in a half hour away. While Baltimore was in the process of healing after the nearly two weeks of riots earlier that month, here they were building an all new community, planned to be the better way to integrate people of all races and faiths. Anthony had his doubts about the project, as did plenty of people, but citizens don't get much of a vote on how millionaires spend their money. Still, he held out hope that good intentions could be used to pave roads not exclusively to hell.

Hope was something Anthony reserved for things he knew little about. As he listened to Chuck Thompson announcing the Orioles as they took on Boston, he held out hope that Brooks Robinson and Frank Thomas would hold up as they got a bit longer in the tooth, but Davey Johnson had been fairly consistent the last two years. Hank Bauer as manager hadn't been as inspiring, but the season was still young.

As Anthony imagined himself at Memorial Stadium taking in a game this summer, his thoughts drifted out to 33rd street, then Waverly, then further downtown, until he was standing in the middle of the street trying to drag his buddy Ruben away from the approaching cops. To his left was a burning Mercury Monterey that looked like it hadn't run in years anyway. To his right were kids jumping on an assortment of run-down cars, swinging bats and boards at the windows like they were pinatas at some anarchic birthday party. He couldn't tell if it was one guy up on the roofs moving up and down the block, training his rifle on protesters, or if each building had their own volunteer sniper. Either way, he wasn't looking when he heard the loud crack that he assumed was a shot to his face.

Unlike when that all happened originally, Anthony came to back in the Ambassador. He dabbed the tears around his left eye, which had started to overwater because of the wind blowing in the car. It was mostly scar tissue from his nose to the middle of his cheek, and his eyelid had melted so taut he couldn't close it anymore, so he was stuck with what his doctor termed a "leaky faucet" from his tear ducts. He rolled his eyes around to spread the moisture, then noticed Father Tate looking at him.

"You went somewhere else for a minute there," Tate said in a bad attempt at not sounding concerned.

Anthony straightened up in his seat. "I was just getting lost in the game."

"Okay. I just don't see people jump that way for a walk very often. They should probably put in McNally." Father Tate turned up the radio a bit as Anthony rolled up his window.

They passed a construction site that was starting to take the shape of a small shopping center. Anthony knocked a knuckle on his window. "What do you think of all of this?"

Father Tate didn't bother to look. "New community means new parishioners. We'll see other denominations come in, of course. But I'd like to think after a hundred years in the area, St. Mary's is going to be just fine. Busier than ever, in fact. After all, you found us."

The construction left in the distance, Wilde Lake itself slid into view. "I'm trying to get out of the city. Maybe even go on missionary work. Get out of the country for a while. That's what Father Lawrence said you were known for, right? It's just weird to see houses and stuff getting in the way of scenery like this."

Father Tate laughed and finally looked over. "The lake? They put that in last year. Who knows how much it cost? But somebody thought a lake would be a nice start for a community, so there you go. God created the world, God created us, we create lakes just like he does now. Everyone tries to become their parents at some point, and we all try and become nothing like them at some point. I'd rather have houses and families and a lake in my neighborhood than a military base."

Anthony was a bit surprised. Father Tate was hardly old, but definitely of at least one generation past. "You're against Viet Nam?"

Tate was getting more amused by the moment. The young recruits were always so surprised that priests were people with actual thoughts about things outside of the scriptures. "I'm against war. I have nothing against any country, or its people. If the leaders are A-holes, I have my problems with them, but I don't think bombs are the way to change minds. Just landscapes."

The borderline swear, as intended, helped loosen Anthony up. "I don't know. Seems like a quick way to make a lake."

"That it does. 'Into every crater, rain must fall.' Jacobiah 21:14," Tate rattled off as he turned onto Bonnie Branch Road.

"I like that." Anthony took in the lake one more time in the rear-view mirror. "I get what you mean about war. I just don't get this one. They say the spread of communism on the news and all, but if that's the case why do we have to go all the way over there? Seems like we're the ones spreading out all over." The lake gone, Anthony looked to Father Tate. "You made up that quote, didn't you?"

"That I did."

"I didn't think priests were allowed to lie."

"Who lied? I said something thoughtful, and actually fairly nonsensical, to be honest. Then I added a name and some numbers to the end. I never claimed it was in the Bible. Let that be lesson number one. We can read all we want, but leadership and faith come from more than that. People come to us for answers, so we do what we can. But in the long run they will hear what they want to hear and see what they want to see. Just don't do it in mass. Stick to the book and save the creativity for the homily."

Anthony dabbed some more seepage from the corner of his eye. "I don't think I'll be holding mass. I might just stick to hearing confessions. If I even get through this."

Father Tate turned onto the gravel driveway that lead to the lower housing building of St. Mary's College. The rocks crunched in the same uncomfortably satisfying way a good long back crack will. "Anthony, you have six years of schooling and training to be a priest, if that truly is your calling. Or leave if it isn't. We hope every one of our pre-ordained makes it, of course. If not, we hope you at least pick up some good ideas and inspiration along the way." Tate eased on the brakes in front of the boarding house, but never shifted to park. "This is where you'll be staying. Go settle in, unpack, look around. Start introducing yourself. Dinner is at five."

The door of the Ambassador creaked open until it popped into place. An older priest, Father Samuels, turned at the noise and put out his cigarette. "Tate, we have oil. Fix that thing. Who's the kid?"

Anthony climbed out of the car, dragging his modest suitcase with his left hand, extending his right to shake. "Anthony Cornuto. I'm here to try and start a new life."

Father Samuels took his hand and gave a long, firm, testing grasp. "'What's past is prologue.' There are no new lives, but welcome to this leg of your journey." Samuels released his grip and gestured to Anthony's scarring. "Whatever happened here is a part of you. Denying it derives no lesson. Alan Samuels. Head on in, we'll get started on the paperwork." Samuels popped and swung the car door shut with a groaning slam. "Fix this, Tate."

Anthony, uncomfortable with the casual addressing of his scar, nodded and rushed into his housing. Generations back it had been a tavern, and still had enough of those bones about it. He came here looking to redeem his soul for the mistakes he had made, cleanse his conscience in the eyes of God, and it was unnerving how everyone else seemed so fucking casual about it all.

The first few days at seminary were a strange blend of what Anthony imagined summer camp would be like blended with the first week of college. There were greetings and well wishing, but he knew he had some time before he fit into the different cliques.

The younger priests and students tended to talk more about politics. On social issues they all seemed to get along when it came to race, but on matters of personal morality there were some who had to talk in whispers. Red meat on Friday was rarely a passionate debate, but some preferred the ceremony of abstinence on it even though the reasons were far outdated. The older clergy, had they strong opinions on these subjects, generally kept to themselves. Anthony suspected it was more out of boredom on the matters, the same groove worn on a record until it was bordering static.

Mornings were spent helping out on chores. This encouraged the new students to start feeling like part of the school rather than just visitors, as well as force socializing and familiarity with the layout. Anthony volunteered for the kitchen, having grown up in the culinary community of Little Italy. He was disappointed to find that the food was accepted at a blanketly tolerable level. Everyone had their tastes, and so to feed the masses meals were best served as simple and inarguable as possible. Some jokingly referred to lunch as "Our Daily Bread" because it was by far the most popular item on the menu. Opinions on bread don't vary widely.

In the afternoon, usually in one of the small courtyards, Anthony would read. He had yet to be given any official assignments as he had come to campus towards the end of a session, but was given some suggested readings by Father Tate. He also figured it would be prudent to start reading the whole Bible. Having grown up Catholic, he was familiar with many passages and readings, and obviously the major rules and ideas, but like most had never sat down and read it cover to cover. He'd considered just starting with the New Testament, but with six years ahead of him he dove in on Genesis. It was interesting to get some back story on all of those "begats" from the Gospels. Maybe he wouldn't breeze through those like everyone usually did.

At dinner he would try and eavesdrop on students to get a sense of what was coming, but rarely interjected. At an early age it was made clear the value of being quiet. One could disappear in a room, become almost invisible, and be witness to all sorts of secrets and truths. Even if you were noticed, if you remained quiet you remained trusted. Quiet people, by nature, don't talk. His brother Chris was far from quiet, and therefore was often silenced then sent from the room. Some adults even considered the justified crying of a seven-year-old as an annoyance, so Anthony learned the art of suffering in silence. He'd rather get to know everyone well enough that he'd feel comfortable when they inevitably asked about his injury, something until now they were clearly shying away from. "What tragedy befell you?" is not a polite ice breaker in most circles.

After dinner things generally quieted down. Some of the older folks would enjoy a nice whiskey, some wine, occasionally a beer or two. The younger set generally held off for some reason, likely that the conversations veered toward nostalgic for days that predate any contributions they might have. It didn't hurt that they had evening studies assigned by those same elders. Anthony was happy to again go off on his own and dive into more reading, but as the light grew dimmer, he struggled more and more.

While his face around his left eye was disfigured, the eye itself was mostly unharmed. Anthony was pretty sure the owner of the burning car had to scrape off that eyelid days later, unaware of what it was by that point. Reading for too long can be generally exhausting, more so if out of practice, and especially if one was never much of a reader. When one of your eyes is regularly either bone dry or flooding itself, the strain is exponential as the evening wears on. Still, the eyepatch he was given itched terribly so he wore it as little as possible. When he finally felt sleep was overtaking him, he'd put it on and hope to be off to somewhere else before the irritation was too much.

It was around ten in the evening on Anthony's second week there that Father Samuels knocked on his door. Anthony opened it and immediately apologized for staying up so late. Samuels shrugged, came in, closed the door, then sat down.

"You can't sleep, I can't sleep. You're hiding in here, I wander around. We all have our ways of trying to clear our heads." Samuels pulled out a cigarette. "May I?"

Anthony nodded, then looked at the pack. "Sure. I didn't

know we were allowed. May I?" Samuels slip the pack to him then let his match linger lit for Anthony. "This is the first one I've had since..."

"I thought that looked like a burn. I've been curious, but didn't want to pry." They both took long drags, then each followed their exhalation across the room instead of making eye contact. "Well, that's the most I'll ask on the matter. You really shouldn't read in this light."

"I feel like I'm way behind everyone else, and I can't sleep. What else am I supposed to do?" Anthony said, self-consciously placing his bookmark. He set his Bible down on his night stand, and Father Samuels slid it out from under his hand.

"This is where we turn for stories, parables, The Word as it were. This is here for us to help find our way and show others theirs in this world." He set it the Bible back down on the dresser, not next to the bed. "But those questions come from being out in the world. You've been out there. It's done a number on you. Going back to your corner is fine, recover, catch your breath. But you can't hide forever. Especially if you plan on missionary work, which Father Tate says you had in mind. You'll need to explore now, before you get sent to who knows where."

"I don't have a car, and there's nothing around here, really." Anthony looked to the Bible now as an escape from this conversation, and in that moment realized how little he'd been connecting to the material. He'd just been reading to get through it, know the details, study. Somewhere in the past week he had already lost his connection to it, save for it shielding him from anything else.

Father Samuels stood and went to the window. He opened it to a refreshing Spring evening. The only sounds were of nature. "You came from the city. Listen to that. No cars, no fighting, no music. Take a flashlight, but there's plenty to explore. I used to all of the time before my knee started to trick me up. Find someplace quiet. Take nothing with you. See how long you can be alone with your thoughts. For me it was at least a month before I could stand more than five minutes in my own head. But you'll learn to meditate. Process what you've read. What you've been through. Then they'll overlap and the scriptures and your pain will flow in the same train of thought. The knots will unkink. Have you ever read up on Buddhism?"

Anthony's face squinched up. Was this a trick question? "No, I was raised Catholic."

Father Samuels smiled and walked to the door. "While there's much to the religion and practices, Buddhism is also a philosophy. There's plenty to take away from it. Also, there's no harm in reading up on what everyone believes. You'll find that for the most part we all come down on the side of making the world a better place. The problems come from getting lost in the details. And that's usually the fault of those not curious enough. I'll drop off some books tomorrow. In the meantime, it's a nice night. Maybe go for a walk."

Anthony looked to the window. Some sort of bird made a noise he'd never heard, at least consciously. Father Samuels left the room. "I assure you; the neighborhood is safe."

For the next several nights, Anthony took Father Samuels' advice. At first, he only wandered the nearby woods, but kept on campus. He wanted to make sure he had an eye line to at least one building so he wouldn't get lost. Within a week he was wandering further and further out, now more familiar with certain small landmarks in the area.

There was a small grotto with what was once somebody's hobby fish pond. The rocks were placed in a rough circle, and the hole was at least a foot into the ground. He initially mistook it for a rain-filled fire pit, caked with algae, until after days of no rain he saw the skeleton of a fish no bigger than his hand, nothing someone would've caught nearby and cooked on a camping trip.

Several trees started to stand out as well, knotted in strange ways. This fascinated him. In the city, the trees were only allowed to grow so large before they were a threat to pipes and sidewalks. They were regularly trimmed to keep out of traffic, until passing trucks did the job just by passing through. Were the knots scars from lightning that the tree had to grow around? Was it some form of plant cancer, or maybe a sap clot? He didn't know much about botany, didn't even know the word botany, but found he could get lost in speculation.

One night he found a couple making out about a hundred yards from a pull-off area on one of the main roads. They had cheap beer and a transistor radio playing some new British band. Anthony tried to leave them be, but stepped on a twig and set them in a panic. After a moment of fight or flight, Anthony stepped out to apologize. The light from his flashlight cast up on the worst of his face, sending them screaming into the night. It took him a moment to piece it together, until he realized he looked like a monster. His self-pity was broken by a moment of wondering if that's how people see him, then realizing he probably just launched a new urban legend. He was still laughing when he got back to his room, the long release of humor he hadn't felt for over a month now.

The evening walks got longer and more relaxing. Even though he was getting to bed later, he felt more rested each morning. He hadn't meditated on his issues, but instead finally was able to put them aside to think about anything else. Samuels was right about letting his daily readings soak in. He would turn them over and free associate with other passages. He knew fully well he was starting to mangle some of the details, but that's what future studies would be for.

One night he came upon an old tunnel. It was long and didn't seem to have been in use for some time, but was amazingly lacking in graffiti and garbage. There was a sense of respect around the place, perhaps apprehension. The other end was visible in the moonlight, but Anthony didn't venture down. Perhaps it was the darkness in between, but he had no urge to visit that light, just focus on it. It was a point of reference, something he could concentrate on, meditate towards. Rivers and trees were too dynamic to really let go of one's awareness, but that single point of light seemed to be exactly what he needed.

Anthony didn't visit the tunnel every night, but on the nights he did he found himself staying out later and later. It was about a twenty-minute walk from the college the way he'd been traveling. There might be a shorter path, but he was content taking the time to go the way he knew. Instead of taking in and marveling at nature, or thinking about that day, he started to truly go blank. He would lose all sense of the now. Then images and voices started visiting him from the past.

He would hear his mother yelling at neighborhood kids while she worked on her all-day sauce. He could smell it cooking. He could feel the rough grain of their dining room table, never properly sanded or varnished, stained by hundreds of meals. He could hear the muffled sound of his father listening to a Colts game, the AAFC version. Once Baltimore joined the NFL his father got season tickets, always taking work friends or neighbors. They didn't have a dog, but Anthony heard one barking. He was brought back to the tunnel. Somewhere nearby the barking continued, so he made his way home.

Each visit the memories would delve deeper, sometimes threading moments of his life through loose dream logic. He would be rushing to class before tripping on a curb and taking out a tooth on a neighbor's stoop. As he wiped the blood, he could smell gasoline, hear people running, then gunshots. He turned, but the crowd was marching a parade to celebrate Columbus Day. Ma was nowhere in sight, the bands were too loud, then there was the burning car again. He stared into the fire, brighter, brighter, until it was a birthday candle. Before he could blow it out, it flickered, blurred, then came back into focus as the end of the tunnel. For a moment it appeared as if a man stood up at the end.

He continued to stare. There was a man shaped shadow for sure, but he couldn't recall if it had always been there or not. It wasn't moving. Neither was Anthony, but suddenly he felt afraid to move in case the shadow did. Having never explored the tunnel itself, he realized he had no idea how long it was and therefore how tall the man was. Figuring the clearance needed for the tunnel and how close to the top the shadow reached, if it was a man it was a fairly tall one. This shape, he was pretty sure, hadn't been there on other nights, but tonight the moon was out and hardly a cloud in the sky, so it could be something on the other side casting the illusion.

"Hello?" Nothing. "Is somebody there?" It didn't budge. If it was a person, no matter their intent, it would've likely responded in some way. This didn't calm his nerves, but did present him with enough of a logical conclusion to satisfy. He backed away until he got to the main road before looking away from the tunnel. The shape never moved. He made his way home, tonight taking the main roads instead of wandering the woods. It took longer, his unease growing, but was better lit for the most part. Also, he reasoned, they'd be far more likely to find his body near the road than deep in the woods. He tried to laugh off that thought, but for some reason couldn't. He didn't feel alone, even when he got into bed and put on his eyepatch.

For the first time in two weeks, Anthony did not sleep well. He had a hard time shaking the image of that man at the end of the tunnel. He thought about asking around, if anyone else had noticed a man-shaped shadow at the end of that tunnel, but understood that in all likelihood the odds of it were low and the question would seem foolish. Still, it haunted his nightmares. Several times through the night he would get up, pull off his eyepatch, and pace his room. Once he left his room to use the bathroom, but could not resist inspecting every shadow.

Throughout the next day he had a feeling he was being watched. Sometimes he would catch a glimpse of someone in the distance, perhaps a detective, or the family of his friend Ruben, but why would they come looking for him now? Would they hold him responsible? He was here to serve his penance. Maybe they were following up and making sure.

The discussion of angels in the Old Testament is much more vague than he'd assumed. He considered skipping ahead to Revelations, which if he was remembering correctly had the most passages about the ones who punished mankind for our sins. Since he never saw anyone, but constantly felt them, perhaps he was being haunted. He also understood it could be his own guilt haunting him.

Why now, though? After so much time bringing himself towards a more tranquil and thoughtful place, to take such a self-punishing turn seemed counter-intuitive. Maybe in his exploring his feelings and new philosophies, he had opened a door to his personal demons and had no bait to lure them back into seclusion. As he imagined these demons, they grew more and more grotesque with each memory. They would snarl "abandoner, coward, racist..." as rows of teeth grew in front of each other, then began to sprout down their spine. They would squinch their face as if smelling a rotten soul, and their skin would crack like dried mud, leaking black and watery blood.

In the middle of one of these flashes, Father Tate placed a hand on Anthony's shoulder, startling him back to the present. "You looked lost in your head again. It doesn't seem like you're very fond of things there."

Anthony took a deep breath and dabbed his eye. "I was thinking about inner demons. But they're just a metaphor. I'm trying to get better at looking at myself. That's all."

Father Tate sat down on the bench next to Anthony. "Sure, they are. But just because they don't exist doesn't mean what they represent is also a fantasy. That's how metaphors are supposed to work, right? There isn't a magic sword to slay them, just hard work, honesty, and reflection. You're just getting started, but as seriously as you're taking things, I think you'll get there. And be stronger for it."

Anthony pulled out a cigarette. He'd taken back up the habit for his walks, but was already down half a pack since breakfast. He lit it, took a long drag. When he exhaled, for a brief moment, he saw the shadow man in the smoke. "Something is after me. I don't know how or why, but it is." He took another drag and blew it around, trying to recreate the vision.

"You sound paranoid. You just said your demons are metaphors. You have a lot weighing on you. You haven't socialized much in your time here so far, but you've been withdrawing even more lately. Come say confession this afternoon. Get some of these demons off your soul. Bottling them up just makes them more dangerous when they break out. I mean that more in a Freudian sense, by the way. If you want, I some of his works. I don't care for his views on monotheism, but he has some interesting ideas otherwise."

There was no trace of the shadow man. Anthony took another drag. "That sounds good. I could use some more non-Biblical reading. I think I'm obsessing."

"You're absolutely obsessing. Confession and book club. Come by around three." Father Tate stood up, slapped Anthony on the shoulder once more, then wandered off. The courtyard was full of wandering students and faculty, but as far as he could tell every shadow was attached to a person.

Confession, especially for the lapsed Catholic, can easily turn into a therapy session. While most people prefer the semi-anonymity of the small, dark, screened confessionals you find at most churches, many in clergy take part in the sacrament face to face. The illusion of secrecy is done away with in favor of a real discussion and real reflection. Anthony and Father Tate sat in his office for nearly a full hour, all the time Tate had available.

Before deciding to enter the priesthood, Anthony had not been to confession for several years, enough to not have a firm number. He wasn't sure where to begin. It would make sense to go chronologically so he didn't miss any, but so many poor decisions blended together. He had certainly stolen, lied, and fornicated. Tate nodded and asked if he renounced that behavior and understood the harm such acts can do to one's self or others. He did. He was surprised that the priest made an allowance to combine all of these into a single confession to absolve, as long as he didn't feel the need to explore any of them for a particular guilt. While certain incidents weighed on him more than others, none seemed to be a crushing regret that would manifest as a lingering terror.

Tate could tell Anthony was holding something back, from confession and from himself. "I know there's something you are leaving out. Since the day you got here. I'm assuming it's why you made your way here. You have to come to it in your own time, but you do need to come to it at some point. We can offer sanctuary, we can offer forgiveness, we can offer a new direction, but offering does nothing until one accepts."

Anthony glanced out the window. Two students were walking to the dining hall. Behind them, for just a moment, he thought he saw the shadow man. "Can we come back to it tomorrow? I'd rather clean out my junk drawer on the rest of this right now, if it's okay."

"As I said, in your own time. Prune the branches before you cut down the tree."

"I guess so?" Anthony finished out the session with a few specific stories of youthful indiscretion. One of them, involving a stolen shopping cart, got a solid laugh out of the Father. He ended up with a tally of five times through a rosary. Tate then provided him a rosary and a packet of instructions, just in case. The Apostle's Creed, Our Father, Fatima Prayer, Hail Holy Queen, Rosary Prayer, and of course Hail Mary were mimeographed in English and Latin, either would be fine. The English would be more reflective, but the Latin would be more difficult, so he encouraged trading off between them.

Immediately after dinner, Anthony returned to his room and began his penance. The repetition was relaxing, helped him focus on anything besides his shadow. He wasn't sure how to pronounce Latin per se, but he'd learned enough Italian that he assumed he was in the ballpark. The second rosary he started getting bored and could tell he was just going through the motions. He pushed through, had a cigarette, then started his third rosary driven by the guilt of not taking his penance seriously. The fourth time through he really concentrated on the words each time as he said them. He was connecting the Latin phrases, hitting those with extra inflection now that he believed he understood them.

The fifth and final time through, he concentrated on a different incident of sin for each prayer, truly asking forgiveness. He relived those moments outside of himself, watched as time after time he violated not just the laws of God, but the happiness and well-being of his fellow man. He imagined details he may have never actually seen, like the grocer doing inventory, coming up short, having trouble paying the bills, and so on. He began to hate this person he saw enact cruelty after cruelty, both small and large. When he reached the end, after two hundred and sixty-five Hail Marys, thirty Our Fathers, and all the rest, he added a special personal prayer that God could find a way to forgive him, and show him a sign as to how to forgive himself. Exhausted, he lit a cigarette, slipped on his eye patch, and drifted to sleep.

When Anthony awoke the following day, he felt a bit better. He could still feel something watching over him, but much of his guilt had been faced. His spirit felt as if it had been massaged - raw and tender but relaxed. His senses seemed sharper. He could smell the lingering traces of his cigarettes. He could hear the muffled grumbles of conversations in the hall. The sun coming in the window was brighter than any day he'd been here yet. So bright, in fact, he took his eye patch with him and wore it any time he went outside.

Before dinner he went for another round of confession, where he more recounted his experience with penance. Father Tate encouraged this reflection and follow up. Just because you repent for your sins does not mean you throw them away. You should hold them in your heart as lessons. Just like Anthony wandered the woods taking the wrong paths until he found the right ones, so too are the journeys of morality. He pointed out the many stories of

Jesus holding the repentant sinner in higher esteem than those who had always taken the path of the righteous. To know temptation and reject it is harder than to never be tested at all.

Anthony didn't offer his most troubling confession, nor did Father Tate pry for it. Real progress was being made. The memories danced on the side of Anthony's consciousness, but he didn't feel it was quite right yet. By the end of the session they were more talking about philosophy than specific sins. With nothing new presented to repent, there was no new penance assigned, though Anthony expected he may say another rosary tonight for good measure. He wasn't taking his walks any time soon, so this could serve as his new meditation.

On his way to the dining hall, Anthony stopped for a cigarette. His old vice had fully taken root again, but as vices go, at least this one was not a sin. He started to think about the specificity of the Ten Commandments, and all of the other supplemental laws the Good Book provided. Until Jesus, shellfish were disallowed. After He dies for our sins, shellfish was not only back on the table, but often used as sustenance on Fridays, when meat was now disallowed. Creatures of the sea were animals, so he wasn't sure why there was a delineation. Certain fabrics were technically out, and though never specifically later allowed, those rules had been mostly dismissed for all but the most orthodox. The Word of God has been interpreted from language to language and generation to generation enough, he had to assume if smoking was ever to be a sin it would've been written in by now.

The sun, still bright, had at least started to retreat behind the tree line. He flipped up his eyepatch to get some depth to his view of a gorgeous day. At first everything blurred and was washed in an intensely dynamic contrast, his left pupil overstimulated while his right had already adjusted. He looked around in vague circles to get his eyes in sync. Once he stopped, there he was. The shadow man was standing at the edge of the courtyard. For the first time, he could simply be seen. There was no question of mirage, except he seemed semi-transparent. He was black from top to bottom, not like Ruben, but like coal. His clothes, his skin, everything about him seemed to almost part the light from him like Moses parted the Red Sea.

Anthony stared at the man, afraid to look away. This was confirmation. It existed. He was being followed. The longer he ignored his sins, the closer this specter came. Was it an angel or a demon? If Lucifer and Saint Peter both hold judgement and punish the wicked, did it truly matter? He had already confessed that day, but perhaps Father Tate would see him again?

The cigarette had burned down close to the filter, but more painfully to the knuckles that had been absently holding it. Anthony swore and dropped it, then inspected his burn. It might blister, but wasn't too bad. He refused to look back to where the shadow man had been standing, and instead stared straight ahead to the dining hall where he would sit quietly, appetite now replaced in his gut by a rock of dread.

A second confession for the day was not an option for Father Tate. He had a discussion group to moderate that centered on retraining older clergy working with parishioners still adjusting to Vatican II. While it had been in place for almost a decade, there were still many holding on to the traditions they grew up with. Tate did take a few moments to talk to Anthony, sensing his urgency.

"Let's assume you're penitent. Let's assume you've given this confession some deep consideration. Say three rosaries tonight and really roll it all over in your mind. That way, when we talk tomorrow, you'll be able to really get it all out. This clearly means a

lot to you, so I'd like you to prepare. Consider this home work."
Tate then placed his left hand on Anthony's shoulder and shook
his right hand and smiled. Anthony stood quietly for long enough
to make anyone else uncomfortable, but Father Tate waited.
Finally, with a nod of surrender, Anthony let go of Tate's hand,
releasing him to his other responsibilities.

Walking to his room, Anthony started at the ground. He
could sense prying eyes in the periphery. Maybe the shadow man,
maybe students. He was sure by now there were rumors about him.
Between the scars and the solitude, why wouldn't there be? Maybe
they'd even started hearing rumors of the woods monster that
scared off young couples making out nearby. If only they knew
what monsters were afraid of.

He prepared for bed, then pulled out his rosary. Adding to the
ceremony tonight, on every large bead he added a cigarette to the
Our Father before beginning the next decade of Hail Marys. After
the first rosary, the room was thick with the smell of smoke. He
kept squinting his watering left eye, dabbing at it. A break was
needed, he put on his eye patch then opened his window. His
throat was a bit parched, so he set down his rosary and headed to
the bathroom.

At the sink, he downed a glass of water in two long pulls. He
flipped up his eye patch and splashed his face, toweled off, then
flipped the patch back down. Glass refilled, he went back out into
the hallway.

The shadows seemed different tonight. He didn't see the
shadow man, just an extra darkness in the corners. He sensed the
shape of this stalking presence at the end of the hall, but even
squinting didn't reveal it. Since his left eye had adjusted more to
the darkness under the patch, he flipped it up for a better view.
The shadow man wasn't at the end of the hall.

He was ten feet away.

Some students rushed out when they heard the glass shatter on the floor. There stood the new guy, face frozen in fear, tears running down his cheeks. The offered support, help, questions, but Anthony didn't respond. As his dorm mates came up to him, they walked right through this translucent thing staring him down. It had impossibly long eyelashes. Its face was a rictus of impatience. It said nothing. It was not there to speak, but to listen. To judge. To punish. The others didn't see this because this was his demon. Should he open up, burden them with his truth? Would they be complicitly cursed? Not ordained, they weren't cleared to offer absolution.

Two students started cleaning up the glass. Another was snapping his fingers in front of Anthony's face. Finally, one grabbed him by the shoulder and pulled down his eye patch. With that, the vision disappeared. Anthony vomited a stale breath held for almost a minute then started hyperventilating. The others had no idea what to do, and he had no idea how to explain it, so he let them lead him back to his room.

He didn't say his other two rosaries that night. He just stared at his ceiling knowing that thing was there. Only his left eye could see it. It was hiding behind that eye patch. Every time he tried to hide from it, the thing came closer, refusing to be ignored. His conscience.

Around three in the morning, when everything was left to wandering deer, raccoons, bats, and the ghosts of settlers if you believe in such things, a branch on the tree twenty feet from Anthony's room finally gave in to its age. It snapped off, then crashed to the ground. It was enough to wake anyone sleeping on that side of the dormitory. Anthony bolted up so fast his eye patch slipped off. He stared at the ceiling for a long moment. He was afraid to look out his window as people gathered outside and in the hallway.

Finally, curiosity won. He traced a path on the ceiling over towards the window, to the top of the frame. The air ripped in through his nostrils was cold. The window was open. He swallowed nothing, his throat dry but reflexive. He looked down.

People were crowding around the branch, looking up at the tree. Everyone had a theory, none a solution. It was dark, but none of the figures below were that complete blackness that comprised his conscience. It was just scared students and faculty.

He reached absently for his cigarettes, his matches, and lit one up. A few younger students took direction from the older ones and dragged the branch to the middle of the lawn, a location just as useless a resting place. There was no storm brewing, no ominous wind. No large birds fleeing the scene. The branch just decided tonight to give in to destiny.

Anthony stubbed out his cigarette and turned towards his bed to go back to sleep. There, in front of his door, was the shadow man. He didn't move. He didn't blink. He squinted in a way that moved his eye lashes in almost a wave hello.

After staring far longer than he had at the looming figure, Anthony moved towards his bed. The figure remained still. It didn't move away, nor towards him. It just watched, judging. Having judged. Knowing. Knowing he knew. Anthony slid into bed. He fumbled around until he caught the strap of his patch on his ring finger. Slowly he raised his hands to his head.

The figure finally moved. It rolled its back from the base of the spine up, slowly, becoming taller but leaning back. In animals this often serves to present dominance. In this gesture, it was clearly getting comfortable. It wanted him to put on the patch. It wanted him to sleep.

Anthony stared, refusing. He set down the eye patch. He

refused to look away. This was his past, his guilt manifest. He needed to accept his life. It was just too hard to think about anything but this thing in front of him. He tried to recall the Latin versions of the Hail Mary, but it came out jumbled and meaningless, rote but broken. He asked it questions, expecting and receiving no answers. It just stared at him. Eventually the winner of the staring contest was exhaustion.

That night Anthony dreamed of his childhood. His father had returned from World War II, defending the American Way against Japan and avoiding the European complications of his heritage. He married his high school sweetheart, who hadn't waited for him, but the timing was such she never told him otherwise. They wanted a robust family, generations of exponentially larger holidays. Instead they were blessed with a single son who showed little promise. As a child in the dream, he thought ahead to his life and how as a priest he would deny them at least grandchildren.

He went to play with his toys, but as he dug through his collection each figure took the shape of the shadow man. He went to read some comic books, but the villain in each turned black and just stood there, challenging the methods of his heroic but violent heroes. He sat down to watch football with his father, but the referee took the form of an unblinking magistrate.

Anthony awoke completely dehydrated. His face was buried in his pillow. He grasped for his eye patch and put it on, knowing this was what it wanted but not wanting to face it. It was there, and that was enough. He went to breakfast, ate in silence, went to the library, ran his eyes over passages in silence but retaining nothing. Eventually lunch rolled around. He dropped an adequate serving into a disinterested stomach. Finally, it was time for his daily confession.

The riots broke out all over the city. All over the nation as well, but Baltimore had an especially visceral reaction to the assassination of Doctor Martin Luther King, Jr. Anthony didn't really follow the news. He knew the civil rights movement was happening, but had never seen the issues. His buddy Ruben from Locust point always seemed happy enough. They worked together, had lunch together, would have drinks together in bars closer to where Ruben lived. He didn't see many black people in the bars back in Little Italy, but ascribed it just as much to being a "local bar" thing as the rhetoric from his neighbors that was less than welcoming.

When people started taking to the streets, his community took up arms. He didn't begrudge people like Ruben wanting more than they were given, but when it came to destroying or taking from his family, he was ready to protect what they had.

Everyone had their radios on. The television coverage had images of destruction, but the real play by play was on the AM news stations. People were calling in and giving their reactions and updates. As far as he could tell, chaos was reigning supreme. Ma was scared. Dad was angry. He didn't fight for this country to be overthrown by its own people. He thought they should be happy to be in the best country in the world.

Then they heard the crowd. It was chanting, shouting. Glass was breaking. Sirens could be heard from other neighborhoods, but nothing as close as the approaching storm. Anthony watched from the windows. The crowd looked passionate, angry, but not bloodthirsty. They didn't look like the enemy.

His father threw a bottle from their second-floor window. It hit a girl that couldn't have been twenty years old. The man next to her caught her on her way to the ground. Two other people stepped in and helped them to the side of the procession. Dad had more than enough bottles of all sizes, like he had been stockpiling for such an event. His next two throws weren't aimed, just absently side armed like skipping stones off a river of people. One bounced off the shoulder of a man in a suit, the other skipped off the hood of their neighbor's car.

It soon became as casual as a carnival game, something you played at the boardwalk for a cheaply made stuffed animal. The whole family was taking turns tossing bottles at the people marching through their neighborhood. They were littering the streets with more glass than the rioters, but at least it was their streets to litter, or protect, or whatever. Looking down the block there were more than enough easy targets flowing through.

Then a shot rang out. It popped into the window of the bakery down the street, a warning shot. The crowd scattered, but only really had forward and back to run. Anthony took this as a challenge. Now they were moving targets, so he started whipping bottle as fast as he could. He missed, missed, missed, hit.

A twelve-year-old girl fell halfway to the ground, held up only by her father's hand. He slung his arm around her side and lifted her like luggage. He looked around in broken rage, tears pouring down his face. He cleared the crowd and got to the sidewalk, then brushed the glass from her, digging some of the cuts further.

Anthony backed up. He lost view of the girl. Of the crowd. He backed out of the room. Of the apartment. He saw the stairs, and just went down, wandered to the door. A crowd was gathered, ready to barricade. He moved to the front, pushing aside an older woman worrying about the deli around the corner. He had gone to that deli uncountable times, pocketed sodas at least once a week. But that girl was hurt. He didn't think about anyone else out there on the street until the explosion.

The Mercury Monterey was hit by a Molotov cocktail. People were starting to throw rocks into and from the crowd. Windows were being smashed. It was utter chaos. He helped the others with the barricade, should anyone try and come in. Another shot blew out a car window out of view. The crowd was scrambling in all directions. One of the rioters ran up to the door and looked Anthony in the eyes. It was Ruben. He was terrified.

Ruben pounded on the door and pleaded to be let in. One of the rifle shots caught a man in the middle of the street in the shoulder. More bottles were raining down from the floor above. Anthony's neighbors were shouting racial slurs new and old at Ruben. Anthony was frozen. As Ruben was tearing up and pulling at the door, yet another rifle shot caught someone in the knee. A wine bottle appeared from the heavens and took Ruben down.

"I know him," Anthony said too quietly to be heard. He tried to open the door, but everyone fought against him. He turned and shouted. "I know him! Let me out!" His neighbors backed up. Anthony opened the door and was immediately shoved out. The door slammed shut and the deadbolt clacked into place. Ruben was on the ground, blood covering his face. His eyes had rolled up into his head, and he was breathing like a fish out of water.

Anthony looked around for any safe harbor. He saw the girl across the street being tended to by her father behind a postal box. He grabbed Ruben by the arms and pulled as hard as he could, but Ruben was mostly dead weight. After what seemed like an eternity, they were halfway across the street when the police arrived. Some children had jumped onto cars and started smashing windows. One car's window exploded under a ten-year-old while his bat was still in the air as the snipers continued to fire off more dangerous warning shots. Smoke was filling the streets.

Anthony let go of Ruben in the middle of the road. He turned back towards his home and one of his neighbors gave him the finger. He danced back and forth, looking for someplace to run, but everywhere was pandemonium. A chip burst from the road n front of him. In the smoke, the snipers probably couldn't tell who was black and who wasn't. He stumbled back and fell onto his tailbone. Seeing stars, he reached up to someone walking past.

Instead of a friendly hand, his wrist was cracked with a riot cop's night stick. That was followed by another to the right side of his head, spinning him towards the burning Mercury. The heat of the door flash fried the left side of his face like a slab of bacon. He fell to the ground screaming so long and hard, he wasn't sure if he passed out from the pain or lack of air.

When he came to in the hospital, his family was not there to visit him. He asked about Ruben, but the staff had no information. He described what Ruben had been wearing, a green button up shirt, but it really wasn't much to go on. One of the nurses said she'd ask around, because there were still two John Does at Mercy Medical. He had no idea how to ask about the young girl.

Anthony never received word on if Ruben had lived. He never received a visit, even a call, from any of his family or neighbors. The chaplain at the hospital was the only one who came to visit, and that as part of assigned rounds. Still, their talks were long and helpful. After a few calls and setting up admission out of semester, they lead Anthony here to St. Mary's college once he was discharged.

Releasing his guilt over leaving his friend to probably die, over hitting that little girl, Anthony felt a weight lifted. He wasn't proud, he hadn't forgiven himself, but he had accepted what he had done and that he had to be better than that for the rest of his life. Walking up to the edge of heroism means nothing if you're still a coward enough to back off when it suits you.

He had considered describing the shadow man to Father Tate, but after getting out his shame he felt it wasn't necessary. He went outside and had a smoke. Father Samuels walked by and joined him. It was mid-June and the Orioles, while more miss than hit this season, had just beaten the Washington Senators in back to back games. There were rumors floating that Hank Bauer might be getting replaced as manager, and Earl Weaver was a top contender for the spot. They were taking on the Minnesota Twins tonight, who had just a few years back been the Washington Senators themselves.

After dinner, Anthony thought about taking a walk for the first time in a long time. He was drawn back to the tunnel, and amazingly felt no apprehension. The closer he got, the more confident he was that he was truly starting to heal, to face himself and be a better person. If he could keep up his studies and his introspection, he thought he might be an excellent missionary, preaching the word of God through personal growth and happiness rather than the bullying he'd heard happens in many parts of the world.

When he reached the tunnel, he saw nothing. He felt nothing. It was just a tunnel. This was no portal to another world, no magical place of self-vengeance. It was just a tunnel. He flipped up his eyepatch.

The shadow man was so close he could feel the tips of his long eyelashes brushing against his skin. He pulled the eyepatch back down.

Once again Anthony backed up to the road, but this time took the long and wandering path back to the college. He chain smoked the whole way, knowing he had a half a carton back in his room from a run into town Father Samuels took him on. The entire time, even with the patch down, he could feel those eyelashes tickling his cheek.

He crossed the campus engaging with nobody. He listened to every sound, took in every smell along the way, all the while staring at a middle distance and not seeing anything at all.

Once he reached his room, he got out his carton and his Bible. Going against the plan, he skipped ahead to the Book of Revelation, the Apocalypse of John.

"The Revelation of Jesus Christ, which God gave unto him, to shew unto his servants things which must shortly come to pass; and he sent and signified it by his angel unto his servant John: Who bare record of the word of God, and of the testimony of Jesus Christ, and of all things that he saw. Blessed is he that readeth, and they that hear the words of this prophecy, and keep those things which are written therein: for the time is at hand."

Anthony smoked and read for hours, going back over this same book as soon as he reached the end. His left eye watered, but he dare not wipe it and risk removing the eyepatch for even a second. He fought to ignore the tickling eyelashes, scratch at them, because they too were under the patch.

After two packs of cigarettes he went for a glass of water. He swallowed it like he was fresh from the desert, then immediately vomited it up. He had another that settled better.

By midnight his room smelled like a truck stop. He kept reading and smoking until sleep finally and without warning took him. He slumped forward, his smoking hand dropping to his lap, to his Bible.

The Bible is a very long book. Typically, the font used is smaller than most books to make room for all of the text. The pages are also made from a much thinner paper than usual. Many an agnostic drug enthusiast has used these pages to roll a joint because of how well the pages burn. This many thin pages, fanned out from repeated reading, introduced to a burning cigarette, will act as very efficient kindling. The rest of Anthony's reading projects stoked the inferno.

Within minutes the room was engulfed in flame. Within an hour the Southern House, once the Ellicott Hotel and Tavern, was burned to the ground, exactly one hundred years after St. Mary's College, founded as Mt. St. Clemons College, had been built.

Anthony Cornuto woke up from the heat immediately. He didn't scream, though the pain was unthinkable. He didn't move. As people outside began to scramble, to bang on his locked door, he just sat there. His body burned, and just before the life left him, his eyepatch burned away as well. He smiled as the shadow man reached for him, knowing it would be denied the pleasure of its vengeance.

REMAINS TO BE SEEN

By Josef Richardson

The following story was reconstructed from tapes, notes, and files left behind after the death of Doctor Boyle. It is not the only disturbing story found within those files, but it is the only one that appears connected to the mystery of the Blink Man.

I can no longer close my eyes without seeing them. A wall of human taxidermy. Innocent children murdered and posed to look like a captive audience to whoever comes upon them. Their skin is still supple, the expression in their eyes still liquid. The sickening odor is beyond typical cadavers decaying in jungle conditions. I suppress a gag but taste bile anyway.

A leg moves.

I wrench my eyes open and they're gone. Even through sunglasses, the grating sting of daylight on exasperated nerves is immediate. Eye drops help less and less. I'm three weeks and two thousand miles from that gruesome tableau. The dull ache in my gut tells me time is running out.

I allow the overstimulation of Baltimore's hectic airport to crowd out the corrosive urge to panic. Best refocus on the mission. Short-term memory continues to deteriorate. Without the miracle of nourishing sleep, soon it will all be gone.

I reach into my jacket for the written instructions and finger the final packet of powder. Before leaving Central America, I tried every substance I could get my hands on to stay awake. Worried about addiction to street drugs, I paid a brujo to cook up a stimulant to keep my eyes open with as few side effects possible.

This reminds me to check if I'm sweating heavily. I am. Not a good look in the dead of Baltimore winter. I'm pretty sure I smell bad, too. I clean up in the men's room as best I can, but the bags sagging beneath my bloodshot eyes can't be fixed. Gotta remember to cough when I'm around anyone in uniform.

Pretend I have a bad flu in the event they force me to remove the shades.

The next instruction says to take a train to Ellicott City. From the ticket counter to the platform, no one makes eye contact. I find a seat on the train and return to the directions.

Doctor Christoff Boyle, Psychiatrist. According to an Agency resource, he does hypnosis on people like me, who've seen horrors in war too overwhelming to process. If he can't make them go away, I would rather not exist anymore.

The train crowds up before departure. I give my seat to an old lady who somehow looks more fatigued than me. The train lurches forward. I tumble into the guy behind me. He absorbs my fall and restores me to my feet without looking away from his newspaper. I glimpse the headline. Walter Mondale thinks he stands a chance against Reagan, with a woman running mate no less.

The rest of the ride, no one looks at me except a young girl I estimate to be around age four. I ignore her until I can't. I might as well close my eyes. They're watching me through her.

The train screeches to a stop at the Ellicott City terminal. From the platform I look up the winding, narrow, main street boxed in by lofty stone buildings reminiscent of old-world Europe. It's a real trudge to the office, and another up four floors of rickety spiral stairs.

Doctor Boyle sees me through the open door and beckons me in. I pocket the sunglasses, expecting him to wince at my haggard condition. Instead he nods and says, "It's good you chose to come."

He gestures to a sturdy leather settee, closes the door, and draws the blinds. The darkness is a cooling salve on a hot wound.

"Should I lie back?" I ask.

"Please."

I haven't laid down flat in over seventy-two hours. I recline belly up, facing a large black and white poster of a spiral tacked to the ceiling. A creaky notebook is opened. Expensive pen scrawls across expensive paper.

"So, tell me Zed, what brings you here?"

No point in dancing around it.

"I honestly don't think I can handle one more day," I admit. More scrawling.

"One more day of…?"

"Them. I close my eyes and it's always them looking back at me."

"And who are they?"

"Kids. They were kids." Here comes the nausea.

He hands me a cool cup of water. I gulp down my revulsion. I know his next line of questioning, so I save him the trouble.

"I'm a soldier. I teach non-violent warfare to some of our less, shall we say, mature allies."

"Non-violent?"

"How to recruit locals, keep disparate groups organized, disrupt enemy supply chains and communication. Things like that. A few months ago, my buddy and I were supervising a squad of Sandinista rebels, typical teenagers, marching them through rainforests and making alliances with rural populations before the government does."

My mind retrieves a cache of sense memory. An incessant chorus of wildlife, overlapping aromas of life and death, and the healing green glow of sunlight through magnificent vegetation.

"Of course, some first contacts go better than others. At best, they smile and offer you refreshments, maybe a place to rest your aching feet. Other times, blank expressions that could mean anything. In places like that, they see a uniform and expect you to loot, torture and/or kill. I can't tell you how frustrating that gets, but you can't blame them. Not if you know what they know."

"Tell me about the children."

I don't want to, but it is why I'm here.

"On a day not too long ago, our little crew came across a small village of men, mostly old timers. They were friendlier than most, and that meant the boys were in a better mood than usual. Everything was going great. They even laid out an impromptu feast of eggs and some milky-green cocktail that tasted better than it looked.

"The Agency gives out pills that prevent us from getting drunk in case we have to break the ice with the more cautious natives."

"Dihydromyricetin," he says. "Please continue."

"Well, whatever we were drinking, by sundown I was blacked out. Next thing I know, I'm on my back in the middle of the jungle in the dead of night, and I can smell a rainstorm fast approaching. My watch says it's almost 3:30 am. I called out, but there was no answer."

The doctor stops writing and looks over at me. Maybe he senses this is where it gets weird, and he'd be right.

"I had to get my bearings before clouds covered the moon and stars. I didn't see any available high ground, so I found a tall climbable tree. I got high enough to spot a distant firelight about a half-kilometer away. Using my compass, I charted a course and headed towards it.

"The change in barometric pressure set off a few old wounds, and within minutes it was raining hard. Bushwhacking my way through the jungle, the whispers started."

"You said whispers?"

"That's right. I figured it was the sound of water splashing in weird ways here and there. At night, every jungle has its share of unexplainable noises.

"After a while, I noticed the whispers closing in, no matter which direction I moved. It wasn't long before I could feel them passing from outside my head to inside. The rain was hammering down like the whole world caught under a waterfall, but I could barely hear it beneath the typhoon roaring inside my head."

"Could you understand them, or was it only whooshing?"

"It started out as gibberish, but as I slogged on, things became clearer."

"What did they say?"

"Regresa a nosotros." I get a chill repeating their words.

"Come back to us," he says. "Were you aware of what that referred to?"

"Not a clue. A part of me was thinking I was on some hallucinogen, either dosed by the villagers or exposed to some mind-altering fauna or flora. I'm well trained to ignore unwanted signals to the brain, so I relegated everything to background noise and stayed on task.

"I made my way up a ridge to reset my bearings. Less than fifty meters away, a fire illuminated the southern edge of a clearing. It wasn't the village though. The firelight revealed ancient stone ruins, scattered across an open field. I needed shelter from the pounding rain, and the warmth of a fire sounded nice too. I had no idea what or who to expect down there, so I unholstered my sidearm and descended with caution.

"I was now close enough to see the glow through the dense greenery. I crawled the last few meters to the edge. The flames were in front of me, close enough to destroy my night vision. From the safety of the foliage, I surveyed as much of the field as the firelight permitted, detecting no sign of life whatsoever.

"To be safe, I circled the clearing before entering at the side opposite the fire. Again, no movement. Using the ruins as cover, I advanced across the field towards the light. It didn't take long to realize this was no structural blaze. It was a pyre. At first all I could make out was livestock. This far out into the sticks, no sane person would destroy such a precious commodity.

"Somehow I knew what I was about to see.

"Entwined with the animals were people. Around thirty human corpses, piled up and used as tinder. The whispers became shrieks of agony and terror. And something else."

"Do you know what that something else is?"

"Rage. Primal, ravenous, volcanic fury. I couldn't resist getting close enough to see the details. I saw a familiar face. My partner. I could only imagine one rational possibility, an ambush.

"Now the voices were shouting recuerda. I was thinking this was the worst thing I'd ever seen in my entire life. I closed my eyes to keep from losing it completely. Big mistake.

"I could feel their fingertips, at first running up my body, then turning me around, forcing my lids back open. I gave it everything I had to close my eyes before they settled on what was in front of me."

My throat muscles are clenching, making it hard to get enough air to speak out loud. What escapes is almost a hiss.

"It's them. The children. All of them. Staring at me."

"Try to relax. Take slower, deeper breaths."

I do as he says, and it helps.

"There was a steep staircase, must have been a seventy-degree incline. I was reminded of theater seats. Five rows filled with children of every age, all knifed in the belly then posed to look like some demented doll collection."

My body wants to cry, but it can't produce tears anymore so it only trembles.

"I could tell they were fresh kills. Skin was bloodless, but they weren't stiff yet. Maybe it was the flames reflecting in their eyes, but I swear, there was a look of expectation in every one of them."

"What did they expect you to do?"

"To remember."

"Recuerda," he says to himself.

"Even now, if I close my eyes, they're right in front of me, getting closer. They're demanding retribution. From who or what, I can't say."

"You said, 'getting closer'. What do you suppose will happen when they reach you?"

"Something far worse than insanity. Something that can follow me beyond death."

He writes in his notebook, slaps it shut, and situates it on his desk. He scoots his chair over, positioning himself so his right hip practically touches my left. He gazes down at me and I detect kindness beneath professional confidence.

"As you know, I focus my work on patients like yourself. What you attribute to a chemically induced blackout may well be something else entirely. Fortunately, you and I have an ace up our sleeve called hypnosis. It's no magic cure, and there are no guarantees which enigmas we may unlock."

"I just need to know, Doc. Can you make them go away?"

"That's what we're here to do." He says it as if for the thousandth time. As if he's a surgeon assuring a child there is life after tonsillectomy. "Let's start by relaxing your whole body, one bit at a time."

He talks me through the loosening of every muscle, head to toe. For the first time in years, I am completely free of physical tension.

"Now we're going to apply a kind of mental anesthetic so we can see things and not feel harmed by them. I want you to stare straight up at the spiral image above you. Stay relaxed and at ease as you focus on the very center."

I concentrate on the black dot. The illusion of motion increases.

"Now listen very carefully to the sound of my voice. We're going to close our eyes, and when we do, we cannot be harmed by what we see, no matter what it is. We will not be afraid, we will remain relaxed, and at ease."

I am aware what comes next and that's okay.

"Take a deep breath, and as you exhale, you will permit your eyes to close."

I draw in the aroma of antique leather, decaying books and musky cologne.

I sigh the air out, releasing my grip on tortured eye muscles. My eyelids descend and the relief is the most exquisite sensation I've ever felt. I wish this sensation could last forever.

In the next moment, the hideous menagerie is back. This time I meet their gaze unafraid. We cannot be harmed by what we see.

"Do you see the children?" he asks.

"I do."

"Okay, now I want you to imagine what you see is videotape being played on a television. Can you imagine this?"

"Yes."

"Next, I want you to imagine it also contains a recording of everything that happened a little before and during your blackout period. Do you understand?"

"I understand."

"Excellent. Now, find the rewind button and take us back to the beginning of the recording. Can you do that?"

"Yes."

I do as he asks. When the VCR chugs to a stop, I say, "Done".

"Okay, now hit PLAY and tell me what you see," the doctor says.

After some static and wavy lines, the program begins.

"I'm with the guys and the villagers, finishing dinner. My buddy and I are translating every joke we can remember into Spanish. Everyone is laughing and having fun.

"I ask what's in our drinks. Our host says it's a ceremonial brew he learned from a Rama medicine man. He says it frees your spirit to express what is in your heart. I thank him for his hospitality, and he pours me another.

"I excuse myself to get fresh air and relieve myself. I am walking back. I notice something in a patch of mud. It's a little girl's shoe. I take it back to the house and ask the villagers where its owner is. They all avert their gazes, except the host. He politely asks us to leave.

"Distortion emerges on the edges of my vision, and all colors are over saturated. Maybe the VCR's tracking is off?"

"I am adjusting the tracking remotely," the doc says. "Please continue."

Whatever the doctor is doing helps some. I continue.

"Our host no longer looks friendly. I draw my knife and demand he take us to the rest of the villagers. He refuses. I tell him to look up. He does and I slash his throat.

"I turn to the others. Nobody speaks or moves. I yank a random villager out of his seat. I hold up the shoe in one hand, my blade in the other, and I tell him to choose. He looks at his comrades, at me, at my blade. I set the tip over his heart, then slam my palm against the butt, driving it in to the hilt.

"I draw my sidearm. My buddy gets up and walks over to me. He keeps telling me to calm down.

Another glitch. For a second, he has a lizard head and claws for hands.

"I ask him to stay back. He doesn't. I shoot him in the forehead. The living start to panic. I kill as many as I can until my pistol is empty.

"The survivors are running away. I toss the pistol and fetch my rifle. From the deck I pick them off, one by one. The sun is about to set. I scramble to the top of the roof and use binoculars to scan for any hidden footpaths leading into the jungle.

"I spot a trail through the trees, the entry well camouflaged at ground level. I reclaim my blade from the villager's chest. Except for a flashlight, I remove everything on me that isn't a weapon. I reload my guns and I collect as much extra ammo as I can carry.

"I locate the trailhead and start down the path. The trail is three meters wide and perfectly level. The flashlight reveals animal and human footprints, along with at least one set of wagon tracks. I'm jogging down the trail."

Doctor Boyle's soothing voice emanates from the night sky: "Please fast-forward to the end of the trail."

I press the FF button on the VCR until I reach the clearing.

"I'm at the temple ruins. The tracks cross the ground and terminate at the ancient steps. I walk around them and see a massive stone partially blocking an underground passage behind the staircase. I scan the ground with the light. The wagon wheel impressions continue on into the jungle.

"I follow these to their end and see two horses grazing next to a small pool of water. Not far is the cart, half hidden by low hanging branches."

The sky speaks again: "What happens next?"

"I return to the passageway and descend underground. At the bottom I shine my light around. About the size of a crypt. There's a simple stone altar at the far end. I push and pull it from every available angle. I dig my fingers in where the back meets the wall and tug at it like a door. It swings right open.

"The flicker of candlelight is just strong enough to reveal women and children clustered into what looks like a burial chamber.

"I tell them in Spanish I am here to rescue them, but I'm too big to reach the chamber. I set the flashlight on the threshold, aimed at them. I lean in to show them my hands are open and empty. I keep repeating the words, 'you're safe', calm and gentle.

"The first one through is a woman in her twenties. Once past the flashlight, I pull her out the rest of the way. I ask her to assure the others it's safe to come out, which she does. I insert the tip of my knife into her medulla oblongata. She collapses instantly. I catch her dead body, then drag it to a dark corner in time to greet my next victim."

"Fast-forward to the staging of the children, please."

"At wacky speed, I snuff out one innocent life after another. I haul the corpses up to the clearing and pile the women off to the side. I use the horses and cart to fetch the men, along with any flammable liquids. I complete the stack of adults, set them on fire, and use the plentiful light to perform my work on their children.

"I count the steps, estimating how many could fit in each row. I place the youngest on top and work down from there. I make sure all eyes are open, and postures look comfortable. I step back to take in the whole of my creation.

"There is beauty in what I have done, but it only lasts for a moment.

"The distortion around my vision is disappearing bit by bit. Now the hyper saturation is going too. I drop to my knees and vomit until my stomach is empty. I lurch to my feet and stagger into the jungle. Now I'm running in no particular direction.

"I leap over a network of tree roots, but land on something slippery. My foot arcs high in front of me. The back of my head slams against something solid."

The tape ends and with some mechanical effort, the VCR ejects it. The TV screen erupts into pixelated disorder. I stare at it, awaiting further instructions. Time is passing, but without markers, I cannot establish duration.

"Zed, I'm going to count down from three to one. When I say 'one', you will open your eyes and return to the here and now. Every muscle, every tendon in your entire body will remain perfectly relaxed and at ease."

There's a new, yet familiar articulation behind his voice. Yes, there it is again. Primal, ravenous, volcanic fury.

"You will do only what I tell you to do, and nothing else. You will obey my commands even while unconscious. Do you understand?"

"I do."

"Excellent. Now sleep."

Yes. Thank you. All things dissolve into peaceful nothing.

"Awaken."

Awareness returns in a sudden rush. It's nighttime. Skin, muscle and bone sting from severe cold. I stand paralyzed in front of a short railroad tunnel, eyes fixed on the hazy, moonlit other side. The rustle of parched leaves accents the ambient drone of insects. Earthen perfumes and the stink of exhausted industry blend in my nostrils.

Next to arrive is memory. My name is Zed Moranna. I live in America. I work for the government. I have committed atrocities on the innocent. I wish to be delivered from my demons.

The crunch of footfalls on gravel advance behind me. They stop. The doctor's breath is hot on my cold neck.

"You're not the first of your kind to sit on my couch, and mine is not the only office entrusted to remedy your particular disorder." He pats me twice on the shoulder and steps to the edge of peripheral vision. My eyes strain to track his movement but remain fixed forward.

"You might be interested to know, I've spent a fascinating career dissecting every aspect, every knowable expression of evil. Co-founded a powerful Order dedicated to understanding and explaining it. But we soon recognized the truism, that even the most detailed map can never adequately impart the territory it depicts. So, we created a mechanism for confronting your malignancy face-to-face."

I get it. I didn't find Doctor Boyle, his Order found me.

"Quite the dark journey, but along the way we kept

encountering Nature's reaction. The Di fu ling in China, Chindi to the Navajo, the Preta of East Asia, and now one of those children you slaughtered in the jungle."

If I had been thinking straight, would I have seen this coming? Is he even a psychiatrist?

"They're everywhere Zed. Their kind exists because your kind creates them. Born from profound trauma, they are the ideal solution to your kind. For example, Peeping Tom who lives on the other side of this tunnel. Quite famous to those in the know. Back when, he assisted my first state-side disposal during Viet Nam. Now, we do each other regular favors. I bring him food, and he eats it."

I fight to move even the tiniest muscle. I remain inert.

He checks his watch and says, "To meet Tom, you must first invite him. You do that by staring down this tunnel from midnight to one without blinking. In a few seconds, you'll be at the fifty-eight-minute mark. Please be sure to let me know the instant he arrives."

I'm starving to beg for my life, thirsty to plead my innocence. I cannot say why I slaughtered all those unsullied beings in such a sickening manner. Okay, that's a lie. I've prayed for such a precious opportunity my whole life.

The deaths of the family pets were anything but normal. My first girlfriend didn't run away from home, never to be seen again. Mom and Dad didn't die in a burglary gone wrong. I didn't enlist out of patriotism, or stumble into Reagan's killing fields by mistake.

A tall, lean figure in a top hat uncoils with theatric finesse at the other end of the tunnel. The forest goes silent. My brain is overheating the way it did the moment I found that little girl's shoe.

"He's here," I am compelled to say. I try and fail to sneak in the word 'mercy' while my speech is still unlocked.

"Then allow me to make introductions. Zed, meet Tom. Tom, meet food. Now blink."

Lids close. This time I am frozen on the steps, the dead gathered on the grass before me.

Lids open. The figure in the top hat has advanced half the distance. For the first time, my warrior self is impotent, denied a voice to articulate defeat.

"Blink."

The victims of my massacre chant in atonal rhythm, "Volver al infierno, demonio."

Half the distance again. The space between us is a measure of my fundamental sanity.

"Blink."

I am a human being. I am a human being.

Maybe five meters. He is separating the human from my being. How is it possible to experience this much suffering?

"Blink."

Their chants are not an insult. They are casting an hechizo with the authority and potency only the murdered can invoke.

Conjecture, empathy, animosity absent in his glare. Eyes reflect the most brutal of truths. Nature annihilates the innocent and the wicked with equal indifference.

The universe does not hear our prayers for mercy, solace, or the strength to persevere. No matter who we are, we meet our end in one final, unwelcome

"Blink."

THE LIGHT AT THE END

By Megan Morgan

The tale was told directly to author Morgan by Iris Jain, the narrator herself. Mrs. Jain is now married and a middle-school teacher in Baltimore County. It is printed here with her permission.

It was on TV a Saturday morning in Spring. Ms. Foster was dead. She'd killed herself, the reporter said. There was no reason for it to have an impact on me. She was just my biology teacher, after all.

It's not like she paid special attention to me. But I guess at least she didn't treat me like a freak, so that must have meant something.

My dad and my sister watched the reporter talk. He stood outside my school, as if that place was what represented her life. The wind ruffled his hair and lifted the collar of his beige coat. Then the image cut away to a forest, all gray vertical lines softened by amorphous green buds. People walked around in the image. Crime-scene tape crisscrossed around trunks. My eyes traced their back-and-forths, then honed in on the black tarp. No way.

What horror had happened in that place?

Dad turned off the TV, and hugged Liz, who was crying loudly. "Oh honey, I'm so sorry." He patted her back, like she was a baby, until she pulled away and sat up. She lifted her chin, and seemed about to say something really mature, to convince him that she was totally fine.

Then she looked over at me, and her eyes got really wide. She looked, just then, like a fox caught in a flashlight beam.

"Iris, you're crying?"

Dad looked over, and came around the couch so fast I couldn't quite trace his movement. He leaned down and looked at me as if seeing me for the first time in years. One hand rested on my shoulder, but I shrugged it off. And then his face changed, somehow.

"What's wrong?" he asked. And his voice was like a cat stepping across a floor strewn with broken glass.

"They're wrong. She didn't kill herself."

"Iris. Don't get wrapped up in this. It's not something for you to worry about."

I opened my mouth. They were wrong, and no one was saying anything about it. I had to—"

"Remember what Miss Julie said?"

Behind Dad, I saw Liz clutching a pink and tan paisley pillow to her chest. Oh. Of course. I'd forgotten to hide that face I made. I'd forgotten to pretend to be like them.

"I'm sorry. I didn't mean to upset you," I said. The line felt tired, like I'd pulled it up on a thin fishing line from the bottom of the Mariana Trench. I looked at Liz. "Do you have my CD you borrowed?" She nodded. "Can I have it back?"

My dad still stared at me as Liz ran up to her room to get "The Visit". I looked at the wall behind his shoulder.

"This won't be like last summer?"

I pulled on my shirt sleeves.

"I'll do my best, Dad."

I listed to All Souls Night on repeat, my CD player on the floor beside me, the squishy foam of my headphones against my ears. Enclosing me in sound. There in the quiet of my room I could rock gently while I did my homework without anyone noticing or saying anything. And I thought about Mrs. Foster. I thought about her untidy desk, and the way she'd brought wildlife she'd captured into our classroom, as if we were in second grade. Small things, like tadpoles that became tiny tree frogs, and newts, and monarch caterpillars. The room smelled of milkweed for weeks during the fall. Sometimes there were feathers, teeth, animal skulls.

She'd told a bunch of boys to stop calling me Spaz-Dance, once. No one had been able to do a damn thing about them taping up posters all over school with the Flash Dance movie cover with the title changed to my nickname and my face pasted very badly over Jennifer Beales's.

There was no reason for me to be so worried about what happened to Mrs. Foster. But I knew the truth, and it ran hard against what they were saying. It gave me a prickling feeling all over, like when you put cold hands under hot water. I couldn't stand it. I had to do something.

The house was very still as I finished my math. Liz had track practice, although it sounded from her phone conversation just before she left that they wouldn't be running much. Dad had write-ups for whomever in town was getting a divorce that month. Mom would get home too late to start dinner, and we'd have to go out to eat. I had some time.

I threw a jacket on over my hoodie, ran down the stairs, and paused at the door just long enough to call to Dad that I was going to the library.

I pulled my bike down off the rack in the garage, then stood in the driveway, shifting the weight of my backpack from one shoulder to the other. My house was way up on top of the hills sheltering Ellicott City. I could look down and see the entire town below me, stone and brick and window. Shops and streets. I saw a lot of people out on main street. So many. I didn't want to, but there was no other place to start. I couldn't just walk into the police station. Or at least, I didn't think that would work.

"Suck it up, Iris," I said to myself.

I kicked my bike into the street, and let it drift down the hill, sweeping around the snake-like curves. Air rushed around my arms, filled my ears.

Be normal. Be normal.

What does that mean?

Be like them.

I could do that, until I couldn't.

There were even more people out on main street than I'd thought there would be from my perch up above. I leaned my bike up against a sandstone wall in an alleyway, so quiet and dim, and stared with something very much like horror at the people who were talking talking talking on the sidewalk. I took a step forward, towards the light. Just one step. And then stopped.

What did I think I was going to do, exactly?

I could walk, and listen to what people were saying. To find out if anybody, like me, thought that Ms. Foster hadn't meant for this to happen. I didn't have to talk. I could just listen.

I turned around and took a step back towards my bike. Stopped again. Sweat prickled on the back of my neck, and heat swept through me, even as my hands trembled. Someone would notice, someone would ask questions, and then I wouldn't know what to say. And everyone knew about me.

I remembered sitting on a rug in primary colors in third grade, and my teacher telling me a little coldly that it would get better. I would learn. Someday I'd brush all the awkward off, and stop getting so loud when things got overwhelming, and I'd have friends. People would see the good things about me. How I could find answers the other kids didn't have the patience to dig up. How I remembered everything, when I wanted to. That had never happened. No. It only got worse from there.

Now I had a reputation.

I turned around and took a step to the light, and the people, and again I stopped. A woman in a black coat looked at me. And her face fell. Her eyes flicked me up and down before she looked back at the man she'd been talking to. Whatever she said next, he looked over at me, too. Then he looked away, fast, like someone who'd seen something they weren't supposed to. He took her arm, and pulled her around the corner out of my sight.

There it was. The reputation. Who knew, now, what I might find out by poking my nose into things. What I might say when I found the truth.

I went back to my bike, and walked it the other way out of the alley. It was at the back, behind the buildings, that I heard the story.

"It was Illchester the Molester who got her."

Two boys and a girl stood at the back of a restaurant, taking a break from whatever crappy early-twenties jobs they were doing to smoke cigarettes that had to be eating a huge amount of their very low pay away. Could I stop without them noticing too much? I decided to try. I stopped and pretended to check one of my tires.

"Oh my god, that's such kid crap," the girl said. But the boy who'd spoken first looked incredibly serious.

"You've never been over there late at night—"

"Yes, I have!"

"—look, there's something there. And I had her when I was in school, she went walking all over the place, all the time."

The girl shook her head. "Ms. Foster did not get killed by a ghost. She got killed by herself. I would've too, if I ended up stuck in this place for the rest of my life."

"Don't say stuff like that," said the second boy, very softly. Then he looked over at me. "Hey, kid, do you need help?"

I stood up. I shook my head. I should say words, a lie, something, anything.

The girl took a drag off her cigarette, and the end glowed red. "See, this is the kind of bullshit that happens when someone can't cope. Every kid in that class is damaged, now. Pathetic."

"I'm not damaged!" I said, louder than I meant. The first boy, who wore glasses, looked surprised. The girl rolled her eyes. The second boy, who had the blondest hair I'd ever seen, just looked sad. Well. I'd started now. Might as well keep going.

"Who's Illchester the Molester?" I said.

The blond boy put out his cigarette, and he looked me up and down, as if by looking he could see something important about me. But I was just a little girl whose skin itched because something was wrong. I shrank under his gaze, whether I wanted to or not.

"He's the Blink Man. Kind of like a ghost I guess who lives in the train tunnel. Sometimes he gets lonely or something, and he calls people up to the tracks, and they just stand there staring at him, way down at the other end of Illchester Tunnel. And when that happens, they see him, forever. With every blink he gets closer. Until at last he gets them. That's what the kids in my class always said, anyway."

"You don't get called there; it only happens to people who are dumb enough to stare for an hour."

"But no way can you stare for an hour without blinking, it's impossible. When people see the Blink Man, it's because he wants people to see him."

I looked over at the girl, and she looked back at me. They weren't serious, were they? She shrugged, then turned away to go back inside.

"Why would he want Ms. Foster to see him?"

The boy with the glasses scuffed his boot on the ground. "Because she had a tragic life. It's always people who've had a bad

162

time that he gets. Lost souls."

"Because he doesn't like people who don't understand loneliness. He needs people who can really see him and get him. There's a mutualism to the sick relationship he has with his victims, you know? It's like how Macbeth needs Lady Macbeth, and she needs him to be more like her. And then everybody dies."

"Man, don't pretend you've read Shakespeare," Glasses said.

They started to argue, and I'd already heard enough. I hopped back on my bike, and left them to fight out who'd read the most iambic pentameter of a man long dead.

My mom had always worried that I should have taken a bus, or found a ride, instead of biking to the library myself. But I liked it. I liked going fast by spinning my own two feet on the pedals, even when it was cold out. The outfits I wore to keep warm always made my sister shake her head, but I had my priorities.

The librarians were used to the way I showed up, red-faced and a little sweaty, so they didn't mind or stare. I went straight to the microfilm index. So many tiny pages of newspaper, there to scroll through and zoom in on, rolls and rolls of them. Comic books, too. I'd read the history, how messages were originally shrunk down so they could be transported by carrier pigeon during the Franco-Prussian war. And now it was scroll-scroll-scroll through hundreds of tiny, perfect newspaper pages, made large on a projector. With patience and scrolling and zooming and sharp eyes, I could find almost anything.

Ms. Foster had won a teaching award a few months earlier. That would be a good place to start. I found the microfilm for the right month, and started scanning page after page of newspaper, turning the knobs and dials on the projector, watching shrunken images made large flash by.

THE LIGHT AT THE END

After ten minutes or so a librarian came up behind me and commented on how wonderful it was that a kid these days knew how to use microfilm. I ignored her. Pages flashed by. I was on a mission. Birth announcements and wedding announcements and sports and human-interest articles and front pages and classified ads flashed past. It was like walking through a world I had known once, but everything was accelerated. I could sense that I was getting close. A glimpse of a familiar comic strip. A front-page photo that felt right. And then there. A photo of Ms. Foster, smiling and very much alive, standing in front of a series of aquariums on a bookshelf.

I stopped and stared at her grin for a long time. I had this sense that I knew more than I thought I did, and also less. There was something at that moment happening in me that I couldn't quite understand at the time, because of course I didn't have context. But part of me just knew she hadn't left behind her life on purpose. And another part of me had this very scary understanding of the fact that I had no idea what it was like to be an adult. Her life was outside of my comprehension. Her burdens were things I could neither see nor understand.

Like I said, at the time I didn't know that's what I felt. All I had was an overwhelming sense of awe and confusion. And that prickling feeling of heat driving out cold.

I read the article. Ms. Foster had started teaching at my school six years ago. That was all I needed. I went back to the drawers, and pulled out a new roll of film. Then I scrolled and scrolled and scrolled through what seemed like endless lines of text. This time wasn't so easy, and I had to go through months of papers before I found it.

Ms. Foster had come to Ellicott City in 1987. She'd moved to Maryland from California. She was looking forward to a fresh start, and couldn't wait to meet the students in her new home. She loved biology and hiking.

I wound the microfilm back up, and put it away in the drawer. I didn't even have a city to start with in California. It was a complete dead end.

I left the microfilm room, and went to the card catalog, keeping my head down as I went. It's what you do when you have a reputation. You don't make eye contact. Then I went through the tiny paper cards. I tried in the "B"s first, looking for Blink Man. Nothing. Then Peeping Tom. Definitely not what I was looking for. The only thing under "Ilchester" were books about Maryland history.

I went to the history section with my little notecard with its lines of tidy block lettering. I pulled down all six of the books that had mention of the Ilchester Tunnel. They didn't tell me anything that I didn't already know.

"Is there anything I can help you with?" The same librarian who had talked to me while I looked at microfilm stood beside me. She wore her glasses around her neck, on a string of brightly colored beads. I supposed it was practical enough.

"No, ma'am."

"Are you sure? It's just – the last time you spent so much time in the library, it's because you were upset about something."

I definitely scowled, and I slammed the last book back on the shelf. "I wish everyone would just forget about that. God!" Then I realized that I sounded like Liz, which was too much for me. I brushed past the librarian, and out to my bike.

I pedaled home as fast as I could, still prickling all over with the wrongness of everything, and now I had a swirl of anger and shame in my belly to go with it. Even the library wasn't safe. Nowhere was safe. And not for the first time, I wished I could get away. Go somewhere else. Or stay and be someone else.

The worst part was that the thing everyone reviled me for had seemed like the right thing to do at the time. Even by the time Ms. Foster died, even after months of therapy, I still didn't see how I'd done anything so terribly wrong. Was I doing the same sort of thing again? Following my instincts instead of the rules? Building and building, one brick at a time, some catastrophe that would leave me ashamed, and known to everyone as that girl?

I biked almost the whole way up the hill to my parents' house. By the end of the summer, I'd be able to do the whole thing for sure. Mom's car sat in the driveway. The air was starting to cool. The sun sat on the horizon, a blazing red ball. I could hear Liz's music, The Cranberries singing "Linger". I could live with that. I hung my bike on the rack in the garage.

There was another place to look, of course. And I didn't need the library.

Inside, I found Mom and Dad cooking. Both of them. Together. I stood in the dining room and stared at them as they moved around the kitchen. Not exactly laughing, but talking more than I'd seen them talk in a long time. Mom smiled a little, and Dad smiled a lot.

I guess I stared a little too long and they felt it, because Mom looked up abruptly as she pulled some spices out of the pantry. Her face went all weird, the way it had ever since that thing no one in the world seemed to be able to forget.

"Hi Iris. How was the library?"

"It was good."

Dad peeked around the corner. "You were there a really long time. Did you get sucked into a good book?"

I shrugged. If I told them what I'd really done, they would both freak out. Because it sounded a lot like what I'd done before. "I'm gonna go wash my hands, okay?"

"Sure, sweetie," Mom said. And I had to run away upstairs, away from that hesitant and hopeful little smile.

Because I knew I was going to keep going. Even though it had been so much trouble before, I would keep going, because if I didn't my skin prickled.

I went into my room and started my Loreena McKennitt CD again. Then I crept down the hall to my parents' room. That was where they kept the extra phone, and also where they kept the phonebook. I had my notebook with me. I flipped through the pages. I found her name. I wrote down her address. And it was really that easy.

I crept back to my room, with my notebook tucked into my jacket pocket. I trembled. I couldn't really do what I was thinking about doing, could I?

"Girls! Dinner!"

"This is going to be so bad," I said to Loreena McKennitt. "This is not going to go well."

I heard Liz going down the stairs, so I turned off my music, and followed her.

Mom and Dad had made their specialty pork balls and cabbage and rice. It was my favorite meal of all time.

Oh, I was such a bad daughter.

I sat down at my spot. Liz sat at hers, right beside me. Mom sat at the top of the table, and Dad sat at the side closest to her. I wanted to go back to my room. I wanted to say I was sick. But Mom looked so concerned, and so – hopeful? Was that right?

"I was really sorry to hear about Ms. Foster, girls. And I just thought that maybe it would be nice if we had a real, good meal together. And everyone could, you know, have the chance to talk."

I remembered Dad that morning, comforting Liz, and silencing me. Because Liz accepted what they said, and I didn't. I'd wanted to talk, then. I sure didn't, now.

Liz got up, and went over and hugged Mom, and then Dad. I forced a smile. "Thanks."

Then Dad put his napkin in his lap, and smiled around at all of his young women. "Eat up!"

I tried, I really did. I cut my pork ball, full of mushrooms and meat and soy sauce, into small pieces. I nibbled on some rice and cabbage.

"Coach said that they'll be sending therapists to our school to help us all. And everyone at practice was a total mess, we hardly ran at all. Does anyone know why she did it, Mom?"

Mom looked so concerned and engaged. As if something about all this had sort of snapped her back to her old self. And I felt bad about that, too.

"I don't know. Sometimes people get really sad or upset, and they don't think that they will ever feel any better. They just can't believe that other people care." Mom took Liz's hand. "It's a really sad thing. She left a lot of people behind."

Dad joined in on the teaching moment, too. "However much pain she had inside her, now there are so many people who knew her who are hurt. All the people who cared about her are going to miss her."

Liz nodded, accepting what they were saying as crystal clear fact. As if, should she ever feel sad, she could pull this memory out of her pocket, and then she would know that sadness didn't last forever. And there were people who would be sad if she left them behind. So simple. I could have printed it on an index card. "She was a really good teacher. I didn't realize until today how many students someone like her has. Almost everyone at track had her for class at some point."

My skin prickled all over.

"Ms. Foster didn't kill herself."

Mom and Dad looked at each other. A united front again. Why had they picked today?

"Why do you feel that way, Iris?"

"Because I know she didn't."

Liz looked over at me. "It's natural to be in denial."

Since when had everyone in my family become an expert in psychology? How was it possible that they were talking about any of this, while every inch of my skin crawled.

"I'm not in denial. Something else got her." I don't know why I said that. I'd spent so long in front of the microfilm, and I'd found nothing. But the blond boy had seemed really sure.

"Iris, is that what you did all afternoon? Were you trying to find out more about Ms. Foster?"

No one was eating, and everyone looked at me. I just nodded. The quiet got heavier.

"Sweetie, it isn't healthy—"

"I was right last time, though," I said softly. "Dad really was having an affair."

Mom went all white. I'd never seen anything like that, the way the blood drained out of her face. Liz clapped her hands to her mouth. And Dad – there were tears in his eyes.

"I think that maybe you should go to your room, Iris," he said.

"Why? So you can pretend I'm not here? So you can finally move on with all of your lives?" I realized that months and months of anger were boiling over. "I bet you all want to sit down here and pretend that you didn't have that shame around. But you know what – I didn't do anything wrong!" And until I said it just then, I hadn't truly realized it. It wasn't my fault, what happened.

I thought that maybe Dad would get to his feet and start shouting. I thought that maybe Mom would start crying. I thought that maybe Liz would run away from me. But none of those things happened. Dad just buried his head in his hands and said, "Go to your room."

I did stand up. And leave the table. But I didn't go up the stairs to my room.

THE LIGHT AT THE END

I went out the front door. I got on my bike. It was getting dark out. I kicked my bike out of the driveway and into the road. I coasted down the hill, letting the wind pull at my hair, and brush my face. It flowed under my arms and filled the folds of my jacket. It made everything light.

I kept alert. I'd left in too much of a hurry, and I was wearing the same dark clothes I had earlier. Cars wouldn't be able to see me.

I made the sharp turn off Church road and onto Main Street. The restaurants and bars were busy as I biked past. I went under the train bridge, and over the Patapsco river. And then, before Main Street became rugged wooded floodplain, I turned up Westchester Avenue.

The address I was looking for was not far. It was one of the smaller houses on that road.

It was where Ms. Foster had lived.

If I was right about Dad, then maybe I was right about her, too. Maybe some train tunnel ghost had haunted her steps. I wouldn't find out in the library, though.

The thing about Ellicott City back then was that even if people locked their doors (which a lot of people didn't), they sure didn't lock their windows. It was how my family got back into the house, if we ever accidentally locked ourselves out. My parents would help either my sister or I in through one of the windows, and we'd just go unlock the front door.

It turned out Ms. Foster locked all her windows.

I stumbled around outside the house in the dark for almost fifteen minutes, and not a single one of the windows budged. I was about to go home, when I looked up, and saw that one window on the second story was open just a crack. And there was a drainpipe right next to it.

I didn't even hesitate.

The next few minutes of my life were some of the longest. The drainpipe creaked and cracked and swayed as I gripped it with hands and legs and feet. It was only by some miracle that it didn't break entirely and dash me against the ground. But then at last I was there at the window. And I pulled myself up over the side, scrambled over a bookcase, and into Ms. Foster's bedroom.

A bed, a dresser, a bookshelf, two nightstands. It could have been my parents' room. But it wasn't. It was a thing all shadow and deeper shadow, so familiar and so unknown. For the first time that day, I was afraid.

With a trembling hand, I reached out to turn on the lamp I could see beside the bed. It clicked on. Then I could see that Ms. Foster had no sense of decorating style at all. Her comforter was blue, and some of her pillows were red, and some of them were green. A floral quilt lay at the foot of the bed. Everything was a random jumble.

Now what was I looking for?

I pushed aside books on the shelf, read every spine. No ghost stories or urban legends, just romance novels and biology texts. I opened drawers in the nightstand, but found only an assortment of empty Chapstick tubes and random keys. The top shelves of the closet were stacked with scarves, the floor lined with shoes. I turned around and looked back towards the window through which I'd climbed.

There was a little black notebook there under the lamp. I snatched it up, as if it were a snake. And then, I sat cross-legged on the floor, took a deep breath, and opened its pages.

It was her journal. And in it, she mostly catalogued the hikes she took. There were pages filled with her descriptions of trails all over the county, and well beyond. She'd even done drawings of some places. On a few pages she'd taped in leaves.

And there, a couple months ago, was a drawing of the

Illchester Tunnel. It looked even more threatening on the paper than I remembered it.

Below, she'd written about the legend of Blink Man, almost exactly as the blond boy had told it.

"He will always win, because you must always blink! He hardly needs the eyelash trick, because it will happen eventually, anyway. The most important thing is not to stare down the tunnel in the first place, ha ha. I like to imagine Davie and Julia would have liked this. They'd be old enough, now, to appreciate the creepiness of it."

I stared and stared at the page until I knew for sure I could remember it, even copy it out, later. It was a good trick, and not one I let anyone else know about.

And then the next entry was about a different trail. Then another. And she never wrote about Blink Man again. But for a while she wrote the names Davie and Julia more. And then, from the dates, she either started hiking less, or she started writing about her hikes less.

The door to the bedroom opened, and I'll admit, I shrieked. And a bright light caught and held me, and I froze. I didn't even think of running. I just crouched there in the flashlight's beam, my dead teacher's notebook open in my lap, not sure if I was terrified or defiant.

A police officer stared down at me, half his face silver in the light. He opened his mouth, closed it. Opened, while his throat worked, and closed it again.

"How did you get in here?" he finally got out.

"Drainpipe," I said.

He rubbed a hand over his head. "What did you touch?"

"Just this," I nodded at the notebook.

He muttered something to himself that I couldn't hear, then looked at the windowsill, and the bookcase under it. The book in my hands. He shook his head, and sighed.

"Your name?"

"Iris." I clutched the notebook, still splayed open, against my chest.

"Whole name."

"Iris Jain."

"You were one of her students?"

"Yes."

"What the hell are you doing in here?"

Her handwritten words were there in my hands. And the knowledge that they didn't mean anything, in the end. The book held no answers. Not ones I wanted, anyway. Everything was muddier than ever.

"Because she didn't kill herself, and I wanted to know what did."

He looked up to the ceiling. "Your school is bringing in therapists, you know. There are going to be people you can talk to about this."

"I've been in therapy. I know how to run circles around someone doing a five-minute session on grief."

He looked over at me, his eyes searching for whatever it was I'd been in therapy for. Bulimia? Cutting? An acute obsession with Jonathan Taylor Thomas that went too far? Where was the black lipstick, the scars, the pain in the eyes, all the expected things?

People didn't realize that a lot of the time, it didn't show on the outside.

"Okay, kid. Why do you think she didn't kill herself?"

This time I was the one who opened my mouth and no sound came out. There wasn't a good answer. It was just a feeling. She'd been alive, just yesterday. She'd smiled during class. Yesterday! She didn't smile in class and then a few hours later take her own life. That wasn't how it worked.

"There was the Blink Man," I breathed at last.

The police officer rubbed his face and actually groaned. "Jesus, not that again. No, kid, some tunnel ghost did not kill your teacher. She went out in the woods, and she – oh man, I'm not good at this. Look, I'm sorry. These things happen. And we don't see it coming."

"But she wasn't unhappy! She did good things!"

And the police officer looked right at me. "Doesn't matter. Everyone who does this is a good person, and a happy person. Sometimes. But she had things in her past, and they caught up to her. Those are the real ghosts. Not some guy in a tunnel."

I still held the notebook. But he was talking to me in a way grownups never did. "What things did she have?"

"She had kids, back in California. But there was a really bad divorce, I guess, and she lost custody. She could only see them a couple of weeks every year. She did her best. But she got news earlier this week that the kids didn't want to see her this summer. She thought that was all she had. So here we are."

"Davie and Julia."

He nodded. I closed the notebook. The prickling feeling on my skin had faded. It was replaced by something else, something hard in my stomach.

"Hey. You're Iris Jain?"

My reputation. Ms. Foster's ghosts. It wasn't fair. I nodded.

"You're the kid who shouted at your dad's mistress right on the courthouse steps."

I hung my head and started to cry. I'd never wanted to vanish so much in my life.

"That was the most amazing thing I've ever seen."

I looked up, with tears still streaming down my face. "Really?"

"Yeah. I mean, you definitely shouldn't have done it. You shouldn't have broken in here, either." He extended a hand. "The notebook."

I passed it over. Then he gave me a very awkward shoulder pat. He looked embarrassed about it, at least.

"Let's get you home. Your parents are worried sick."

He put my bike in the trunk of his squad car, and he let me ride up in the front. It was, at most, a two-minute drive. It was long enough for me to feel ashamed. It was long enough for me to feel sorrow. It was long enough for me to feel anger. It still didn't make sense. I'd liked the idea of Blink Man better.

The car stopped in front of my house. The police officer looked at me.

"If I ever find you breaking into another house, ever again, there's going to be official paperwork involved." Then his face softened a lot. And I think he was looking as much at Ms. Foster as he was at me.

"It doesn't get easier, Iris. But you do learn to carry it better.

OBLIVION'S CURTAIN

By Paul R. Sieber

This story was discovered in a journal, in an antique shop in Ellicott City. No names were included in the journal and many relevant details were blacked out. Author Paul R. Seiber has fleshed it out into a clean narrative, but names and certain details have been created to give the fragmented journal a coherent structure. We have been unable to verify the events within.

"O Time! Thou fatal wrack of mortal things,
That draws oblivions curtains over Kings"
From, "Contemplations"
— Anne Bradstreet, 1678

Time.

I had to look up the author. I remember reading it once, maybe it was back in high school. I'm not sure. I know I remembered hearing it even if I wasn't sure of the exact words. I think that my new obsession with time now was due to how limited I saw it. I'm still not sure why this poem had hit me. Strange.

I'm not a poetry guy. I'm not even much of a reader. I just don't have the time for it. Well, maybe I don't make the time for it.

Time.

Should I regret not having time to do things before now? I hate the idea of regret. No matter how much it permeates my existence, I still don't like the idea of focusing on it so much.

Maybe I should have made the time.

It's almost 8:00 and pretty soon Pete, the bartender here at O'Houlihans, will be putting on the Caps game. Predictable. This place always reminds me of Cheers but without all the witty banter. I come in. Pete knows what I drink and gives it to me. I don't have to ask. I put my money on the bar, he takes what the drink costs and leaves my change. I don't have to say anything. He knows me but he also knows not to strike up some weird conversation to ask me about my day or to talk about the news or relationships or any of that bullshit. I like that. It's comforting in some strange way.

I look around here and see familiar faces, Some I've seen before and some are types I know. They are having the same drinks. They follow the same routines. It's pretty predictable. I know them even if, like with Pete, we have never talked.

I don't know their names but still, I know them.

That guy in the corner works at the hospital. Pretty sure he's the guy that sweeps up all the blood and shit. He's wearing scrubs under his denim jacket and a name tag. He's drinking some cheap rotgut. Saw him in here with a girl once. She looked too good for him. They fought. It was a pretty loud one, too. Haven't seen her since.

That girl at the end of the bar works in some office. She's dolled up and is wearing some pretty expensive designer clothes. I used to think she was some kind of executive but now I think she's probably more like a real estate agent. I think in her job she walks and stands a lot. She shouldn't wear those shoes, though. She probably does it to be fashionable but they hurt her feet. She pops them off of her heels as she sits on the barstool but only if she thinks no one is noticing. Wouldn't want to ruin the look. She likes white wine. This is a weird place to order wine.

Then there is that couple back in the corner table. If you can call them a couple. He's way too old for her. He looks like he could be her teacher or her dad. She was probably pretty once, but as my grandma would say, she's been "ridden hard and put away wet." Worn out for a young gal. She's probably been a pro for a while. Shame. I think they're still negotiating a price.

I guess this place isn't like Cheers after all.

I always wondered why I cared about this crap. Why I notice all this. I always have. It's a natural thing for me to study people in their surroundings. It makes me good at my job. My lieutenant calls me "the closer" because I'm really good at reading people and getting them to fess up. I like getting confessions. Dammit, I'm good at it. Maybe I should've been a priest. If this had happened in a confessional maybe I wouldn't be where I was right now.

I don't know.

Nah, I like getting laid. Priests don't get laid, unless it's an altar-boy. Priests can't smack around someone who's unwilling to talk either. I don't mind doing that when I need to. I'd never admit it but I actually enjoy that, too. Shit, I just admitted it.

Priests can't smack people around. Can they?

I can't seem to focus. Seriously, what the fuck difference does that stuff make now? There wasn't any reason to spend time dwelling on stupid shit.

Time.

I should have been focusing on the last few days, but I couldn't seem to do that. I lifted the glass of whiskey to my mouth and breathed it in. I loved the smell, somewhere between fresh cut wood and sugar. I downed it and swallowed hard. The slight burn in my throat radiated outward, enveloping me in the sensation of warmth. It made me feel like I'd just been covered with a blanket that someone had just pulled out of the dryer or I'd just sat down in front of a fireplace with a roaring fire. For a brief moment, that made me feel good. No, good isn't the right word. Maybe it just made things feel normal.

I finished the drink and before the glass even hit the bar, Pete was ready to refill it. He poured me another round of liquid courage and grabbed five bucks from the handful of cash I had sitting in front of me. I downed that one pretty quickly, too. I don't think normal is what I wanted to feel after all. I wanted it to make me feel numb. I needed to feel numb.

I don't think there's enough fucking whiskey in the world for that though.

Pete grabbed the remote to turn on the tube. It was time for the game to start. I wish that made me happy. I like the Caps.

Time.

It was 10:05PM, February 4th, 2003. I remember the exact time, because I was five minutes late for my shift. I was always late when I worked nights. It screwed up my sleep schedule. Then again, maybe I was just being an asshole because I hated having to work all night. I guess I shouldn't get pissed off, it was my own fault. I mouthed off and the lieutenant wrote me up and stuck me on nights for 30 days. That really pissed off my partner Tina. She hated working nights, too.

The Lieutenant told her, "you can join him on the graveyard shift, or you can both break in new partners."

She'd stuck with me. I'd have done the same for her.

You know what's funny though, I can't remember having to work nights because of her being an ass.

Yeah, I'm a gem to work with.

I walked into the squad room and Tina was already at her desk reading a case file. She greeted me with a glare, letting me know she wasn't pleased with being here at night or with me showing up late.

"What do we have tonight?" I asked, before the look she was giving me could bore through my head.

"M.P." she said. "Possibly more."

An M.P. was what we called a missing person. M.P.'s wouldn't usually come to the graveyard shift, unless there was more than just finding someone. They gave us cases like that when they thought the M.P. might be in danger or dead.

"Gimme the story," I said and sat down on the edge of her desk.

She said the story was that the Maryland State Transportation Administration was looking at ways to alleviate traffic in the area and was considering creating bus ways for mass transit, to take the busses off the main highways, and let them get from A to B faster on dedicated roads. They were considering updating the old B&O Tunnel in Ellicott City. The tunnel and the old bridge would be used for one of these bus ways over the Patapsco River from River Road to Catonsville.

Good idea, I guess. I never used busses.

"They sent a couple guys out to survey the tunnel and bridge to see if it was viable. That was on February 1st. The guys never reported back in." Tina said.

"Why are they sending us on a two-day old M.P.?"

"Around sixish, they found one of the surveyors down by the bank of the river. He was covered with blood, and tar, and muck. Looked like he wasn't injured much, just scratched up, dehydrated, and bruised," she said.

"Just the one guy?" I asked her, suddenly finding myself interested.

"Just the one. Found their survey equipment under the bridge, all smashed to shit, covered in blood and muck, too. He wasn't talking much, just mumbling and shaking. They took him over to Saint Agnes."

I reached over and took the file from her and began to look it over

"Davis!" I could hear the Lieutenant from across the squad room.

"DAVIS!" he barked, again. He did that a lot. I usually deserved it but I wasn't in the mood today. I was hung over and his voice seemed louder than normal. "Can you ever get here on time?"

"Traffic," I said, and smiled. He looked at his watch. It was almost 10:30PM. I don't think he was buying it.

"The hospital is releasing this survey guy to us…"

"Matthew Pearson." Tina pointed the guy out to me in the folder. I pretended to keep reading the file, so I wouldn't have to look the lieutenant in the face. It got so red and puffy when he yelled, made him hard to look at.

"Pearson… yeah." The Lieutenant hated being corrected. Just glad I wasn't the one doing it this time. He grabbed the file out my hands and dropped it on Tina's desk. "They're bringing him over here."

"OK…" I started.

"I want you to have a go at him," he interrupted me. "The other surveyor is still in the wind. With all that blood on his clothes, we need to consider if Pearson offed the other one."

I flipped the file back open. There were pics of the surveyor's equipment all busted to hell, Pearson's clothes stained to all hell and a couple snaps of where they found him down by the river. I flipped past them to a pic of the guy when they found him. Jesus, he looked scared. Perps usually don't look like that. My instincts said that maybe this guy hadn't whacked his buddy, maybe they were both hit and he was scared he'd get in hot water for ratting out whoever did it? Maybe. Can't tell a lot from a picture but it was always a place to start.

"So, he hasn't said anything at all so far?" I knew the answer, but asked anyway. Partly to get clarification, and partly to be a pain in the ass.

"Nothing. See if you can get him to talk, I want to get this handled before the morning. Before the press gets wind of this, hate when they grab hold of these things, and we don't have any answers. Need to know where the other fella is, dead or alive."

"Press? Why the extra push, boss?" He hated when I called

him boss.

"There's a lot of controversy about that tunnel being redone. Historical people are all up in arms that it be declared a historic landmark. Other folks want practical use of existing infrastructure like it."

"So?" Tina's turn.

The Lieutenant's face started doing that red puffy thing again.

"So." He took a deep breath. "So, my bosses do not want the press to make this into some political thing, with someone trying to kill to save a historic site, that kind of crap. OK?"

"I guess, but…"

"We do not want this as tomorrow's top story, unless it is to say case solved, get it?" He was pretty flustered. Someone must have chewed his ass out about this already, so of course shit flows downhill.

"Find out what happened to the other guy…" He paused. He sucked with names.

"Patrick Dean." Tina said. The lieutenant frowned at her. I was a bad influence after all.

"Yeah, Dean. Find out where Dean is, and what the fuck happened."

About a half hour later, two uniforms brought Pearson in. He was cleaned up, and wearing some hospital scrubs. His clothes had gone to the lab for testing.

"Put him in interrogation four, I'll be there in a couple minutes."

I wanted to let him sit in there alone for a bit. Make him stew. That always worked for me, to get them out of their element.

I always used to laugh when I watched cop shows on TV. The interrogation rooms looked nothing like they do in real life. They always showed these big rooms, with two-way mirrors, and big tables that you could chain the dangerous suspects to, so Sipowitz and the cast of NYPD Blue could talk them into full confessions that they'd happily write out and sign. The real thing wasn't like that at all. The rooms were small, usually only had three chairs. There was a window with blinds but not the giant one on the TV shows. They'd have a small table or desk that we could throw a notepad and pencil on. There was a video camera up in the corner. The camera was there, supposedly, to keep guys like me in line. If I smacked around a guy the camera would see and the lawyers could argue that I "coerced" the confession. Tapes got erased accidentally a lot. Must not be a very good recording system. Never seemed to find one where I did that. Funny.

I stood behind Tina as we flipped through the rest of the file. Then I leaned forward to get her two cents. We had been doing this for 5 years now. She was good on the numbers and finding the little things that I might miss. I was good at getting folks to talk. We closed a lot. That was probably the only thing that kept me from getting fired. If I hadn't been good at that, they'd have canned me for my mouth a long time ago. When I was a kid, I got a job at a McDonalds. Only lasted 3 days. I called my supervisor an asshole in front of the customers and they canned me.

Did I mention I smacked him in the face too? Yeah, that was probably a contributing factor.

"What do you see?" I asked her.

"Report says he had blood on his clothes, mud from the riverbank and some sticky stuff. Lab guys are testing it to see what it was." She liked lab reports.

"Sticky stuff? Like what?"

"Tar-like substance is all it says."

"What was he doing, rolling around on a new road patch? What about the equipment, that survey-scope thing…" I flipped to the photo showing it.

"It's called a Transit."

I looked at Tina, always a wealth of info.

"My dad used to work construction. They use the scope to

look through to a target at the other end, can let them know distances, if stuff is straight..."

"I seriously don't care." I cut her off. "Did they find any tissue, or anything on it?"

"Just blood, like it was handled by bloody hands and more of that tar. Nothing more than that. Looks like he may have smashed it on the rocks by the river."

"Could he have thrown it off the bridge?"

"They found it too far away, looks like he carried it over there and then smashed it."

I told Tina that after we talk to Pearson, we'd have to swing over there and check out the tunnel. She let me know that there were some uniforms over there now searching the area, seeing if they could find anything. Good. I hated clue hunting. She loved it. I could sometimes picture her like Sherlock Holmes with a big magnifying glass, exclaiming "Eureka!" when she found a clue.

I leaned back against her desk and she closed the folder. I sat there for a few moments, thinking of how I wanted to go at this guy. My mind kept going back to that picture of him. He looked scared. How could I use that? Should I scare him more? Should I be comforting and try to become his buddy?

It was a couple minutes before I realized Tina had been calling my name.

"Bill... Bill?"

I looked over to her.

"Good cop, Bad cop?"

We loved that routine. I'd come in like a bat out of hell and she'd swoop in like a guardian angel and then they'd blurt everything to her to avoid my return.

Never hurt that she was hot as hell. Well, that worked with the straight male perps and a few of the female ones. I was thinking about this one case where we did that. This guy was a horny bugger and Tina really got him going.

"Bill? Good cop?"

I told her I didn't think we should go that route yet. I needed to get a feel for this guy. I guess in my head that picture kept making me think he was scared. Bad cop might completely close him off. I let her know that we would start with a soft-sell and see if he gave us anything. I could always go bad cop on him later.

It was about 11:25PM when we walked into interrogation room four. Pearson sat on the floor in the corner. He was a big guy, about six foot maybe 250 pounds. Right now, though, he was in the corner curled up in a ball like a frightened child.

"Matt Pearson? I'm Detective Bill Davis. This is my partner, Detective Tina McGee. Is it OK if I call you Matt?"

Pearson didn't even acknowledge that we had come into the room. He sat there in the corner, his eyes wide, mumbling. I couldn't make out what he was saying. Probably gibberish, I thought. I reached out to grab his shoulder. His face snapped up to look at me. He looked like he did in that picture. This guy was scared. I hadn't seen that kind of scared before.

"Let's get you up in this chair, Matt. Detective McGee and I just want to talk to you for a bit, is that OK?"

Pearson nodded. Well, at least I knew that meant he could hear me and understand what I was saying. I helped him to his feet and got him to sit in the chair. He pulled his knees up into his chest and sat there rocking.

"No one is mad at you, Matt. We're just trying to figure out what happened to you and…" I looked over at Tina.

"Patrick Dean, your partner." Tina said.

"Yeah, Patrick." I nodded at Tina for the save. I was lousy with names. "If Patrick is in trouble, we need to get to him as soon as we can. Right?"

Pearson started sobbing. Not like a little cry kind of thing. I am talking big-time, full sobs. He got all raspy and out of breath from it. I looked over at my partner. I hadn't seen anyone ever cry that way before. It was either the worst acting of all time or this guy was falling apart right in front of us.

Tina sat on the chair in front of Pearson directly across the table from him. She put her hands on the table.

"We just want to help Patrick," she said in the most comforting way possible.

Pearson's sobs began to turn into some sort of laugh. Not a happy go lucky thing but the kind of laugh that someone would have when given horrible news. "Congratulations, your mother's cancer is gone but she had a stroke." That kind of news.

Pearson put his hands up to his face. I thought he was going to wipe away his tears. Instead he used his fingers to pry his eyes open.

"Can't... don't," he whispered.

"Can't what? Can't help Patrick? Did someone hurt Patrick? Was that his blood on you?" Tina questioned him, pressing a bit harder than I intended to at this moment.

"Can't... don't," he repeated.

Tina leaned back in the chair and looked up at me. This was a first for me. I was starting to question the lieutenant's thoughts on this. Why'd they even let this guy out of the hospital? He should be in a psych ward.

"Can't... don't," he said again.

I was about to ask him what he meant when there was a knock on the door. Pearson nearly jumped out of his skin. I put my hands up.

"It's OK, Matt, just stay calm."

He started rocking again, his hands on his face. His fingers prying his eyes open and then that mumbling.

Yeah, that crazy mumbling.

I opened the door. It was one of the uniforms.

"Lieutenant wants you."

We told Pearson we'd be back. Not sure if he heard us or even cared. The lieutenant was standing outside the interrogation room.

"They found Dean."

It was about 12:30AM when we got to the tunnel these guys were surveying. The file said it was the old B&O tunnel and bridge. I didn't realize they were talking about the Ilchester Tunnel. I remember playing here as a kid, everyone did. I didn't live in the area, but my grandmother did. She lived in this awful old yellow house that needed a paint job. You know the kind, where it looks like it has needed a paint job since it was built. The tunnel was a great place to hang out as a teen. We'd go there to drink beer, smoke, tell ghost stories, and that kind of shit. Bunch of urban legends about it and now a real story to tell.

They had put up crime scene tape at the far end of the tunnel to block the area off. Several patrol cars had their lights flashing all over the place. This was pretty close to some residential areas. We were going to draw a shitload of attention pretty soon.

No press so far but no doubt they'd be there shortly. Thank God. I hate dealing with them. I always piss them off because they're fucking leaches. Only good thing about a reporter is when they flip you a couple bucks for some info. I usually feed them bullshit so they don't ask me anymore. The annoyance wasn't worth the money.

There were a bunch of uniforms here. One kid, I am betting she was a rookie, was bent over the side of the bridge. Looked like she was sick. Another cop was patting her on the back. What was funny to me was if you'd see some rookie get sick at a crime scene, the veteran officers would usually make fun of them or get pissed off at them. The other cop didn't seem pissed. Weird.

There was a sergeant standing in front of the tape blocking off the bridge. I knew him. Good guy. He seemed uncomfortable, too.

"Hey Davis, McGee." He spoke to us, but quietly.

"What's going on, Sarge?" Tina asked.

He just nodded his head and lifted up the tape for us to pass under.

"Sarge? You alright?"

He turned toward me and nodded. A strange look in his eyes. Reminded me of the picture of Pearson in the file.

We walked across the bridge, and through the tunnel. It was dark as hell and I wish I had more than just this shitty flashlight in my hand. Funny, when we partied here as kids, I didn't seem to care as much about this being so dark. We lived for that. It was great to get wasted in the dark tunnel and try to scare each other. Then we'd get to grandma's house at about 3AM and she'd be freaking out. Always told us Tom was going to get us over there. Loved those ghost stories.

The cops at the other end of the tunnel had grabbed some extra flashlights so we could see that they were centered in the middle of the tracks at the far end. Jesus, if the dead guy was lying right there in the middle of shit why did it take so long to find him? They'd been here all day. I just hope they hadn't moved everything around before we got there. I needed Tina to do that Sherlock Holmes shit.

As we got to the end of the tunnel, I could see that they had a tarp lying over the tracks.

"What the fuck is wrong with you guys?" I blurted out. "You don't do anything to my scene until I get here, that includes this fucking tarp!"

Tina held up her hands for me to calm down but if they disturbed anything I was going to really be pissed. One of the uniforms, his nametag said Everett, came up to me and handed me an industrial-sized flashlight. That thing could light up a football field.

"We found the vic about an hour ago." Everett told me.

"Yeah," I said. "Sitting right in the middle of the road, that's why it took you all day?"

"Prick." Everett whispered.

"Anything look like an obvious cause of death?" Tina asked a question to diffuse the situation, before I tore into Everett.

Asking some uniform a cause of death was a waste of time. All this guy was probably qualified to do was write traffic tickets.

Yeah, he pissed me off.

"Coroner said he won't be able to tell anything till the crime scene guys get him out."

"Out?" I blurted.

Everett gestured toward the tarp. As we walked over to it, I thought to myself that it looked almost flat on the ground, like there was nothing under it.

Everett lifted the tarp from one side. I turned on the big flashlight. Everett pushed my arm until the flashlight focused on it.

It was a hand.

Sticking up through the gravel between the railroad ties was a hand. It wasn't like a severed hand, it was attached to the arm like the body was buried in the gravel under the tracks.

It wasn't just that but it was how the hand looked. The fingers were curled up, like you might imagine a drowning person reaching up out of the water as they go down for the last time.

"What the fuck? Did someone chop off his arm and plant it like a shrub?"

Like a magician revealing his assistant had disappeared, Everett pulled away the rest of the tarp.

I've seen many a body in my years as a cop. Like that rookie kid on the end of the bridge, I threw up once or twice and I've seen plenty that made the bile move up in my stomach.

But not like this.

Not like this.

It wasn't just an arm planted in the gravel.

Dean was in there. All of him. The hand came through the gravel rail bed in the space between two railroad ties but behind that, projecting just out of the gravel between the tracks…

Behind that was his face.

His face was frozen in a moment in time. Sticking out of the gravel, mouth open like a man gasping for breath above the water while being pulled under by Jaws or a giant octopus or something.

His face.

I don't know exactly what I saw. Desperation, fear, panic. Black tar and blood look like they had been squeezed out of his mouth and puddled on the ground around his face. It was locked in his face, that open mouth and his eyes. Where the fuck were his eyes? If fear could be captured at the moment it occurred, it was captured on his face.

"I am sorry, detective," Everett's voice, "Crime scene guys asked to cover it up. They had to send for special equipment."

I gestured that it was OK. I wasn't going to chastise him for covering this up. Besides, this guy was buried in the gravel beneath the railroad tracks. I don't think they could have disturbed any of that with a tarp.

Now I know why all they did was report they found him, with no details. How the hell could you explain this?

I looked over at Tina, my Sherlock Holmes partner. She was bent over, turned the other way. Nothing made Tina sick. She eats raw fish for Christ sake. I was still not sure why I wasn't sick. Maybe I was in shock.

"How...?" I searched for my words. "If they dug a hole by hand, it would have taken one heck of an effort. To do it without disturbing the ties, or the track..."

I patted Everett on the shoulder. He was shaking. I moved over to Tina and walked her back down the tunnel to our car. I stayed on site until the crime scene folks returned. Excavator was on the way. I called the coroner and let him know this was a priority. As soon as they got him out, I needed some answers.

I returned to the car and drove Tina and myself back to the precinct. Neither of us said a word.

It was close to 3AM by the time we got back. I had asked them to leave Pearson in the interrogation room. The lieutenant wanted to put him in lockup until we got back, thought it might scare him into talking. I told him that I thought that was a bad idea. He was scared enough already.

Now I was sure about that.

Thankfully, the lieutenant had listened to me. Pearson was still in the room. Tina and I decided to regroup with him and explain the situation so we could decide what tactic to take with this guy.

After a detailed description of the crime scene, the lieutenant looked up at me.

"So, how are you gonna get him to confess to killing Dean?"

What the fuck? Had this guy not heard a word I had told him? There was no way in hell that Pearson killed Dean and buried him like that. Whoever did it had scared the shit out of him, too. Was it some weird kind of organized crime thing? Was there some mob money that could be made if they did or didn't revamp that tunnel? Hell, we were talking about construction work and if any business had links to the families, it was construction.

That and waste management.

I told the lieutenant that my gut said this guy didn't do it.

"I don't give a rat's ass about your gut feelings. They found this guy with a potential murder weapon, covered in his friend's blood…"

"They haven't matched the blood and we aren't even sure about cause of death, yet, lieutenant." Tina chimed in.

The lieutenant grumbled over that. He knew she was right, but he was sure he was right, too.

"We are going to have everyone on our ass about this in a few hours. I want answers. If he didn't do it, he knows who did. Push him. Do what you do best, be an asshole."

Great. The one time I didn't want to push a suspect. The one time he is asking me to be an asshole is the one time I don't want to be.

Another uniform knocked on the lieutenant's door.

"Davis, got you some stuff back from the lab. On your desk."

I thanked him and turned back to the lieutenant.

"I think if I push this guy too hard, he'll fold. If we could have more time…"

"Two hours." The lieutenant gestured for us to leave his office. He followed us to his door and slammed it shut behind us.

Fuck.

Tina and I went over to my desk to see the stuff we got back from the lab. There was a plastic bag with Pearson's clothes in it and another larger bag with that transit doohickey.

Tina sat down and started reading the lab report. Sometimes they wrote that stuff in gibberish. Well, gibberish to me. Tina could decipher.

"Blood is definitely not his. Don't have a type to cross match with Dean yet but it's not Pearson's."

I took a close look at the clothes. There was a ton of tarry stuff on them, more than I expected. Even more than there was blood. It stunk, too. Sour, but oily. I know that smell, but could not remember from where.

"What about the tar?" I was hoping they had identified it. I didn't know if it would be relevant to the case, but I still wanted to know what it was.

"Let's see." Tina scanned the report. "Huh. Creosote."

"You mean that shit that cakes up my chimney?"

"No. More like a liquid version that they use…" She paused.

"Use for what?"

"To treat railroad ties."

Now I was confused. That bridge and tunnel were old. The wood was all dried out. How could that much creosote have gotten from that onto his clothes and the transit.

The transit.

Son of a bitch. Something was wrong here. The early pics I saw showed it as broken. This thing was intact.

Did they have more than one of these? Were both tested? One was broken, the other not broken.

I grabbed the evidence and headed toward the interrogation room. Tina could barely catch up with me.

If Pearson killed Dean, it had to have been with this one and not the broken one, right? If I had to push him then I was going to do it with the murder weapon in hand. It was time to be an asshole.

I turned to Tina.

"Bad cop." I entered the room, leaving her outside.

I slammed the door shut behind me. Pearson sat on his chair exactly where I had left him hours ago. I slammed the transit onto the table.

"Would you like to tell me what this is? How many of these did you guys have with you?"

Pearson would not look up. I then noticed his eyes were tightly closed. He mumbled and rocked.

"Look at me." Pearson didn't even acknowledge my presence.

"Look at me!" I shouted and shoved the transit into his face.

Pearson slowly opened his eyes and saw the transit in front of him.

"How many of these did you have?"

Pearson slowly lifted his hand and indicated one.

"But it was broken!" I shouted at him. "You smashed it?"

Pearson nodded. Now I was confused.

"Is this the same one you smashed?"

Pearson nodded again.

"That's not possible!" I lifted the transit to my face and moved it to look into the eyepiece.

Pearson jumped from his chair. He snatched the transit from

my hands, slamming me back against the door with a loud thud. He grasped the tool and retreated back into the corner, hugging it tightly against his chest.

"Can't... don't," he said again.

Tina and one of the uniforms barged in when they heard me slammed against the wall. I signaled them that I was okay and motioned for them to not enter the room.

I knelt down in front of Pearson to get as close to eye-level with him as I could. I showed him I was calm and lowered my voice to a near whisper.

"Can't what? Don't what?"

Pearson's eyes grew wide.

"Blink..." he mumbled.

"What?" I asked.

"Blink..." he said louder. He began to stand.

"Blink..." He got even louder. "Blink... Blink... BLINK! Can't Blink... Don't Blink!"

I stood up and began backing out of the room as Pearson stood there tightly clutching the transit.

"DON'T BLINK!" he shouted as I closed the door.

The uniform turned to look at me, and asked if he should go and retrieve the transit. I said to leave him be for the moment. I walked away from him and Tina and sat at my desk.

Holy shit.

Tina came over and sat on the edge of the desk next to me.

"What was that all about?" Tina asked me.

"Peeping Tom." I laughed as I said it.

"This guy is a peeping Tom? I don't get it."

"No, that's not it," I told her. "It's an old urban legend we heard as kids around there. Hell, my grandmother..."

"The one who lived in the little yellow house?"

I chuckled. She remembered the story I told her.

"Yeah, that one."

Tina looked at me, confused.

"She used to tell us scary stories about Peeping Tom, the Blink Man of Ilchester Tunnel. Mostly to try and scare us away from partying there, I thought."

"So, what's that have to do with all this?"

"If I remember the story right," I explained to her, "It goes something to the effect that if you can stare down to the end of the tunnel and not blink for one hour, you'll see the Blink Man, Peeping Tom. Then afterward, every time you blink, he will get closer and closer, and then eventually so close he'll kill you, or something like that. Christ, I can't remember the whole thing."

"No one can keep their eyes open for an hour without blinking."

"Yeah, I know," I replied. "But as kids, we sure tried."

"So," Tina stated quite clearly, "you're telling me this guy is saying that the Blink Man killed his partner and is going to kill him?"

I nodded.

"By doing something that is physically impossible?"

"Yeah," I replied. "That's exactly what he's saying."

"I'm calling psych."

I nodded. I could not explain all of this. There was no one who could. Did the lab guys reassemble the transit to see if they had all the pieces? Yeah, they might have done that and yeah, maybe someone dug a hole and buried Dean in it and maybe Pearson is just nuts.

And maybe I need a drink, 'cause this was starting to freak me out. Two and two were not adding up for me.

As I sat there, pondering my fate and how all this fit together, I saw Tina talking to the lieutenant. He turned to look at me. I knew that look. "His office, now." Yeah, he didn't even need to say it. I stood up to go to his office and it hit me.

I stuck my head in the door but didn't enter. I should have

entered.

"The transit," I said. "It's like an eye."

"What's your point?" Tina asked.

"It doesn't blink." I replied, smiling.

Tina shook her head. I think she knew where I was going but didn't like it. She turned toward the lieutenant.

"Davis," the lieutenant spoke softly, "we are calling in psych. This guy is off his rocker."

"I am so close to…"

"I think you're getting a little too wrapped up in this," the lieutenant said.

"Just give me one more chance with him…"

The lieutenant sighed.

"Just until psych gets here. Then I'm done."

Tina shook her head in disapproval. The lieutenant sighed again and told me to go ahead but I'd only have a little time since Tina had already called for the consult.

I went back to the interrogation room. Pearson was back on the floor in the corner with the transit.

I knelt in front of him again, calmly.

"It was Tom," I said quietly.

Pearson nodded.

"Did he hurt Patrick?"

Pearson nodded again. There was a knock on the door. I stood up annoyed and opened it. It was Tina.

"I only have a few more minutes, can you let me go?" I was pissed, she could tell. She's seen me pissed before.

I left the room and slammed the door behind me, only afterward realizing that I may have scared Pearson with that.

"What the fuck is it?"

"I thought you might like to see the coroner's report on Dean, asshole."

I snatched it out of her hand. She was right to interrupt and I was wrong to get mad but I wasn't going to let her know that. I don't like to admit when I'm wrong. I should've learned to do that.

I opened the file and began to read. Once again, gibberish. I showed it to Tina, she knew I needed a summary.

"Dean had numerous broken bones and contusions, as well as the, um…" she hesitated. "The thing with his eyes. But almost all of that was post-mortem."

"Okay, then summary please!" I was losing my patience. "What did he die from?"

"His lungs were filled, in essence he drowned."

"So, someone killed him down by the river, then dragged him up the hill, to the end of the tunnel, to bury him?" This scenario didn't make sense to me.

"He didn't drown in water," Tina paused. "His lungs were filled with…"

I knew the answer.

"Creosote."

I pushed the coroner's report back in her hands and turned to open the interrogation room door. Tina grabbed my shoulder.

"Walk away from this one." Tina looked deep into my eyes. "Please."

It was my turn to sigh. In any other reality, that look from Tina would have sent me into a frenzy, to get the hell out of work and back to her place. Of course, that hasn't happened before.

Well, not this week.

My problem is that I hate leaving stuff unfinished and I was still kinda pissed that no one was taking my side on this.

"I'm not done with him."

I left Tina standing in the hall and closed the door behind me. I had to know. Yeah, this guy might just be some crazy asshole but none of this made sense anymore. What did he see or what did he think he saw?

Or maybe I was losing it. Was I actually trying to prove

someone was killed by Peeping Tom?

I sat in a chair in front of Pearson and bent down to get closer to him.

"What happened to Patrick?"

Pearson sat there rocking; his eyes wide open.

"We..." Pearson mumbled. "Surveying the tunnel... taking a while, so dark, hard to see markers... Patrick was at the other end... Patrick... Oh God!"

"What happened to Patrick?"

Pearson started to tear up.

"I was looking through... through..." He gestured to the transit. "I saw, I saw..."

"You saw Tom, didn't you?"

"Saw him... rise up... pulled Patrick down... I couldn't... I wanted to... I ran... grabbed his hand, then his eyes... Oh God!" Pearson began deep heaving sobs, almost taking his breath away.

I put my hand on his shoulder. I meant to comfort him. At first, he stopped moving, so I thought it did. Then I felt cold, unreal cold. I can't explain it. He grabbed my hand and pushed it off of him.

"Don't blink!" He closed his eyes tightly and started rubbing his cheeks as if trying to rub something off of them. "He's here! I can feel it!"

Pearson started thrashing around. He shoved me to the floor and started swinging the transit wildly, with his eyes closed, not knowing where he was swinging it, smashing it against the wall.

"Don't Blink!" he shouted.

I could hear the banging on the door. I could hear them, yelling for me to open it. I can't lock it from my side. Why can't they open it?

I ducked.

Pearson swung at me again. He was screaming at the top of his lungs, his eyes tightly closed.

"No! Don't Blink!"

I grabbed at the doorknob and tried to open it. It was jammed. It never jammed. I started to beat back on the door when it hit me.

The transit struck me on the back of the head. It struck me so hard I could taste blood in my mouth, as if my head had burst open.

After that, everything else was a blur… I saw Pearson, I saw him open his eyes and scream. Not a normal scream. Not even like something from a horror film but some kind of unearthly thing and I swear to you and to God almighty, if there is one, I saw his eyes… it was like invisible thumbs crushed them back into his head. I saw his neck twitch. He slammed against the wall then catapulted to another wall like someone would throw a rag doll. Then I heard what sounded like bones snapping and that smell, that sickly sweet, oily smell.

I'm not exactly sure when I passed out.

I can remember waking up in the hospital. My head hurt. I went to reach for my head, when I realized I could not move my hand. I was handcuffed to the bed. What the hell?

No, they did not end up charging me. Doc says that the injury to my noggin would have made me incapable of killing Pearson. Coroner ended up declaring that Pearson killed himself. I guess they thought a crazy guy could throw himself around like that.

They did take my badge and gun. There would be a misconduct investigation. I may have used "extreme" interrogation tactics on Pearson that pushed the poor guy over the edge.

Yeah, blame me.

Of course, there seems to have been a malfunction with the recording system in that room. Tape was blank.

Never happens, does it.

I got out of the hospital the next day. Still had a headache. Hearing would be next week. I needed to call my union rep. Still not sure what I was gonna tell him.

"Sorry, I didn't rough up or kill the suspect, some supernatural force was in the room and did it instead of me. Blame Peeping Tom."

Yeah, like I was even sure of that myself. Doc says the blow to my head gave me a concussion. I could have been hallucinating everything.

Yeah, that was probably what happened.

Well, that's what I thought at the time.

Saw a package in front of my door when I got to my apartment. One of those big padded envelopes, you know the kind. The ones that would be big enough for a video tape.

Looks like my partner made sure the recorder malfunctioned.

Note said she had my back. Christ, she thinks I did something.

Maybe all I needed to clear myself was on the tape. I cracked open a beer and sat down to watch the blockbuster film of the week. I put the tape in.

Nothing special here. Quality was shitty, apparently the wall-mounted video camera wasn't much of a cinematographer. Picture goes in and out once in a while. Heck, it's old equipment.

As I was watching through, I noticed the screen getting staticky several times when we left Pearson alone. Each time he seems to be freaking out the picture gets all fuzzy. Then it clears up right before we go back in.

I'm getting nothing here except weird static. I fast forward, to our last visit.

"You saw Tom?"

"Saw him... rise up... pulled Patrick down... I couldn't... I wanted to... I ran... grabbed his hand, then his eyes... Oh God!"

I watched as I put my hand on his shoulder... the picture... static again...

"Don't blink!"

"He's Here! I can feel it!"

Still Static…

"Don't Blink!"

I could hear the crashing in the room, the thrashing about, but could not see anything… just static…

Hell of a time for the camera to fuck up.

Shit. This was a waste of time. I paused the tape and took a swig of my beer. No way was this gonna clear my name. I sat back and grabbed the remote. That was…

What the fuck is that?

The screen is filled with static but I swear to green apples that's an eye. The static looks like an eye. Right in the goddam middle.

Okay, that's weird. My head is still not working right. I'm paranoid and tired.

I turn off the TV and lay back on the couch. Sleep came surprisingly easy. I probably would have slept all night too, if the static from the TV hadn't woken me up. My cable must be out.

But I turned it off. Didn't I?

What time was it? Midnight. Time to go to sleep in my own bed.

I turned the TV off again, went to my bedroom, pushed the dirty clothes to one side and climbed in. Again, sleep came quickly.

If it just wasn't for the static from that damn TV. I sat up on the couch. I could hear Pearson on the TV.

"Don't blink!"

"He's Here! I can feel it!"

I went to shut off the VCR. It was off. The tape was on the table, where I left it. That's right… I took the tape out last night. Why didn't I remember that until just now?

"Don't blink!"

Was that an eye again? Oh fuck. That voice. It's not Pearson. Whose voice was it?

"Don't…"

This isn't real. I was having a nightmare, right?

"Blink."

I threw that big damn 70's ashtray, you know the heavy glass ones that your mom would put out there, must weigh five pounds, right at the goddamn TV screen. The glass smashed. There were a couple sparks. Nothing like the explosion when you break a TV on a TV show. Nothing is ever real, is it?

This wasn't real and I broke a perfectly good TV.

I had to report to Internal Affairs with my union rep to be questioned under oath. They asked me to take a poly. My rep said no. I also took the fifth on everything they asked. Pretty much a waste of their time.

Towards the end of the interview, they brought out the TV and tape player to ask me why this tape, marked for that day, was blank.

I told them I had no idea, no way I could have done anything to it. I was in the fucking hospital.

"Explain this." They asked. "It's like the machine wasn't turned on at all."

Static. A blank tape, as expected.

"Don't…"

You have to be shitting me.

"Blink."

This time I know I saw it. Damn near filled the screen. I fell backwards out of my seat. Union rep asked the I.A. pigs to leave. I asked them to take that fucking TV with them.

"Are you on drugs?"

Nice. Especially coming from my rep. I asked him if I was done and when he verified I was, I got the fuck out of there.

I stopped at a local sports pub to get drunk. I figured this whole situation deserved getting drunk, right?

You know this kind of place. Pool tables, dart boards, and like twenty TVs.

Yeah. I didn't think that through, did I?

I walked in and started to head to the bar. Whole damn place went static. Lots of games were on, and there was a lot of bitching. Was the eye on the screen again? I don't really know, I ran out the door so fast, I practically don't even remember going in.

I had to catch my breath. None of this is real. I have a head injury, after the weirdest interrogation in history. That's what this is.

I struggled with my keys to open my apartment door, then closed and locked it behind me.

Sure. If I am being chased by a monster out of a horror film, a locked door will save me, right? I pressed my forehead against the door, for a brief moment I felt safe.

Brief.

I must have left the TV on.

You know, the one I smashed with an ashtray.

"Don't"

I knew the voice on the TV now. It was mine.

It was 7:59PM on February 8th, 2003. I sat at the bar at O'Houlihans downing my fifth whiskey, when Pete switched on the game. Caps were playing Pittsburgh.

Shitty picture. Pete slapped the side of the TV, hoping to clear it up. I lifted my glass to my lips. I inhaled a sickly sweet, oily aroma.

"Fucking cable company." Pete exclaimed when the picture went out completely. Nothing but static.

"Blink."

TRAVERSE

By Steve Toase

K. Patrick Glover mentioned this project to me because of my interest in Forteana. A couple of weeks later I met with an old friend from my archaeology degree who now works for a university archive. While we were having a beer, the Ilchester Tunnel came up in conversation. Once they realised it was the one in Maryland not Somerset, they told me about a research project studying 19th century temporary worker camps across Western Europe and the United States. It seems that the project stalled after a training excavation in Ellicott City went wrong. Although she couldn't get me the project records, she was able to let me see the site diary and the personal diary of the archaeologist in charge of the work, Jenny Calburn. I'm not sure exactly what happened here, (Jenny has recorded a lot of unprofessional practices and there seems to have been a real tension between her and Ewan), but I passed them on to K. Patrick Glover. I thought they could add a bit of background to the history of the tunnel.

– Steve Toase

Missing Person Unit
National Crime Agency
Public Liaison

Dr Samuel Brentford
Head of Dept
Department of Archaeology and Prehistory

Dear Dr Brentford,

Thank you for your recent letter requesting an update into the case of Jenny Calbourn. I can tell you that as of this point in time we have made no further progress. As a result, we are pausing our investigations, and have returned the site records mentioned in your letter, including both the site diary, and the Jenny Calburn's personal diary.

With kind regards,
PC Faith Mayweather
Public Liaison Officer

Jenny Calburn's Personal Diary
15th October

Not a good start. First all the hassle getting the equipment through customs (something that the university was supposed to have sorted out). Then when we do get through and get all the surveying kit cleared, there's no one from the Historical Society waiting to meet us. Ewan was even more snappy than usual. I know that he doesn't want to be here. It's not my fault that the Archaeology Department doesn't think I'm senior enough to run the excavation on my own. Like I told him, sexism affects us all.

We finally managed to get a minibus taxi sorted out and get to the accommodation (at least the university managed not to mess that up). I'm just writing this now before I get some sleep. Jetlag is kicking me to bits. I'm glad we programmed in a rest day tomorrow, but I want to get started!

Jenny Calburn's Personal Diary
16th October

Slept late. Far too late.

Still no sign of our contact. I've tried ringing the local historical society, but no answer. I've told the students to have some time off. Go and familiarise themselves with the town. Ewan wasn't too happy about that. I believe his exact words were, "The last thing we need is that lot laid up with hangovers." A bit hypocritical, considering.

Update

The local contact Sarah McSanders finally turned up at 6:30pm, full of apologies. Barely stopped longer than five minutes. Some kind of ongoing family crisis, but promised to meet us on the site at 8am tomorrow.

Site Diary
17th October

First day on site.
Contact Sarah MacSanders met us at the entrance.
All required permits to allow work to begin in order.
Introductory talk about the history of the location delivered, with a focus on the relationship between the camp and the nearby tunnel/bridge.
Short tour of the area directly around the site to put the project in context.
Health and safety talk delivered.
First job tomorrow is to clear the undergrowth that is obscuring the earthworks.

Jenny Calburn's Personal Diary
17th October

I thought Ewan was going to lose it. There's always one

student. He should know that by now. One who chooses to mouth off. When Sarah had finished talking about the background of the area, and asked if there were any questions, James Sandhaven put his hand up. I didn't show it, but groaned inside. Anyway, he started talking about how he'd been reading up on the area, while Sarah nodded along, then he pointed behind us in the vague direction of the tunnel and said, "I've heard something about Peeping Tom. What do you know about him?"

For a moment she looked like she was going to say something, then smiled and muttered about paying attention to real history rather than rumours. Ewan ended the whole thing quickly, before any of the other students decided to play up. I mean they're only first years. Barely out of school, and they just need to let off some steam. Tomorrow we have some local volunteers joining us. That should help keep things a bit calmer.

We moved all the equipment into the house we're using for a site hut. I was led to believe that there would be power, but there's no evidence of this either. No time to hire a generator either. I really need to have a word with the department. Sending us halfway around the world only partially resourced. At least they packed the step-down voltage convertors.

It was a good opportunity to observe the students actually doing some work together. Usual mixture of first years with a handful of second years supervising. Most just here to get a free trip because it sounded more interesting than doing their practical in a field in Doncaster. Some keen (maybe a bit too keen), others lazy as fuck. We'll see how they cope with the site clearance tomorrow.

Site Diary
18th October

Arrived at site early. Divided into three work groups to enable us to circulate students around different tasks.

Morning spent cutting back vegetation.

Navvy camp foundations starting to emerge.

Starting to define stone footings for Navvy camps' more permanent buildings.

All undergrowth removed and stacked. Initial site photos taken.

Basic training in using the cameras delivered to each group.

Students started recording visible features.

During this stage, some graffiti was found carved into the stonework. At first glance they seemed to be surveying marks; a circle with a line running through them. While Ewan led the teams in further scrub clearance, I created a photographic record of these marks.

By the end of the day had identified over 27 spread across the site.

Three first years were trained in locating the surveying benchmark to bring in for the topographic survey working from the plans provided. All the work they did back in England was using Ordnance Survey benchmarks so it took a while to find the US Geodetic Survey plaque just inside the tunnel.

Jenny Calburn's Personal Diary
18th October

I sometimes wonder why I bothered getting Ewan this job. He has absolutely no interest in teaching even the basics and his mood is worse because it's not his project. I know that smarts for him. He doesn't say anything directly of course, but watching the way he talks to the students and gets distracted to the point of doing nothing, it's pretty obvious where his head is at. Me finding the graffiti really got his back up. He missed out on funding for the project back in the UK. Again, he won't say anything directly.

Won't talk about it. I tried mentioning it once and he changed the subject so fast I thought he was going to give himself whiplash.

We at least made some progress with the site. All the scrub is cleared and stacked at the side, ready for burning, and we've found the survey point so can bring in a temporary bench mark tomorrow.

I took James Somerfeld, Kath Bryce, and Gemma Tyson to do the surveying. I'll be honest, not because they have the most aptitude, though they're not the worst three on the site, but because they seem to be well liked and it always helps to get to know those ones first.

When we got to the tunnel, there was a load of giggling and I heard Peeping Tom get mentioned again.

I know they're technically adults, but I've still got a duty of care to them, and it's the sort of situation ripe for the girls to be taken advantage of. Turns out it's some kind of urban legend connected to the tunnel. It took me at least four times of asking before Kath finally told me what it was all about. Turns out it's some kind of local Bloody Mary variation. Challenge test. That sort of thing. Stare down the tunnel for an hour, see Peeping Tom. At midnight. I wonder how many of these stories are still going?

When we got back to the accommodation a few of us ended up sitting outside talking about these stories from when we were growing up. Even Ewan joined in, telling us how he stood in front of a mirror at Primary School reciting the Lord's Prayer backwards to try and make the Devil appear, but nothing happened. I told them about my American cousin who made us do Bloody Mary, and then ran out of the house when I crept into her bedroom at night wearing an old Halloween mask.

We were a bit loud, to be fair, but I was still surprised that when the hotel manager came up, he tore strips off us. Not because we were disturbing the other guests, but because of what we were talking about.

I suggested to everyone we go into my room and carry on talking there, but the heart had gone out of it.

Site Diary
19th October

Met Sarah MacSanders on site.

Unfortunately, the local volunteers we were hoping for are not available now. We have a large enough team of students so were able to set them up and working.

First task, clean up all the stonework for proper recording. Once that's done, we can decide the best way of carrying out the topographic survey. This decision is student led.

The students decided that a series of transects two metres apart would give us a sufficient density of points to capture the detail.

Traverse from the survey point to the site to establish the temporary benchmark completed as a training exercise. Ewan took a second team to complete the traverse back. We repeated this training task to train everyone in using the Total Station Theodolite independently by the end of the day.

Unfortunately, a storm came in during this stage. Conditions were completely unworkable and we had to abandon site.

Back at the accommodation I delivered a talk on the differences and similarities in American and British navvy camps of the time.

Jenny Calburn's Personal Diary
19th October

Today was a complete wash out. We got a small amount done before the skies opened, but not really enough to justify any of the effort put in. We had to abandon by 2pm, so we didn't even get the survey started. To top it all, Sarah MacSanders now tells me that the local volunteers have bailed on us, and she admits she's fairly new to the area, so all that local knowledge I was hoping to tap into is not available. I raised my voice. I'm not proud of it, but what do people expect? This project is turning into one broken promise after another. We were meant to be doing a social history of the navvy camp. Trying to find the living relatives through informal conversations and then include that research in our project.

MacSanders has suggested she can speak to some local families. See if they are willing to be interviewed by the students, but that's not my research approach, and they're just not going to open up in the same way.

Jenny Calburn's Personal Diary
20th October 3am

It's three in the morning, and I'm sat here fucking furious. Ewan has just left after telling me he left the Total Station set up at the tunnel when the weather closed in. Several thousand pounds worth of equipment just left there, in the middle of fucking nowhere. Switched on too! So, the battery will be fucked. The spare is charged, but I've no idea if it will work, because of course he couldn't remember if he put on the rain cover.

Honestly, I'm sick of him. I'm sick of his wilful incompetence. How do you forget that you've left the survey equipment set up? He asked if I wanted him to go and get it now, but there didn't seem much point. We're back on site in a few hours, and if it's going to be stolen then it will have already happened. I don't even know if the liability insurance will cover this. That's the department's only Total Station and I had to fight tooth and nail for them to let me bring it over. It's not his reputation on the line. At least we didn't get started on the survey so there's no data to lose. I'm so tempted just to abandon the lot of them, climb on a Greyhound and get lost somewhere.

Site Diary
October 19th

The weather is much better today.

We had an unfortunate incident where the Total Station was left out on site overnight during the bad weather. However, after a new battery was fitted everything seems to be working OK. There are some anomalous readings on the Data-logger, but we can remove those at a later stage.

Once certain the Total Station was working, we began the topographic survey of the site. The aim of this stage of the project is to allow the students to;

each have a turn operating the equipment and working on the staff,

learn the restrictions and limitations of each part of the process,

learn that surveying is a partnership where the person holding the staff is just as important if not more so,

learn decisions have more influence on the quality of the survey.

To facilitate this, we're logging each transect with the initials of students taking the readings so that when we process the data, they can compare their accuracy.

We laid out the test pits.

Our permits are pretty strict. We are only allowed to excavate a total of ten 1m x 1m test pits across the camp.

We can have two students working on each test pit and rotate them out to work on the Total Station, so that they gain experience of carrying out both topographic survey and excavation.

Ewan is supervising the excavation side, training the students in context recording, planning and section drawing.

I'm working on the survey.

By lunch we've completed several transects. All pairs have so far correctly identified a lot of detail is getting missed by taking points every metre, so we're increasing the density of points recorded allowing a much more detailed survey.

Jenny Calburn's Personal Diary
20th October

We actually made progress today, opening up several test pits and getting the topographic survey started. On the whole the students are enthusiastic, and learning quickly, which is the point of the exercise, I guess. I'm still worried about the Total Station. There seems to be a weird smudge inside the lens. I'm hoping that water hasn't got in and damaged the optics. I mentioned it to Ewan, but he just shrugged and said something about it all coming out in the wash.

When I got back to the accommodation, I decided to download the data. Belt and braces. Everything seems OK in the data log. The only issue is a series of anomalous readings between the initial traverse bringing in the temporary benchmark and the topographic survey. Normally we use a letter code so we can identify what we're surveying, but these are prefixed by ⊠

Jenny Calburn's Personal Diary
21st October 2am

I couldn't sleep. Something about those readings. There's only three of them, but they don't make sense. I went through all the menus on the Total Station and there isn't a way to even generate that symbol. Then I, finally, checked the time and date on the readings. They were all taken just after midnight when the Total Station was left out at the tunnel.

Ewan wasn't asleep when I knocked on his door. He pretended to be, but I'd heard him moving around before I knocked.

When he answered the door, I showed him the laptop, and pointed out what he should be looking at.

"So?"

That was his answer. His only answer.

"Someone has messed around with the Total Station after you left it out."

He took the laptop off me and peered at the screen. I'm sure I smelt whiskey on his breath.

"Maybe the internal clock got reset when it got wet."

"Which was your fault," I said, taking the computer back.

"But it doesn't have any effect on the readings. If that's the worst outcome, then I think we got off pretty lightly."

We? We? This is all down to him. He was the one that jeopardized the whole project. He's the one who hasn't an ounce of professionalism in him. I was on the verge of telling him what I thought. Fuck the other guests. Then the hotel manager came out, and just stood watching us.

"This isn't over," I said to Ewan, turning back to my room.

"It never is with you," he shouted after me. "It never is."

Site Diary
21st October

It's unfortunate that I have to record that the research has come to an end. Due to administration problems we are no longer able to continue with the project at this time. It is the hope of all the project staff that we can return to finish off our research at a later date, but it is not felt that we are able to proceed any further this season.

Jenny Calburn's Personal Diary
21st October

It's over. The whole project is fried. The permits were in place, but no-one had actually spoken to the landowner. He was waiting for us when we arrived this morning, leaning on the gate. Claimed he'd never been asked for permission. Never even heard of MacSanders. Demanded we get all our equipment off site straight away.

Ewan tried to reason with him, with the subtlety of a flying brick. I went to help calm things down, but he held up his hand and waved me away. Fucking waved me away! I left him to it and went back to talk to the students who were unsettled. Mostly worried about their grades. I couldn't give them any answers. How could I? Instead I watched Ewan try and dampen the fire of the landowner's anger by throwing petrol on it. When the guy went back to his car and came back with a gun, I stepped in, dragged Ewan away and got the students back into the minibus. There was nothing worth recovering on the site. We hadn't unpacked the surveying equipment yet, so that was safe.

We still have a week before we fly back. I don't know what to do now.

I didn't feel like company so I fired up the computer and started processing the surveying data, and putting it into the CAD programme.

Most of the points actually looked OK. The students had done a good job on the topographic survey, and at least there are concrete results there that they can be graded on. Something odd though. That cluster of anomalous readings prefixed by ⊠. Incredibly dense. When I overlaid them on the base map, they're all around the tunnel. At first, I thought they were some error from bringing in the benchmark but every single one is at the far end of the tunnel. Out of curiosity I opened the data log. They were all taken during that hour after midnight. One other thing. When I first spotted these odd readings in the data, I counted three. Now there are forty-eight. I don't know what Ewan did, but I think there might be some kind of virus in the programme.

Site Diary
22nd October

As we still have three days until our flight back to England, we have decided to take advantage of our spare time, and use it for documentary research. The students have divided into groups and each group has been assigned a different archive to investigate.

While they're researching, the project management team are processing the survey data.

Jenny Calburn's Personal Diary
22nd October

I've refreshed the data several times and the problem just seems to be getting worse. Every time, the number of points around the end of the tunnel increases. All with the same date stamp. I was reluctant to show them to Ewan. I knew he would blame me. He did. Accused me of corrupting the data. Accused me of introducing a virus. I could definitely smell the alcohol on his breath. Saw a three-quarter empty bottle of bourbon by his bed.

We refreshed the data. Reloaded it into the CAD programme. There were more. Like a rash. All in the same place.

"Have you tried rotating the image?"

It seemed so obvious after he said it. Of course, the third measurement the survey records is height. I dragged the cursor across the screen and tilted the image to see the heights of the points. They were still stack upon each other, but rising. Ewan slammed the screen shut.

"I'm going to take this and see if I can sort out your mess."

I grabbed the laptop and he wrenched it from my arms.

"This is a university project and a university laptop. You're not working on this any longer."

What could I do? I'm not getting into a fist fight with him. I let him go. Let him take the computer. I'd got a backup of course, not that I had anything to open the files on.

Jenny Calburn's Personal Diary
30th October

Because of events that happened on the 23rd I haven't had chance to write. With the police interviews and shepherding the students back home away from the press. The university has arranged counselling for us. I've declined so far, but don't know how much longer I can put it off. I want to get the project wrapped up.

That morning, some of the students had been concerned about Ewan when he didn't get up for breakfast. Honestly, by this point I didn't give a shit. They tried knocking on his door, but got no answer. Eventually they persuaded me to get the hotel manager to open up the room.

The smell hit me first. That iron tang of blood. The laptop was at one end of the bed, screen spidered and jagged. It took me a few moments to see Ewan fallen down the far side, duvet pulled down on top of him, only his fingers visible. What I remember, what will stay with me, is the splinters of computer screen glass wedged into his fingertips, clots around the wounds. That image, more than what he'd done to his eyes, is the one I wake up to in the middle of the night. That laptop glass piercing his skin.

And the laptop. I tried to get the police to let me take it, or at least copy the data off it. Not a chance. Lots of talk of evidence, and it being wrecked far beyond saving anyway.

There were too many things to sort out. All the students had to give evidence. Wasn't until we got home, I remembered the back up.

I loaded it onto my desktop PC earlier, to check I had a full copy of the data. The least I can do is salvage the survey transects so the students can get their marks. When I loaded them into the programme, the anomalies were there. I tried deleting them and refreshed the rendering. They increased, still in that spot on the far side of the tunnel, but something strange happened. Every time I ran the programme and tried to shift them, they increased in number. That was all at first. I rotated the view. They were higher each time. Then something changed again. There were no more, but the x,y coordinates changed. Each time I refresh the programme the concentration of points gets closer. I'm on the forty ninth iteration now. The points are still migrating. I've just looked away long enough to write up this diary entry, but I have to go back and check on what's happening. I'm not sure if I will be able to stop looking. I've just refreshed the data again. It's like there's a shadow in there. I'm not sure what will happen, but if you find this, the data is on the external drive. I don't know if we've made an error. If the equipment was defective or damaged. My eyes are stinging now. I've just refreshed again. The points are moving toward me. I need to stop writing now and just watch.

That was the final entry. I've tried to track down some information on both Ewan and Jenny, but there's not much out there. I don't know if Ewan is a first name or surname, so that's a dead end. I did find a couple of mentions of a Jenny Calburn who wrote an MA thesis looking at navvy camps. Everything seems to end in the mid 2000s, and though I called in some favours, I can't find any other papers by her. I even checked the archaeology magazines for obits. She just seems to disappear.

YOU CAN'T SHOOT GHOSTS

By Jacob Le Doux

This story takes place after the release of the film Butterfly Kisses. Its author, Mr. Le Doux, is the actual person described within. The related events happened to him as depicted. He has taken the liberty of putting them into a recreated interview format as best he can remember, and has written up a conversation that was related to him by one of the participants at a later date.

Case Number: 21291311
Date: January 15, 2019
Howard County Police Barracks
Interviewing Officer: Deputy Arthur Collins
Prepared By: CPL Denis Andrews
Involving the vehicular demise of James Thomas and Leena Tuneski

COLLINS: It's January 15th 2019 at approximately 10:15 PM. I'm beginning the interview of one Mr. Jacob Le Doux, who was the first person on the scene of the accident and who believes he has vital information pertaining to the incident. Is that correct and are you aware that you are being recorded Mr. Le Doux?

LE DOUX: ...

Collins: I'll need you to please say that you are aware sir. The microphone is unable to pick up body movements.

LE DOUX: This is a waste of my time and yours. I told you there's more going on with this than you'd possibly understand. I've been trying to tell you already for over an hour.

COLLINS: I am well aware that you have been trying to make your points heard, sir, and they will be. I have also asked you to please contain your emotions. This is all just simply procedure that we are following here. Checks and balances and all that. Are you fully aware that you are not under arrest, nor being detained, and that you are being recorded?

LE DOUX: So I can leave?

COLLINS: This won't take long at all, Mr. Le Doux. If you'll only be cooperative with us, we can all get out of here that much sooner. I'll remind you; it was you that felt we needed to know something.

LE DOUX: I'm aware. Ok? Can we get on with this?

COLLINS: Earlier this evening there was a vehicular accident near the intersection of Bonnie Branch and Illchester Road outside of Ellicott City, which caused the unfortunate deaths of two individuals. You were found on the scene of the accident. Is that correct?

LE DOUX: You know it is! That's where we just came from! We were both there! What is the point of this shit?

COLLINS: Please just answer the questions as they're asked, sir. I'm not interrogating you. I'm just setting up an analysis of the evening. Can you please state for the record what you were doing out on Illchester Road earlier tonight?

LE DOUX: I knew something was wrong. They were taking too long and I had a bad feeling about the whole thing.

COLLINS: So, you are saying that you knew the individuals in the accident personally?

LE DOUX: Jesus Christ, you know I did! Have I been talking to myself this whole time? Have I!? Weren't you listening at all before you hit the damn record button?

COLLINS: Please Mr. Le Doux, you need to understand that this interview isn't being done for me or for my benefit. At some point soon this tape will be reviewed by investigators working on this case. I know that this was a terrible and emotional occurrence and I'm sorry you saw what you did. But I'm going to ask you this just one last time, please keep yourself restrained and your emotions in check. You are not under arrest but I would be happy to modify that situation for you if you insist on these outbursts. I'm trying to understand how you came to be the very first person on the scene of a very nasty accident. And we need to get all of the necessary information cataloged. I know this may seem tiresome and repetitive, but please bear with me. Did you receive a phone call from the victims, or some other form of contact? Were you to meet tonight, maybe somewhere near there?

LE DOUX: Jesus! This is fuckin... Ok... sorry... Look, it was me, I called them, cause it was all making sense to me now. I had to talk to the both of 'em and let 'em know that I understood now. We were supposed to be meeting over at Fish Head.

COLLINS: Cantina? In Baltimore?

LE DOUX: Yeah, I think it's really Arbutus but whatever yeah. We were gonna meet there cause the place has good food and they usually do live music on the weekends. Plus, it's kind of in-between where Otter and Tuna were staying and where I've been crashing. But they were taking too long to get there. I knew something was wrong. I fuckin knew it! I knew something like this was going to happen eventually, that's why I called them. It was only a matter of time, man. I should have seen it sooner. I should have been listening better. But I didn't, and now...

COLLINS: How do you mean you knew this would happen? You somehow knew that there would be an accident tonight? Were one or both of your friends dealing with some kind of problem, perhaps, like maybe depression, or something? How could you have had advanced knowledge of what appears, by all accounts so far, to be a tragic accident?

LE DOUX: I didn't know they were gonna crash. But it was only a matter of time until something tragic happened to him. From what I've heard and been able to put together, it was practically a miracle already that he'd made it this far. You can't stop what killed them. You can't even find it.

COLLINS: Find what?

LE DOUX: Who...

Collins: Who?

LE DOUX: Exactly. It was the fucking Blink Man.

COLLINS: Excuse me? Who is this Blink Man and how is he involved in all of this?

LE DOUX: I don't really know, not really. I just know that there have been others who've faced him and there's even been those who've tried to bring him into the light before. But some things simply can't be unseen. Some things can only be found.

COLLINS: Are you implying that there's some kind of lunatic out there causing deadly auto accidents? This is not to be taken lightly Mr. Le Doux.

LE DOUX: No! No, it's not! But it's so much more than that. Once you see, you can't unsee.

COLLINS: What are you trying to say Mr. Le Doux?

LE DOUX: I'm not trying to say anything. I already told you. You still aren't listening.

COLLINS: Are you telling me this Blink man is something supernatural? Some kind of boogeyman?

LE DOUX: I guess you could say that. He's a Flicker Geist. An ethereal specter of wrath. I don't know the fucking science.

COLLINS: Mr. Le Doux, you are beginning to try my patience. I am happy to hear your story. That's why we are here. To give you your time and try to make sense of this. But quite frankly, it is very suspicious that you just happened to be there, on the scene of the accident, before any of the emergency units arrived. And then, to have you babbling on and on about how you "know" what happened. We brought you here to hear what you had to say. I very much do want to understand what caused this tragic accident, but I'm not going to allow you to sit here and make a mockery of our justice system and waste the valuable time of our staff and men such as myself, who could be putting our time towards the pursuit of finality, rather than dealing with some young punk having a laugh at us. What were you doing there tonight? Why were you meeting this couple and how did you wind up on Illchester Rd?

LE DOUX: I told you that too, man... Look, to understand any of this I have to start back a bit. You gotta understand what happened before. How we wound up here, so to speak.

COLLINS: I truly hope you can shed some light on this, Mr. Le Doux. Because so far, you've given me nothing but a hard time. By all means, go ahead. You have my attention.

LE DOUX: Let me start at the beginning. I moved here to this area in '99 from P.A. I was young. I was on my own and I was a partier. Most of us were, when we were younger, right? Well, when I moved here, I quickly began to make friends. Long story short, A led to B led to C, led to me meeting and becoming friends with a guy named Otter and a girl named Tuna.

COLLINS: Was that James Thomas and Leena Tuneski? The victims of the crash?

LE DOUX: Yeah, I guess it was. You know, even after all this time, I never knew that was her last name. Makes sense now though.

COLLINS: Go on...

LE DOUX: Well Otter, James, he was a tall, skinny, buzz cut, goof ball, with a pension for drugs and rock and roll. He kinda looked like an otter, so I didn't question the name. He had big wet eyes all the time cause of something from when he was a kid. I guess that aided in the naming, too. Tuna, or Leena, on the other hand, well I didn't know why they called her that till now, but with a name like that I never felt like asking her why. Didn't figure there could be a good answer. I took 'em both at face value. Everybody had nicknames when we were younger anyway, so why not.

Otter and Tuna were already madly devoted to each other when we met. They knew each other since they were kids. One from the "Dena", and the other from "Dirty Burnie". I had made a number of friends when I got here, and wound up in a number of different circles, but after a while, I found myself gravitating around Otter and Tuna more than anyone else I'd met. We had similar interests you see. We all liked scary movies and scary metal bands and scary stories. We were lovers of the macabre.

We would venture anywhere that people said was haunted or spooky or just plain interesting by moonlight. We never shied away from adventure, you know. The folly of youth, I guess.

Anyway, our love for the darkled realm eventually led us to the Ilchester Tunnel near Historic Ellicott City. It was considered a cool, spooky spot to hang out, and it was. I think the old tunnel was built a long time ago, at like the turn of the century or something. When people were still just turning the lights on. You know what I mean?

COLLINS: Please continue Mr. Le Doux.

LE DOUX: Yeah, well, we used to go up there to hang out on top of the tunnel and watch sunsets or sunrises. It didn't really matter what we were doing, the main focus was usually tom-foolery.

Drinking, smoking, talking. Usual youthful retreats. We used to go up there just to chill, you know. Get away from work and the daily BS of life.

The Tunnel wasn't the only thing up there though. Just yards away from the tracks was this ridiculous set of steps. There had to be 100 or more and they seemed to lead up at a grade that was almost a straight line. I've never been on steps so steep. Even if you weren't a Maverick man like me, smoking a pack a day, you still wound up winded, just taking-your-time getting to the top of those steps. And a bit beyond the steps at the top of the big ass hill was Creepy College. Or at least that's what everybody called it. I've heard folks call it Hell House and other things but whatever. We all called it Creepy College. I think it used to be some kind of a seminary school or something, some kind of Catholic school, if I'm not mistaken. I couldn't help but feel bad for those poor fools every time I thought of them trudging up and down those steps though.

The school itself was even older than the tunnel. And not only the school but the whole area had a history of lore to go with it. Assuming you yourself are local, I'd guess that you've heard a few over the years. There are so many stories about the goings on in those woods up there and the use of black magic. There's just so many tales. Supposedly a number of people have lost their lives to strange and tragic accidents up there over the years since it was built. And with a place that's as old as that, there's bound to be the echoes of ages past, still present. It was foreboding to say the least but inviting to thrill seekers like us. There was an electricity in those woods unlike anything we'd felt yet.

We had gone up there to the tunnel and the steps in groups a few times, just shootin' the shit, before it became blatantly apparent to me that none of my people had ever actually gone up to the college itself. For all their talk about what lurked at the topp of the hill and all the times we'd gone up there to hang out, I was always waiting for someone to say we should check out the college. But no one ever said it. I now understand why that was. They'd all simply been too scared to go. No worries though, I was fully prepared to rectify that problem. I figured we'd see the college for sure.

One night when a group of like six of us, me, Otter, Tuna, Poole man, and a couple others, all decided to go up and drink some cheap vodka at the tunnel, I decided on my own that it would be the night we finally saw the college. I knew somebody had to be going up there. It stood empty for a long time. Plus, the tunnel and any other good spot that could be found up there was tagged-two-ways-from-Sunday. There was no way that every kid that had rolled up there over the years, to party or doodle, had themselves been too afraid to take a peek.

So, when we'd all made our way over the seven hills, we met just above the paper mill, at that little lot on the hillside. We liked to park up there cause we figured people would just think we worked at the paper mill and not question the cars. Anyway, we got all the way up the road, past the bridge and tunnel, and to the ridiculously steep steps, and I hit the group with my plan of action. We were gonna go up, it was decided. Of course, not everybody was super stoked, but not one of us were gonna chicken out in front of the rest of us. Would've been bad form.

When we finally got up to the college, it was magnificent. It was huge and menacing. It was all that we wanted it to be. Soon as we were able to break our gaze with the old college, we starting making our way around the side of the building. We all walked dreamily past the great building until we came to the first window that was at eye level. We stopped to huddle round and peer through the dirty windows. We were looking through and could see desks and all kinds of stuff still in there. I was interested as hell then, cause I'd thought this place had been empty for decades. You know? I expected moldy, empty, decaying rooms, like some of the old buildings we'd been in on our previous ventures. It was weird though, just seeing everything so untouched like the past was a blink away. But I'll tell you, before we even had a chance to discuss what we could see through those windows, we heard someone yell, "Hey!" at the top of their voice. And before that could barely even register in our brains, we heard a dog bark. When we turned around, we saw a man holdin' a shotgun and a jet-black dog barreling towards us.

There was no thought man. There was no time for thought. Tuna screamed, "Run!", and we all turned our asses around and booked it. We weren't thinking about getting bit, or getting shot, we just had to get away. Right? But then, shit man, all of a sudden there's this huge BOOM and pellets or bee bees or something are spraying the trees all around us, as we're trying to get back to the steps. It was unreal. Sounded crazy as all hell, bouncing around the brush, like angry killer bees just missing their mark. Then of course, there was the problem of the very real killer mutt. It was right on our heels. I was running just ahead of Otter. It got so close to snatching Otters' ass, I figured that dog had to know what he'd had for lunch. It was nuts. But we got away. We got back to the cars and headed home fast and…

COLLINS: I'm sorry Mr. Le Doux, but I'm going to have to stop you there. I'm finding it hard to see the connections here. How does any of this story even relate to this evening's incident?

LE DOUX: I'm not done. I'm getting there, man. You said you wanted to understand. Please, just let me finish and then you'll know. Then you'll see.

COLLINS: I hope so. For both our sakes. Go on.

LE DOUX: So, like I said, we had a close call that night. Scared the bejesus out of us, ya know? We weren't about getting in trouble or getting chomped on. We just wanted to have a little "me" time in the woods. You could say we learned our lesson, cause we didn't go back up there for a long time, not back to the college anyway. We'd heard similar stories from others that shared our experiences up on the hill. Apparently, the guy shot at us with salt pellet. We weren't the first to dodge its spray and I'd bet we weren't the last. It wasn't gonna kill ya, but it'd slow you down or at least slow your desire to return. The old man was said to live there on the property in some shack. He guarded the spot from looky-loos and vandals, or did his best, I guess. It worked on us anyway.

Over the next couple of years we did go back to the tunnel a couple times to enjoy a sunrise or set, but no one ever said anything about a tunnel watchmen or nothin'. There were rumors of people dying up there, but it seemed safe enough. We weren't gonna do anything stupid and fall or nothing. At least no one's dog ever chased us out of the tunnel. You just had to worry about the train, I guess. And with the train, you just stay had to stay on the side. The tunnel was plenty big enough. But after our close call we never had the gusto to head back up those damn steps again. Just wasn't worth it, not to us. We knew that some shitty kids had gone up there with an appetite for destruction more than once. It was burnt at least twice before I ever saw it again.

COLLINS: So, you did return to the college?

LE DOUX: Yeah, but not for years. Like I said we went up to the top of the tunnel a couple times but I didn't go back to the college till we heard about the fires and that the guard was gone and that you just had to dodge the police.

COLLINS: Yes, we took over from there. Too many kids still go there. You and all the others were very lucky you never got hurt or killed messing around up there. Especially with the decay of the area.

LE DOUX: I'm sure. But it's all gone now anyway. So, after I'd heard that the guard was gone, I won't lie, my interest in knowing what was left up there was as fresh as ever. I figured we had to go back. We had to get closer. Otter, Tuna, and me, we all decided we would go back one more time to see what the looters had left behind. We all wanted it to be a special night so when we did finally go back, we decided to drop a little liquid before we went.

COLLINS: You decided mind-altering drugs was the best way to experience a deadly burnt down building?

LE DOUX: As I said, we were dumb young partiers, still getting it out of our systems. I realize how stupid I sound, but there's no better way to experience the soul of nature, than through the eyes of LSD. So, we all got wet and headed to the college.

We made our way up there and parked at the old usual spot. But then we thought about it, what if we have to get out quick. So, we decided to park under the train bridge that led to the tunnel. It was a much closer shot to the steps.

When we got to the steps we paused to spark a J. It always helps to be loose and limber before you go venturing into darkness. When we were standing around, Otter tells us he didn't feel like going up just then. I gave him a hard time of course, cause this was our chance to finally get inside and take a look at whatever wonders awaited us. But he wasn't having any of it. He said he was too burnt out and he just wanted to go hang out by the tunnel. He had the fish-eye look goin'.

What I mean is, Otter had this condition called Lagopthalmos. It was because of some terrible ear infection he'd had when he was a kid. So, he had to put these fancy drops in his eyes all the time. He had a terrible habit of just staring off when we were all fucked up, ya know. Like he was breaking through to some other dimension that only he could see. When he said he was burnt out I knew it was cause he was feeling the eye thing. It got to him a lot. So, in the end, I didn't pester him too much. I figured it was his loss.

So, we let him take what was left of the J and wander off to the tunnel on his own. Me and Tuna were determined to see the college. We slowly made our way to the top of the steps. When we got there, we could really feel the world sway, ya know. At the top of the stairs was a little corridor of trees that you had to get through. The branches hung low and created a canopy of sorts that led you to another small flight of steps. These were nothing like the other steep bastards. It was just a few more really. But going through that canopy was creepy as hell, all messed up like we were. I'd swear you could hear the forest whispering.

Those woods were alive man. It was like the branches were reaching for us every step of the way. Guiding us along with crackling bones of twig. Finally, we broke through the canopy and got up the last little set of steps. Then we were there, staring at the college again. It wasn't the same of course. Like I said, there'd been a couple of fires and the building was more like a half-burnt skeleton that some dying beast left behind in a hurry through the woods. Parts of the walls had caved in and the once great entrance was now an abstract forming of I beams and rebar.

One thing that made the scene just that much better was the moon. The college sat at the very top of the hill. That night the moon was pregnant and looming over the building like a great, big, unblinking, watchful eye in the sky, looking down on the college itself, as the building sat crouched upon the top of the hill, menacing the trees around it. It was practically snarling with its jagged teeth of broken glass. Like I said, there was an electricity to that place. You could feel the moon light on your skin and the whisper of foreboding on the wind. It was magical really.

We stood there for a while just soaking in the atmosphere till finally Tuna broke the reverie and suggested we move on. We decided to go the opposite way around the building than we had years ago. Maybe we unconsciously thought that the dog would still be waiting. I don't know. But we didn't have to go far until we found another window. Just like last time, we could see through the dingy glass. Inside was a large empty room with one door. That door sat just slightly open and it called to me.

I don't know why but I had to go in that room. I had to know what secrets awaited. I told Tuna that I wanted to go through the window and she didn't respond at first but her body language told me that she was not trying to follow. I turned to make my move inside and she grabbed my arm. I looked at her and she was crying, I mean sobbing. She was totally freaked out and she didn't want me to go in. I know it was a little selfish, but I really didn't care. I was gonna go in anyway. I didn't wait all this time to just go home.

So, despite her tears, I turned back to the broken window, determined. I was just putting my foot through the threshold when the silence of the night was shattered. Suddenly a scream, well I guess it was a scream, but at the time it seemed totally alien, burst through the night, totally evaporating all bravado I had just been experiencing. I stood up in stark terror. The sound filled the air. It was like some great, dark, beast, slithering through the woods. A sound I could never recreate, like some bio-mechanical, midnight serpent, tearing through the countryside around us. The noise echoed through the trees and shook us to our core. The door, the window, the whole damn building was instantly uninteresting, forgotten. We ran. We were flying as fast as we could, trying to get back to the steps, to get to the cars, and get the hell out of there. I know we were a bit out of our heads but as soon as we took off it seemed as though the college wanted to keep us. We kept getting snagged on branches, like they were reaching out to grab us as we passed. And out of nowhere bats were swooping all around our heads, screaming shrill little battle cries. It was like something out of a movie, man. We just kept pushing on though, away from the burnt skeleton of the building, through the haunted copse, just straight balling. When we finally got to the actual steps, things got even stranger.

When I came up on the top of stairs, I could see Otter running up them towards us. He was shouting and jabbering about something. I couldn't tell what was wrong but he just kept asking if we saw him. I thought he was freaked out about the noise, but he just kept going on about some figure. Did we see him, did we see him, he was right there, did we see him. I was scared and confused. Me and Tuna were totally freaked out about that terrible sound. I had forgotten all about Otter sitting at the damn tunnel. I didn't know how long it'd been but it felt likes hours and if we looked half as bad as he did then I knew we were in trouble.

I didn't have time or concern for understanding Otter and I just tried to get us all moving towards the car. When we ran down the final hill to the car, Tuna was ahead of us. When I got to the car she was already inside. In my current addled state, it took me a second but I realized Otter wasn't with me. I asked where's Otter, but Tuna didn't know. I figured maybe he fell or something.

I ran back to find Otter and I did. As I was coming up the hill, I could see him standing still as a statue, at the bottom of the steps, with his 9mm pulled out and pointed at the top of the stairs. He seemed to have a bead on something and I shouted. I don't know if he heard me but he sure popped off a fuckin shot, man. I couldn't believe it.

YOU CAN'T SHOOT GHOSTS

COLLINS: I'm sorry, your friend exposed and fired a hand gun? Do you have any idea how unlawful that is? And that's assuming it was a legal weapon.

LE DOUX: I know, I know, man, I couldn't believe it either. But I ran up to him and he was white as ghost. I grabbed his arm and forced it down, took all my fuckin strength. He was coiled tight like iron, he was so freaked out. I got the gun from him and just kept telling him we had to go. We had to get the hell out of there before some crazier shit happened. But he just kept going on about seeing him. Otter wouldn't shut up.

He was there, he was there, did you see his godamn hat? He just kept asking me, but I don't know man. I didn't see shit. I just made us get back to the car and get the hell out of there. Honestly, I don't even know how we got home. I can't remember the ride at all. But we made it safe and sound, none the less. I gave him his gun back but made him promise to never take it on one of our creepy ventures again. He wouldn't stop talking about the man he saw. The man in the hat. I didn't know what to make of it back then. I figured he dozed off, or was staring into oblivion or something, and a train came through, and scared the shit out of him. I told him he'd be fine, that we were all fine, and that we wouldn't go there again. Like you said, I told him we were lucky that the cops didn't show up when he popped off. But he said he saw him over and over, continuing to be the broken record. He said he saw him at the top of the steps. I didn't see anyone. But what does it matter anyway, you can't shoot ghosts.

COLLINS: Alright! Enough! This is clearly going nowhere! You haven't explained one damned thing, Mr. Le Doux. You just keep going on with this ridiculous tale.

LE DOUX: But you just heard the biggest part. The key really.

COLLINS: All I heard is that you are a grown man who has no problem with breaking the law. I've heard that you are a drug and alcohol abuser. I've heard that you have no problem with breaking and entering or illegally entering onto private property. On top of that I have heard that you are willing to laugh off felonies and the use of firearms. All I've heard are reasons for me to further believe that your involvement in this case is questionable. None of this seems to having anything remotely to do with the death of your friends.

LE DOUX: It has everything to do with it. Otter saw it all. Otter found him. Otter paid the price for a condition he couldn't even help but have. It wasn't his fault. How could any of us have known?

COLLINS: I'll entertain your line of thought. You are saying that this blinking man was there at the college that night?

LE DOUX: No! Well, Yes! The Blink Man. He's always there if he's not riding with you.

COLLINS: So, how does he fit into this now? None of this makes sense, you do realize?

LE DOUX: Yes, it does! It will. It's not over. That was just the beginning, man. But I didn't know. I didn't know until it was too fucking late!

COLLINS: Didn't know what, Mr. Le Doux?

LE DOUX: I didn't know what Otter had found. I didn't believe him. I just thought, well, I thought, you know, we were all fucked up, we heard the train, he was confused. We were just trying to have a little fun. It was supposed to be cool. To find the hidden treasures of the haunted house. I never thought that it would lead to this. I never thought... I should have listened.

COLLINS: Did your friends tell you they were having problems with this character?

LE DOUX: No! No, it's not that simple. See, after that last night that we went up there. The night that Otter found him. We started to drift apart. Whatever actually did happen to Otter up there that night had changed him. He was totally different after that. It was like a bad trip that just kept coming. He wouldn't let up about this guy he said he saw. That he kept seeing. It wasn't often. But every now and again the guy would be there, off in the distance, waiting, watching. That's what he'd say anyway.

It seemed like he was just getting further and further from reality. We hardly talked or hung out after that. He just kept spiraling further into a world of fear and paranoia. He was hardly even going to work back then. Tuna said it was hell just trying to get him out of bed.

All Otter ever talked about was his follower, the man who was always there. I couldn't take it. It was all just too heavy for me. I wasn't messing with drugs anymore. I would have a toke every once-in-a-while, but I barley even hit the drink. It was trying to stabilize my life and Otter was just going further off the deep end. So, we barely talked. Hell, we barely saw anything of each other. I did keep talking to Tuna, though. She would call me every now and again to let me know how she was doing or to fill me in on how much Otter had improved, or not improved, I guess I should say. His condition literally got worse over time. Tuna said the Blink Man was getting closer. Otter was growing more and more out of control. He had been fired from his job and spent all his time rummaging through whatever stories he could get ahold of about the Illchester tunnel and the surrounding areas. I didn't understand any of it until recently.

But then it happened. I know there was already all kinds of stories about Ellicott City. But until recently I never understood what was happening to Otter. There was this found footage documentary that came out last year, called Butterfly Kisses. It wasn't until I saw it that things started to make some sense. The movie was made by this guy, Erik Myers, and it's all about these kids who found a way to see the Blink Man. But it was also about this guy who had figured it out too, thanks to those kids, and was trying to tell other people. What it turned into though, was insane. After seeing this movie, I knew that the Blink Man was what was haunting Otter. It had to be. It all made sense.

COLLINS: Not to me it doesn't.

LE DOUX: In order to see the Blink Man, you have to be able to look through the tunnel for an hour. I don't know if Otter got lost in a blank stare or if it was his condition, but he saw him. He had to. It all made sense now. After seeing the movie, I started trying to get ahold of him and Tuna. I had to get them to see this movie. I had to let them know that I got it now and I understood. But they weren't calling me back and seriously, I just assumed the worst. It had been a long time since that night on the hill and I couldn't believe he was still with us. You see, once you've seen him, every time you blink, the Blink Man gets closer. Till he's right on top of you, man. I think, I'm sure actually, that the only reason Otter hadn't already felt the cold kiss of death was because of his condition. But I just kept ringing them and ringing them till finally Tuna hit me back last week. She said they couldn't meet last weekend, so I hit them up all this week. Since today wound up so nice, I tried to get them to meet me at Fish Head for a beer and some tunes. I thought the atmosphere might be a welcome distraction. So, we could talk and maybe try to figure out a next move.

Tuna finally hit me back and said they'd meet me at 8 outside the bar, but she was hesitant. She was hesitant of even trying to go out, but they never showed. They weren't answering the phone. They weren't texting or calling me back. I didn't know what to do. But Fish Head isn't really that far from the college. Maybe 15 minutes or so. And I'm sure you know, there are backroads that'll bring you right to it. There's backroads to weave you all over Baltimore and the surrounding areas. Otter and Tuna were smokers so they preferred less eyes on their travel. I knew they would be coming down route 29 and I had a feeling they would take backroads from the college to the club. So, I headed that way.

You'd think he'd stay away from it, Otter, but I guess obsession works that way. It gets a myriad of ethereal fingers into us and grips and pulls, tearing us into the labyrinth. It leads us blindly like lambs to the slaughter. I still can't believe what I saw. When I came around the corner and saw the smoke, I could have died. I knew it was them. Even before I realized it was their car, I knew it had to be them. It was insane. It was horrifying. I was so scared. When I saw them there, all smashed up, I just sank. I couldn't think. I could hardly breathe. I got out of the car and went to see if I could do something. I knew I couldn't. I just knew it was too late.

They were all fucked up man. His face, the blood...

COLLINS: I'm very sorry for your loss.

LE DOUX: It didn't seem real. It was... God, it was all too real. But it just seemed like some terrible dream. Even sitting here with you, I keep hoping I'll wake up. I won't have to deal with this pain. With this chaos.

COLLINS: Loss is never easy and rarely has any sense to it. It was a terribly unfortunate thing that happened. Did you see someone else at the scene? Is there something you aren't telling me?

LE DOUX: No, man. That's it. The Blink Man had to have caused it. I don't know how close he was.

COLLINS: You said there was no one else there. What makes you think that something else was involved?

LE DOUX: I told you. It's all in the story. Otter saw him. After that there was no turning back. You can't undo some things man. Tuna was just a poor creature, unfortunate enough to have loved a doomed man. She was the truest victim in this. It took me too long. Gavin was right. People have to know. Something has to be done...

COLLINS: Well, Mr. Le Doux. If that is all you have to share with me, then you are now free to go. Thank you for your time and I'm sorry if I was brisk. These terrible events are hard on all of us.

LE DOUX: That's it. I can just go.

COLLINS: Yes sir. Your statement has been recorded and we will finish our investigation as soon as possible.

LE DOUX: So, what are you gonna do?

COLLINS: We will have a coroner's report soon and will put all of the details together.

LE DOUX: You didn't hear a thing I said, did you?

COLLINS: Mr. Le Doux, your friends died tonight in a terrible accident. That is a pain you and their families will have to find a way to heal. I will admit that the circumstances of the crash are strange. There didn't seem to be any reason for it.

LE DOUX: Yeah, they hit the only obstacle for yards.

COLLINS: But from where I'm sitting, there is nothing to blame here except a very sad and cruel twist of fate.

LE DOUX: Slash the circle then. That's why the cycle never ends.

COLLINS: Excuse me?

LE DOUX: Nothin'… Look man, I tried and I'll keep trying. Maybe I'll just disappear into the folds of this mystery, too. But I will keep trying until I do.

COLLINS: Look, Mr. Le Doux, again, I am truly sorry for what happened here and what you saw. But this does truly appear to be one of those terrible and unexplainable things. I will share your story with a colleague of mine who might be interested. But I'm telling you now, to please put these thoughts of haunting specters and vengeful Flicker Geists out of your head. Let yourself have time to grieve. But I will pass your story on.

LE DOUX: You do that. Please. Cause some things can't be unseen, until you finally close your eyes.

END OF TAPE

Deputy Collins closed the door to the interview room. This case was far stranger than it seemed it should be. Sometimes facts simply don't all match up. Sometimes coincidence is just that, coincidence. But sometimes...

"So, what do you think?" asked Lieutenant Tina Mcgee, leaning heavily against the wall outside the interrogation box. Feeling that old flutter of panic again, she knew all too well what Deputy Collins was likely thinking.

Collins took a second to collect his thoughts before he could respond.

"I don't know. It's all so strange. It looks cut and dry but... some pieces of this puzzle, don't wanna fit."

Tina couldn't help but picture another interrogation room filled with doubt and mystery. It seemed so long ago. Best let old ghosts lie.

"What do you think of Mr. Le Doux?" She asked.

"Oddball, that one. But I at least believe that he believes his story. But let's be honest. The guy has admittedly been something of a party boy. I'm not really sure what to think, to be honest with you. Hey, do you think you could get me a copy of this documentary he was talking about? What was it called?"

Tina's breath caught for only a second when suddenly it felt like someone had walked over her grave. Then, in the blink of an eye, the feeling was gone. Regaining the minor loss of composure, she turned to Deputy Collins, and with a knowing look in her eyes she replied...

"Butterfly Kisses."

POSTSCRIPT

By Megan Morgan

This article was written for and accepted by a Baltimore based publication in the aftermath of the release of Butterfly Kisses. For reasons never explained, it was pulled from the publication schedule at the last minute. No other publication would print it. Until now.

Ellicott City, Maryland

I visited the city one Spring day earlier this year – when the buildings had mostly recovered from flooding two years ago, and before they were damaged by even more catastrophic rains over the summer – and I was instantly charmed. The historic parts of Ellicott City have the look and feel of some quaint European village, augmented by Colonial architecture that clings to the steep sides of a river valley. Houses and businesses built before, during, and after the Civil War are stacked almost on top of each other, building blocks of stone and wood. The walls that keep the hill from sliding into the sidewalk have glass marbles embedded in the mortar. Rock outcroppings tempt the brave to climb them (a sign instructs the brave to refrain, though). And every glance reveals some new crooked, mysterious alley.

It was the sort of town where every restaurant is a discovery. Where you could turn a corner and find the cutest of coffee shops, or the most incredible tie-dye t-shirts. Where long-standing restaurants cozied up to brand new shops of geekery. Where you could look up and see art venues perched high on the hill above you. It was all these things without any sense of self-consciousness.

All this, and ghost stories, too – enough to fill an entire

volume, which the author Shelley Davies Wygant compiled in her book *Haunted Ellicott City*. Every building seems to have a spirit or two embedded in the stonework, and uncovering them will give a visitor a glimpse into Ellicott City's history. There's the Civil War soldier who never left, the man who was brutally lynched, Hell House, and the historic train station.

Only one haunting is reported to have claimed victims, though.

Baltimore, Maryland

About four years ago, Gavin York's father-in-law, Bart Hunkeler, went into the basement of his new home in Columbia, Maryland to poke around in the dusty ductwork keeping the house warm. It was an older home, but one that the retired foreman was proud to have. As he made his inspections, he discovered a ratty shoebox under the broiler.

Written on the lid were the words, "Don't Watch." Which was obviously an invitation to watch, right? Because anyone in their right minds with a box of Mini-DV tapes that should never be viewed would just destroy them. They wouldn't bother sticking them under a broiler in a basement after writing "Don't Watch" on the lid.

Mr. Hunkeler and his wife Eve gave the tapes to their son-in-law, a film major working as a wedding videographer.

What Gavin York saw on those tapes reignited his dreams of becoming a filmmaker, and horrified his in-laws so much that they decided to sell their house. The tapes were, apparently, made by a pair of film students working on a project for one of their classes. The black and white footage followed their journey to find evidence of an entity known as the Blink Man.

Gavin's wife, Amelia, supported him as he lovingly edited the footage into a film all his own. This, he claimed, was a real-life Blair Witch Project. With just a little investment, he would finally be a real filmmaker. He would finally break into the business, if only he could get a few other people to hop on board and do some work for free – then they would all have their passage to fame. Amelia was thrilled to see life come back into her husband.

And then the documentary crew showed up. And as dark as the mysterious footage on those Mini-DV tapes was, Gavin's life was about to get even darker.

White Marsh, Maryland

It's a nice day at Red Brick Station. The cool autumn weather pairs nicely with the pumpkin beer they have on tap, made on-site. You can even peek into the brewing rooms through glass windows in the restaurant. And there is the table where Gavin once sat, talking into the documentary crew's cameras, explaining the importance of the footage he'd found. I'm here to meet the people whose lives were left destroyed by the pursuit of Peeping Tom.

Amelia York and her mother Eve Hunkeler are not the sort of women to get willingly embroiled in the kind of mess surrounding *Butterfly Kisses*. They are both family-minded, and their primary concern these days is protecting Amelia's son, Carter. Both, however, get this look in their eyes when they talk about Erik Kristopher Myers. The look of two women who watched a house fire, and know exactly who set it.

For three years they've been silent about what they saw, and finally, they're ready to speak out.

"The documentary crew just showed up at the house one night. Gavin had been talking to the director, Erik, for a while.

And then they just dropped in. Gavin said, 'This is what is happening right now.'"

Amelia York talks about her husband lovingly, if reluctantly. It's been three years since he died of a heart attack, and yet she hasn't had much opportunity to mourn. See, her husband's death, she says, is being sensationalized by Erik Myers' new film *Butterfly Kisses*, and the documentary hasn't given her much time for peace.

"Reality was thrown out the window," Eve says. "It was certainly edited together to promote the filmmaker."

When I ask them what happened to Gavin, they admit that he did become obsessed with the film student tapes in a way that wasn't healthy. He was a desperate man taking what seemed to be his last shot. Was his death directly caused by this pursuit? That's uncertain.

Was he pushed too far by the documentary crew?

Eve and Amelia will tell you, "Yes."

The Ilchester Tunnel, Maryland

Drive along the Patapsco River about two miles from Historic Ellicott City, on a narrow road firmly nestled in the bottom of the river valley. You'll come to a gravel lot shaded by a train bridge. Walk up an access road to the train tracks, and turn left – there, across a train bridge built in 1903 rises an enormous rock face; and in that wall of rock is a tunnel.

Walk across the bridge (make note of the three-petaled flowers in the ironwork) and watch the ground fall out from under you as you walk over the river. You can look down through the grating at the clear water below, patterned by ripples and patches of white where it splits and swirls around rocks. It is higher and airier than you'd have expected.

Meanwhile, the gaping maw of the tunnel looms ahead. At the near end is a stone arch, with the word Ilchester at the top, with the date of its completion split to either side. Beyond is endless black, with a tiny aperture of light at the end. Standing in front of it, there is a sense of both being drawn forward and pushed back. Even for the skeptical, there is a power here, either because the shape of this tunnel taps at some primordial part of the human mind, or because something "other" dwells here.

According to the legend, this is the only place to find a spirit known as Peeping Tom, or Blink Man.

Baltimore, Maryland

They followed Gavin for weeks while he tried to get the word out about the horror film he'd crafted. He contacted ghost hunting groups, authors, and experts in video manipulation to authenticate the tapes he'd found. He reached out to newspapers and radio stations. This was real! Like the Blair Witch Project, but this time insisting the tapes were real was no gimmick – he'd found the footage.

The crew was relentless, catching all Gavin's highs and lows. They interviewed the people around him about the intimate details of their life, exposing the family's money troubles even as Gavin poured all their finances into this work.

He talked to Matt Lake of *Weird Maryland* fame, and there they were, pushing their cameras in the face of the author even as Gavin grilled him about the provenance of the Blink Man legend. One has to wonder how much more desperate a man clinging to his last hope might have grown if his every misstep and foible was recorded by a camera crew. Gavin's excitement withered into desperation, and all the while they watched it happen.

When Gavin was at his most fragile, they put him in front of a speeding train.

White Marsh, Maryland

I ask Amelia and Eve what they think of the tapes. Did Gavin make them himself, are they a hoax played by another party, or are they real?

"The tapes Bart found were real tapes," Eve says. "I can only say that the tapes in the box were real. Gavin came over to the house and showed me some of them."

And Amelia is particularly insistent that Gavin was innocent of any trickery. "I know Gavin had nothing to do with creating those tapes. And because of his level of obsession with them, I think he was really trying to find out."

And just how obsessed was Gavin? Enough to empty out an account set up for his son. Enough to neglect his family's only source of income, his freelance wedding videography, during peak wedding season. Enough, say Amelia and Eve, to miss the fact that someone with ulterior motives was pushing him

Ilchester Tunnel, Maryland

Peeping Tom's origins are a bit of a mystery. It's proposed that he's the spirit of an old blind man struck and killed by a train in the early 1900s, although he is also compared with the Flimmern-Geists, a type of spirit that hangs out in your peripheral vision. You know how sometimes you see something out of the corner of your eye, and then when you turn to look, it's gone? That's Peeping Tom.

Except in this case, it's possible to get the spirit to show up right in front of you.

There are two problems with this:

1. Doing so requires staring down Ilchester Tunnel for a solid hour, from exactly midnight to exactly 1am, a time reserved for bored teenagers and the very determined.

2. Once Peeping Tom is in front of you, there he will remain. And each time you blink, he gets closer. And closer. Until he is right in front of you, filling your vision. And as you stand there, desperate not to blink, his long eye lashes will brush your face – a butterfly kiss that apparently can kill you, because once this Flimmern-Geist is that close, his victims die.

It's a staring contest that's impossible to win.

Washington, DC

They didn't have an ending for the documentary. What had begun as a fascinating character study, and what had taken hours of work by an entire crew to film, wasn't panning out. Gavin's film wasn't garnering much interest. A well-educated populace was calling the image of Blink Man rising up at the end of Ilchester Tunnel fake.

So, Director Erik Kristopher Myers pulled some strings, and arranged for Gavin to be on a DC radio broadcast with Mike Jones. Gavin grasped at the opportunity to get the truth out to the world, at the chance to ardently insist that what he had was the real deal.

The whole thing was a set-up.

Gavin shriveled in his seat as caller after caller decried him as fake and phony. He exchanged barbs as the interview deteriorated. And just when it seemed he couldn't take anymore, the worst blow landed.

It was a call from one of the makers of *The Blair Witch Project*, Edwardo Sanchez. Under any other context, his words were measured and kind, if firm. It sounded like great advice from a filmmaker who's made it in a tough industry. Gavin's reputation was on the line, and he needed to be honest.

Under the circumstances, this genuine advice was the last blow to Gavin York. After the interview with DC 101, Gavin discovered that Amelia had left him. He'd taken money from their son's bank account to finance his movie, and she'd found out. It was more than she could tolerate.

Gavin vanished. Then reappeared at the Ilchester Tunnel late one night. And then vanished again, for the final time.

White Marsh, Maryland

"Watching Gavin progressively turn into someone else – it was upsetting. And we had to protect our daughter and our grandson," says Eve.

Amelia's life since Gavin's death is much changed, though she's done her best to pick up the pieces and move on. She's living back with her parents, and helps her son Carter with his homework every night. They go on playdates. And all the while, the documentary about her husband's death has been moving forward, no matter what she or her family have to say about it.

Their interactions with the director haven't helped.

"We went to the screening, and he didn't come up to us at all. He acted like we didn't even exist."

The burden of Gavin's death, what may have contributed to it, and the way it's now being represented weigh on Amelia and Eve, but they are ever determined to do something about it. All they want, they say, is justice for their family. They want the world to know the truth – that Gavin as he is portrayed in *Butterfly Kisses* is not the sum total of the man. That he had sacrificed much over the years for his son and his wife, and he was passionate about his craft.

As for the director? Eve says, "I'm not somebody who has ill will against anybody, but this guy, he's a murderer."

When we reached out to him about this article, Erik Kristopher Myers responded, "No comment."

Ellicott City, Maryland

The area around Ellicott City is brimming with stories. Tales of injustice, of war, of violence, of fire, of floods. Buildings are built, teem with life, then fall into disuse, and are destroyed – or are wiped out in an instant by some catastrophe. It is a place that is made beautiful and prosperous by the very things that can destroy it.

And just down the train tracks, still in use today, the Ilchester Tunnel waits. A passageway only constructed because of floods that wiped out a viaduct. A dark channel through stone, where a legend lives. And while Blink Man might not be able to ensnare you in a deadly staring contest, you'll certainly find it hard to look away.

AFTERWORD

By Erik Kristopher Myers

My brother went to school with a girl who went to Ilchester Tunnel one night to see Blink Man, or Peeping Tom as my daughter calls him. He's a ghost or a demon that haunts the tunnel next to where Hell House used to be and he can only be summoned if you can stare down the end from exactly midnight to 1am without blinking a single time. Once you see him, you're stuck with him because every time you blink, he takes a step forward until he kills you. If you try not to blink, he has these long eyelashes that tickle your cheeks and cause you to blink so he can get right up on you. If he's real, he's worse than my ex-wife's lawyer, and that guy was an asshole.

— Some Guy on the Internet

1.

Peeping Tom is real.
I can prove it.

2.

He's a (boogey)man of many names, although the one by which you may call him is largely informed by your age, and which playground you were on when you first heard the story. I was nineteen when that particular branch of local folklore pricked my ears, and although too old for the schoolyard at that point (and being, at any rate, the sort of kid who preferred to sneak cigarettes under the stairwell and swap ghost stories with similarly disaffected teenage malcontents), my mind was nonetheless prime real estate for exactly this brand of urban legend to build upon. After all, I'd lived in a haunted apartment building for the first eleven years of my life; I'd performed impassioned classroom presentations on the existence of both Bigfoot *and* the Loch Ness Monster, using SCIENCE to bolster my arguments; and I'd read every book on alien abductions, urban legends, and general Forteana available in the Baltimore and Howard County Public Library systems. I'd once attempted to convince my fourth-grade friends I was a lycanthrope, and later on, a tenth-grade friend in turn tried to convince me I needed an exorcism. *Peeping Tom?* THE LINE FOR ADMITTANCE STARTS HERE, folks. That ticket was purchased the moment I knew there was one for sale, and all it cost me was a trip to nearby Ilchester Tunnel. But that would come later.

Now, keep in mind that this was in the Stone Age prior to the *X-Files* wave of 90s UFO mania. The beginning and tail end of the Great Speculation Boom had emerged almost simultaneously during the 70s, when Uri Gellar was wowing audiences with pretend spoon-bending, and Peter Graves very sincerely informed television audiences that the Patterson-Gimlin film was real footage of a real, albeit unknown, animal; he then presumably cashed his real paycheck with equal sincerity. Magazines like *Fate* still appealed to an audience grown almost intentionally soft after a decade of Vietnam, Nixon, and the Generation Gap; crystals and Disco and Tarot cards seemed defiant in their bland safeness. Two decades later the whole Far Out quest for interdimensional beings and the greater universe existing beyond our own had bled out along with any sense of cultural adventure. We'd seen the top of Everest, and there was no Yeti brought home in a cage. Dinosaurs were dead, whatever blurry and artfully ambiguous photos of

Scottish (and North American!) lakes might otherwise suggest. Spring-Heeled Jacks and Mad Gassers and Mothmen were fun diversions; now the Silly Season had passed. The great explorers were all dead. There was Iran-Contra and "Where's the Beef?" and MTV and turtlenecks. You might find a rerun of *In Search Of...*playing on a Tuesday morning after *Mr. Belvedere* reruns transitioned into the weekday graveyard existing before the start of dramatized court shows and the afternoon news. Thus do the self-proclaimed seekers of Truth go to die on ugly couches: old and doughy and disenchanted, watching midday TV, waiting for the *honk* of a daily school bus, and only vaguely remembering the faded magic of monsters. That's what the next generation is for, so please pass the jelly.

But I was lucky. Part of that was the fact that I was, indeed, among that next generation of kids; I was also hopelessly devoted to horror movies, E.C. comic books, and anything else that promoted the concept of the supernatural as real. More than that, I wanted to experience it for myself. This might sound like Red Flag behavior — particularly when you took into account my near-shocking refusal to apply myself scholastically — but like all things, it came down to location, location, location. A few probing questions from the guidance counselor might have revealed that I'd spent my pre-teen years growing into a scowling art-snot just a stone's throw away from Antietam Battlefield (a perimeter my parents pressured me to circle as part of my semi-mandatory cross country training; today, I'd sooner let a Confederate phantom drag me compliantly to Hell than to even consider a casual jog). As such, ghosts and assorted boogah-boogah were stirred into the regional batter and gave it that flavor I associate now with mountains, woods and streams. My father had long ago informed me, with grave seriousness, that our apartment complex was seated along the traditional Route of the Dead, and conjured for me images of wagons near-toppling beneath the weight of rotting soldiers piled high, leaving behind them a ghastly trail of wheel-tracked gore above which the carrion birds screamed. The Civil War, Hitler's henchmen, Normandy Beach and all that stuff were fascinating to him, and he'd never hesitate to share some gruesome anecdote. Incidentally, I'd be remiss if I failed to mention his complete and total contempt for my love of violent films.

He's also the one who plucked me out of that world of uniformed apparitions and moaning fields where the bodies stained the ground, and where now no grass dare grow. I was eleven when I was transplanted to Columbia, which was seventy miles away but might as well have been a million. Hagerstown was my first painful breakup, and though the mountains may be smaller, and the forests torn down to make room for outlet malls and Taco Bell and Starbucks and Panera, part of me never left, and all of me returns at least once a year. Same state, but entirely different state of reality. The only way back was the highway bridging the Baltimore metro area to that scary building of which all the neighborhood kids spoke in hushed tones, and where I shivered beneath the blankets, eyeballing the closet door and what was lying in wait within; a place where I would capture, years later, an EVP recording of a boy screaming. Sometimes, late at night, I wonder about that cassette tape, packed away deep in the basement where I don't have to see it or think about the impossible sounds magnetized therein, and as my mind goes down dark tunnels, I wonder whether I caught my own voice on tape that blazing June afternoon, reaching back across time and space to preserve that terrified child who would someday grow into a terrified man-child.

Tunnels.

That's what you're really here to read, and I'm late to arrive, like a corpse deemed uncanny by virtue of his stubborn refusal to remain timely. Every ghost needs a grand entrance, it's said. If I'm grinning as I type these words, it's only to suppress the scream. That smile? It's a mask of normalcy draped over a sheer wall of terror from which two eyes stare back from the mirror. If I stare back long enough, they become one.

So: Ilchester Tunnel. Maybe you've been there. Probably not. I could go into the history: how the B&O Railroad was originally built around the side of the mountain, spanning the Patapsco River by way of an aqueduct; the freak storm that destroyed the structure, as well as the station, and killed numerous passengers; the decision for engineers to establish a sturdier throughway by blasting a tunnel straight through the cliff wall, affixing a wrought-iron Bollman Truss leading now inevitably down that midnight road; how the industry abruptly went under following the opening of that passage in 1903, and how the nearby paper mill closed as well; or how prestigious St. Mary's College exploded into sudden flame and burnt to the ground on the one hundred anniversary of the flood that forced men to act against instincts warning them *not to cut through that cliff*, as if they knew some door was just waiting to be opened. I could tell you all of that. But that's what we in the storytelling biz call *world building*; it's salad when what you want is the steak. *Peeping Tom* is the steak in this story...bloody, messy, and very rare.

I mentioned all those names he's collected, like maggots in an empty socket. While *Peeping Tom* seems to be this generation's preferred moniker, there are almost as many Ellicott City residents who still refer to him as *Blink Man*; as if to prove what's Old becomes New again, the title seems to be making a comeback amongst the younger set. I've also heard that *Old Winky* and *Mr. Blink* remain in use by a dwindling population of septa- and octogenarians; these are still far greater in number to the discreet minority electing to use my personal favorite, *Ilchester the Molester*. Anyone who asks *What's in a name?* clearly hasn't been tasked with selling to an audience, as the elements that constitute a good ghost story are no different from any other commercial enterprise: you need the product, you need the hook, and you need the icon. But all it takes is a lousy name to sink the ship, and our malevolent inhabitant of Ilchester Tunnel has had the benefit of decade-by-decade rebranding.

The fact that he's gone by so many different handles is indicative of the Urban Legend framing device constituting his backstory. This likewise props up his validity as a slice of legitimate Maryland history by virtue of Tom's malleability, and sheer longevity. Regional folklore thrives on (and endures in spite of) oral tradition, and as our Kindergarten teachers showed us, long ago, in the same faraway time when ghosts and goblins were as commonplace as making the bed and summer vacation, the game of Telephone functions both as a method of transmission and dissemination of our own embroidered truth. In short, *The Blink Man's* been around for over a century, and he rolls with the times. We allow *him* to allow us the opportunity to introduce a fresh identifying label as New Wave dies, as those *Who's the Boss?* reruns vanish along with the tube TVs that transmitted them, or as newfangled internet chat rooms open the door for unforeseen mechanisms by which to share the horrors lurking in our backyards.

Yet with each retelling, we both add and subtract. If there's a single name by which *Peeping Tom's* lineage can be derived, that name is *flimern-geist*: a term allegedly coined by German alchemists to describe the phenomenon of so-called Shadow People -- specifically the ones dwelling just beyond the periphery of vision. Yet as more evidence finds its way into public consciousness (i.e., the source for such claims, as well as the linguistic and psychological origins), we find that the assimilation of the otherworldly comes with a cultural price. Even *flimern-geist* is flattened, smoothed out, and Americanized; Google the word *flickergeist* to stumble upon content related to the playful spirit of Ilchester Tunnel, whereas the word from which it's derived turns up more or less in passing only.

This is all tangential, though. What matters is the story, and the story endures. Jesus, after all I've written, I still haven't told you the *hook*? Forgive me this bit of dramatic intrigue; after all, what did I say renders a dead man inexplicable…?

Ask an old-time Ellicott City resident, or even a random person strolling Main Street on a brisk autumn afternoon, about Ilchester Tunnel. Query a son or daughter who's returned from a sleepover, about which ghost stories they told after the host's parents had gone to sleep, leaving them wide-eyed and terrified, greedily exchanging allegedly true stories of inexplicable local phenomena as the Witching Hour fell upon them. Ask a teenager who's too young to drink but too old to wander the Mall on a Friday evening, and they'll tell you where the kids go at midnight. They'll tell you about the Tunnel. They'll tell you about The Dare. They'll tell you about hiking up to that spot, shadowed as it is by high slopes that block the stars and smother the valley in darkness. They'll tell you about standing there on the far side of the trestle that spans the Patapsco River far below, and reaches its conclusion at a sheer rock face into which a passage has been opened; a passage through which the occasional train still passes, and whose sad wails echo throughout that haunted valley. They'll tell you about the so-called Staring Contest that no one can seem to win except an anonymous friend-of-a-friend whom they knew in grammar school; who used to babysit their neighbor; who worked at the grocery store down the street back in '89, or maybe it was the gas station…? Hard to say, since no one they know directly who's tried has been able to pull off the superhuman act of staring down the length of tunnel from exactly the stroke of midnight until the bell chimes one, without blinking, remaining focused on that pinprick of bluish-grey light at the far end; but supposedly there are some who have, and have lived to realize they summoned *Peeping Tom* into their field of view; and that no matter where they go, no matter where they look, he is now always there, and takes one step closer with each successive blink of the conjurer's eye until, at last, he's nose to nose with his prey, awaiting that final blink that will allow him to spring. Sometimes they're found dead, these people, apparently victims of heart failure; sometimes they're found hanging from rafters, or lying in bathtubs thick with the blood they've loosed from open veins at the wrist. Better to call it a draw when it's a game you can't possibly hope to win. And the best part was that it was all *true*.

Of course, the story spoke to me.

Of course, I had to go.

Of course, I had to try.

And, of course, I didn't see anything. Not that time, anyway. That would come later. Much later.

At the time, I thought nothing of this beyond it being a ghoulishly fun story in an area I came to learn was ripe with ghoulishly fun stories. I may have lost the rolling hills and battlefields of my youth, but in nearby Ellicott City, the older, Baltimore-based version of Erik found new creaking floorboards to flinch at the sound of. If Stephen King was looking for Castle Rock in Maryland, the historic district of Ellicott City would suit the requirements nicely; nestled as it was between rising cliff walls upon which houses and church spires reached for the sky, while the narrow ribbon of Main Street plunged down to a river that has proven more temperamental than any legendary monster. Besides the unexpected storm that destroyed the aqueduct at Ilchester Station back in 1868, that raging bitch known as Mother Nature hurled the waters against the quaint storefronts on Main Street in 2016, and again in 2018, ousting more than one domesticated spirit from its domicile. Indeed, it seems every shop, tavern, or side alley has a ghost story or three, but none so malevolent as *Peeping Tom*, who has made alliance with the very weather itself.

But come on — if our token *flickergeist* owes its backstory to anything, it's every child's private bathroom terror, The Bloody

Mary. The basic rules are the same: there's an act of conjuring, followed by shrieking insanity. The difference is, the Bloody Mary story can be disproven in about five seconds. All one needs to do is kill the lights, close the bathroom door, say the name three times, and *voila* — nothing happens. Show me a person who's seen a gore-soaked crone appear in the mirror and I'll show you an old woman suffering a messy head trauma. *Peeping Tom* had a built-in defense against this sort of skeptical inquiry, and that's the near-physical impossibility of proving *or* disproving the tale. Pull out the *Guinness Book of World Records* (assuming anyone bothers to read physical content anymore), and look up the world record for staring; then get back to me. Don't worry, I'll wait. Then, once you've done that, ask yourself the likelihood that anyone, anywhere, could focus their eyes on a distant point for sixty minutes without blinking a single time. This isn't even about neurological functions — this is about common sense, for crying out loud.

But someone had to have done it. Right? *Right?*

I confess: I tried. I stood in the snow beneath a full moon, with the silver reflection illuminating the valley as though it were full day. My feet were freezing, and I failed miserably maybe five or six minutes in; that was enough for me to dismiss the story as bullshit. *Clever* bullshit; but bullshit all the same. The fact was, so many of these stories were bullshit with or without a *Mythbusters* crew on hand to explain why Goatman couldn't exist due to the improbability of that specific gene pairing, or why the bizarre feathered dragon-octopus we locals dubbed The Snallygaster was even more zoologically offensive. The problem — for me, anyway — was that as a lifelong devotee of such contestable lore, once you began eliminating one demon, cryptid, or legend from the roster based upon nothing more than its inability to make rational sense in an otherwise rational world, those that remain begin to take on a bit of stink, as well. And that night at Ilchester Tunnel was the first time I walked away from such an experiment, thinking: *Well, that definitely doesn't exist, because I proved conclusively to myself that the odds of keeping your eyes open that long is almost impossible, to say nothing of there being an actual eyeball monster that follows you around until he kills you.* If there was any sense of accomplishment in that moment, it was replaced by a feeling of disloyalty. Either I was growing up, or I was getting too old to see the possibility of magic in a world that desperately needs it. In the unlikely event Tinkerbell needed resuscitation, I was the last person she ought to depend upon to declare my belief in fairies.

The dominoes sort of went over for me after that. We entered a new age of digital analysis, and certain Givens no longer were. The Dinsdale footage of Nessie was a boat; Roger Patterson's pendulous-breasted creature was one of several male actors looking to take credit, and all clad in little more than a fur suit; there had never been a Thunderbird photo; the Flatwoods Monster was an example of mass hysteria; and so on, and further. As my hairline receded, my pride in the twin labels *Skeptic* and *Atheist* grew accordingly. I picked fights on message boards, dropped F-bombs on podcasts when discussing religious charlatans like Harold Camping, or con artists like Ed and Lorraine Warren. There was even that moment when, sitting in the home of *Exorcist* author William Peter Blatty (a staunch believer in the dubious case that inspired his bestselling story), and he presented me with the actual EVP recordings he made that were subsequently turned into pseudo-meta-fiction in his 1983 sequel, *Legion*; and while fourteen year-old Erik would have lost his mind to *actually hear the real tapes* that had now become infamous amongst fans, the thirty-one year-old curmudgeon he had grown into could barely keep the smirk from his lips. Suddenly, I began to wonder about *my* EVP recording that had terrified me so much.

I grew older. I grew smarter. I grew bored.

And then I met Gavin York.

He was a wedding videographer based out of Baltimore who might have sold used cars if his devastated credit had allowed him to purchase one of his own at company discount. About my age, with a smile that was dazzling in its insincerity. He made me nervous the first time we met, despite the very public location (a bar) and my ability to fake a last-minute emergency if things went south. They *would* go south, later on; but that first encounter stoked the coals of my dormant suspension of disbelief, because he claimed he had something I needed to see. It was proof, he told me. It was The Real Thing.

We'd found one another in a Facebook group in January of 2015. I say *group* as a singular because while he spammed nearly every forum with his request for an interested documentary filmmaker to tell his story, I responded only once, and once was all it took. Gavin was cagey. Secretive. Troubled and troubling. And I had to see for myself. I had to see the contents of the shoebox his father-in-law had discovered, one cold November, pushed away beneath the boiler of his new retirement home; I had to see the content on those decade-old mini-DV tapes that allegedly chronicled the death and disappearance of two student filmmakers who, in 2004, had gone to prove the existence of *Peeping Tom* for themselves. It wasn't *The Blair Witch Project*, he assured me. It was real. And he was going to share it with the world.

As a filmmaker, I had two very attractive possibilities: on the one hand, I could present the authentication of real, and local, supernatural data, while a host of experts examined Gavin's findings on-camera; on the other, I could present the portrait of a man in crisis, and examine why desperate people cling to their delusions in the face of inarguable evidence to the contrary. So, I watched those tapes. I wondered whether they were a clever fake on Gavin's part, or perhaps an unfinished horror film long ago abandoned by the kids who grew too bored or too busy to edit the hours of content into a complete narrative. I wondered, and I wondered. I was still wondering seven months later, as I opened a motel bathroom door and found Gavin, naked and caked in dried shit, his corpse cringing in the bathtub with his eyes and mouth wide in the frozen, endless shriek I can only assume accompanied his passing. That was when I knew the truth at last, and all the self-congratulatory skepticism that had built like a callous over those ghost stories I'd loved as I child was ripped away to reveal raw, bloody flesh beneath. Kind of like a steak, you might say.

Gavin's story is told in *Butterfly Kisses*, the documentary I subsequently assembled, and then released to the world in October of 2018. I won't bother to recount it here; it exists, and it's there for you to watch, independent of this writing. I'd simply ask you to take what I've shared with you here, and peer, if you could, just beyond the borders of that film; look very closely, and you can see the Director, just off-frame, beginning to believe again. Stare, if you will, but try not to blink.

Peeping Tom is real.

I can prove it.

3.

Peeping Tom is *not* real. I can prove that, as well.

In November of 2014, I was fishing about for a concept. My previous feature, *Roulette*, had been released the autumn prior, and I wanted something fun and fresh. That love of urban legends and folklore was at a high boil, just waiting for the right mechanism; a desire to say something about belief systems was likewise queued up behind the commercial needs of an entertainment-based endeavor. These are admittedly incongruous elements when lined up just so.

Like all the best ideas, the concept for *Butterfly Kisses* came to me like lightning out of a clear blue sky, while I was on a walk. I'd seen recently a preview for yet another Found Footage movie in release — and if you require a definition for the subgenera, I would point you to the previously-mentioned *Blair Witch Project*, which, while not the first, certainly established the popular formula for "discovered film/video detailing the death or disappearance of the filmmakers in an alleged supernatural incident" — and as is the blessing and curse of creative-minded storytellers, my wheels began turning. I flashed back to that brief period in time, back in the summer of 1999 when, for a few months, audiences genuinely believed that *The Blair Witch Project* was, in fact, a "real" documentary; I wondered whether anything like that could ever happen again. Audiences were too savvy now, I thought. Documentaries, as we know, are biased. So-called Reality TV is anything but. Give ten filmmakers the same footage of a family picnic, and ten narratives will emerge. *The camera doesn't lie*, goes the saying, but it does, and it does so shamelessly.

Hence, *Butterfly Kisses*. My concept was a Found Footage movie in microcosm, featuring fresh-faced actors for maximum suspension of disbelief. I'd wheel out the tropes, the conventions, the clichés. The very concept, involving two Maryland film students in search of a local phantom, was intentionally evoking *Blair Witch*; even if the average viewer had never seen another movie of the sort, what Sanchez and Myrick fashioned was both the template, and the gold standard. It had become universal. Sit anyone down in front of *Butterfly Kisses*, and they'd know the beats, and the plot points. This is true of any genre — once a narrative becomes formulaic, it becomes predictable.

That's where I'd try something different. The Found Footage would serve as the film's core, but wrapped around it would be a reasonably-authentic faux-documentary, featuring real people, playing themselves, who would point out these recycled beats *to* the viewer as they effectively dismantled the content as being hoaxed. These individuals would run the gamut from paranormal investigators, to audio/video analysts, folklorists, film theorists, and even Eduardo Sanchez himself. In this way, I'd employ what I considered a clever bit of misdirection: *No, seriously, folks, I'm not trying to convince you this mysterious footage is real — you're too smart for that! The documentary elements dissecting it, however...*

To accomplish my aims, I needed a local phantom. The mercenary part of me realized I'd do best to create something from scratch, if for no other reason than to retain the copyright should Hollywood (haha) someday come a-knocking. I knew immediately that if I planned to populate the film with real, Google-verifiable experts, I'd find no better setting than Ellicott City, which had the virtue of rich supernatural history, and the added bonus of being cinematic as hell. The question was: what sort of nefarious entity was I going to toss into the cultural pot of otherwise "real" ghosts, and where would he or she rattle her chains?

The answer to the latter spurred the former. Ilchester Tunnel was among the few spots in the historic district with a legitimate reputation, but lacking any specific boogeyman. It's a real train tunnel where real kids go to give themselves real night terrors; pop by on a Friday or Saturday sometime around the witching hour and you'll see faraway flashlights even from the road, or hear screams of terror, punctuated by laughter. It was (and is) A PLACE WHERE WEIRD THINGS HAPPEN. I myself had been up there many times after dark, seeking some experience to take home and add to the list of inexplicable occurrences I have ultimately come to rationalize away; I even filmed a horror movie up there in 2004, back when I was a film student like the protagonists who would spur the *Butterfly Kisses* narrative. It too, went unfinished, though not because I died or disappeared, much to the regret of some.

From there, I began riffing on established tales. *Peeping Tom* would, like Bloody Mary, require a summoning spell that was irreversible; it would also be so close to impossible to pull off that there was no way to quickly prove or disprove it. He'd bear a passing physical resemblance to Jack the Ripper, or Slenderman, or the archetypal Shadow. He and his rules needed to be simultaneously new and familiar, like any good scary story to tell in the dark. He needed a backstory that could be woven into the very real history of the valley, and the creation of the tunnel itself. He needed aliases. He needed to *exist*.

I wrote the script in seven or eight days; and as I began casting about for collaborators, I took things a step further in terms of verisimilitude. Under a variety of pseudonyms, I began generating articles about the legend of Ilchester Tunnel that I quietly seeded online. I did this to entertain myself. My theory was that perhaps I could take the meta-nature of *Butterfly Kisses* to the next level, and experiment with False Memory Syndrome. Maybe no one would believe either layer of my film; but if I took a real place with a real reputation — and one that was begging for a face, a name, and a set of rules — and I began positing the legend as being equally real, then perhaps Ellicott City locals would suddenly misremember having heard the story, long ago, at a sleepover, or riding the merry-go-round at school. Wouldn't that be fun…?

I made the film. It played film festivals, won awards, and was released in North America in October of 2018; worldwide distribution would occur the following summer. I did countless interviews. I told the story of how and why I created the character. I laughed at the stunned silence and patent disbelief these claims generated. *Butterfly Kisses* was a movie, though one that seemed written as much by the grumbling skeptic I had become as the boy who believed in monsters. In this way, I reconciled the two. I argued both in favor and against such weird and wonderful things as ghosts and goblins, and finally put the bow on a lifelong love of the macabre.

That, as they say, was that.

4.

But.

5.

Peeping Tom *is* real.
And as I said, I can prove it.

6.

A curious thing happened leading up to the release of *Butterfly Kisses*; one could argue that I shouldn't be surprised, even now, given the great lengths I took to ensure it. When one attempts a magic trick, they always plan for it to work, but there's always that shock when in fact it does.

Peeping Tom began to take on a life of his own, independent of the film I was secretly ushering through production and release. I'd not spoken a word about the premise, not even to friends; and yet the character's regional fame was growing, a little bit each day. The stories I'd planted were being read, shared and discussed. There were Reddit threads; A Creepypasta entry. One morning I awoke to discover that a Paranormal YouTube channel had done an episode of the so-called "Flickergeist of Ilchester Tunnel," and the host was equal parts stunned and excited that she'd never heard the story before. I wasn't surprised; it would be another nine months before the film was premiered for anyone outside of the production to see.

People were talking. People were sharing encounters they couldn't possibly have experienced. And on and on. Like any good urban legend, the experiences were always those of a friend-of-a-friend.

Like any good urban legend.

I toured the United States in 2018, going from screening to screening. Every Q&A began with the same question: Is the story real? I never had to ask for clarification on which aspect of the film was being referred to.

I read articles about the film in newspapers, where *Butterfly Kisses* was described as a fictional work about a real ghost story. Radio hosts and podcast critics began their spots with the assumption the legend inspired the film, rather than the other way around. Both CBS and FOX interviewed me at the tunnel during the nightly news, presenting the same narrative. Soon Tom had even ended up on the official Ellicott City website, listed among the haunts for tourists to investigate. He exists outside the frame of my creation now, and it seemed wholly appropriate to learn, the week before the movie's Blu Ray and VOD release, that a book on Ellicott City ghost stories had been published almost simultaneously; a certain tunnel-dwelling phantom had received an entire chapter.

I told you, way back at the beginning of this, that the first time I visited Ilchester Tunnel, I saw nothing; later on, I would experience something that would lead me away from disbelief. I did. I saw how legends are born, and how stories bind us. *Fun bullshit*, I called them, and maybe they are. Maybe that part doesn't matter. Maybe we just need the fun, particularly as the magic fades and age descends upon us. The stories outlast us all, and form our cultural heritage.

Butterfly Kisses is my truth, but the legend belongs now to Ellicott City.

Peeping Tom is real.

A Final Note

And that, as they say, is that.

The curtain has been pulled back, the secret has been revealed. The stories contained within this book are fiction. Of course they're fiction. Or perhaps meta-fiction, whatever the precise definition of that nebulous term might be.

I met Erik as described in the foreword of this book, but I didn't go home and find myself drawn in to an investigation surrounding his documentary, I went home and enjoyed his incredibly well-made and entertaining horror movie. It did, however, stick in my mind.

Erik and I became friends. A few months later I pitched him the idea for this book. He was flattered and, I think, a bit amused. He said to go for it. So, we went in search of writers and stories and we came back with an amazing and eclectic variety for you.

I hope you enjoy them.

K. Patrick Glover

COPYRIGHT ACKNOWLEDGMENTS

"Thom" by Shelley Davies Wygant. Copyright ©2019 Shelley Davies Wygant. Printed by permission of the author.

"In The Court of The Yellow King" by K. Patrick Glover. Copyright ©2019 K. Patrick Glover. Printed by permission of the author.

"The Flimm" by William Couper. Copyright ©2019 William Couper. Printed by permission of the author.

"The Shadowghast" by Matt Lake. Copyright ©2015, 2019 Matt Lake. Originally published in *Here Be Monsters* (Parnilis Media). Reprinted in an expanded form by permission of the author.

"Dead in Vegas: One Night Only" by Seth Adam Kallick. Copyright ©2019 Seth Adam Kallick. Printed by permission of the author.

"BUTTERFLYKISSES68" by Patrick Storck. Copyright ©2019 Patrick Storck. Printed by permission of the author.

"Remains To Be Seen" by Josef Richardson. Copyright ©2019 Josef Richardson. Printed by permission of the author.

"The Light at The End" by Megan Morgan. Copyright ©2019 Megan Morgan. Printed by permission of the author.

"Oblivion's Curtain" by Paul R. Sieber. Copyright ©2019 Paul R. Sieber. Printed by permission of the author.

"Traverse" by Steve Toase. Copyright ©2019 Steve Toase. Printed by permission of the author.

"You Can't Shoot Ghosts" by Jacob Le Doux. Copyright ©2019 Jacob Le Doux. Printed by permission of the author.

SPECIAL THANKS GO OUT TO...

Kick Ass Thunder Dudes, Jacquelyn Hardrick, Eric S. Schaefer, Janice Glover, Paul & Laura Trinies, Sandy Kallick, Steve Pattee, Jonathan Williamson, Jeremy Reis, Karl Mossberger, Nick Frisone, Keith Perkins, Abi Godsell, Paul y cod asyn Jarman, Katie Whittle, GMarkC, Nerds from the Crypt, Simon Tierney-Wigg, Lisa M. Gargano, Dre Lotthammer, Lily Mansfield and Taylor Pickett, Tifany Kendall, Jackalope Vollman, Nancy Niche, Stuart Dodgshon, Natalie Peirce, Beth and Mason Doermann, Cameron Callahan, Tia Twigg, Eivind Kjorstad, Rayhne, Benjamin Hausman, Benjamin Radford, Joshua Monroe, Matt Bunker, Ricki Cummings, Antonio Fucci II, Richard Longbottom, Lawrence Waldman, Arthur Green, Aaron T, Luke Renz, Ernesto Pavan.

www.ingramcontent.com/pod-product-compliance
Lightning Source LLC
Chambersburg PA
CBHW020546020726
47494CB00006B/1937